VIKRAMAJIT RAM was born and educated in India. After graduating from the National Institute of Design in 1990, he practised as a graphic designer for several years. His first book, *Elephant Kingdom: Sculptures from Indian Architecture* (2007) was followed by two travelogues, *Dreaming Vishnus: A Journey through Central India* (2008) and *Tso and La: A Journey in Ladakh* (2012).

He lives in Bangalore.

The Sun and Two Seas

VIKRAMAJIT RAM

SPEAKING
TIGER

SPEAKING TIGER PUBLISHING PVT. LTD
4381/4 Ansari Road, Daryaganj,
New Delhi–110002, India

First published in paperback by Speaking Tiger 2016

ISBN: 978-93-86338-01-3
eISBN: 978-93-86338-16-7

10 9 8 7 6 5 4 3 2 1

Typeset in Minion Pro by SÜRYA, New Delhi
Printed at Sanat Printers, Kundli

for
N, V, S
and
R

Part One

1

CADAMBAGIRI

THE PLUME OF WHITE SMOKE SWIRLED ACROSS THE SANDALWOOD ceiling like a great winged serpent, lazily looking for a way out into the night. As faces tilted up and jaws dropped in fright, it dragged behind it a roaring ball of flames which burst through the lattice screens, showering the assembly below with red-hot arrowheads. It licked the brocade banners which burned even as they cascaded as patterned gold nets. It bit the gilded capitals, clawed out the ivory brackets, blistered and melted and peeled the wall murals and, in an explosion which shook the very foundations of the palace, devoured the ceiling in a sea of black-orange; the gold finial in the roof peak fell directly into the fire-pit in the ceremonial dais. Despite the utter devastation of the pavilion, it was a miracle that no one succumbed to the crashing columns and beams. And praise be to Cadamba! said everyone: the fire had started *after* and not a moment before the wedding had been solemnized.

By noon the following day, news of the fire fanned from the citadel into the outlying villages. As the fragrance of burnt woods drifted in the wind to the boundaries of Cadambagiri, so word travelled further afield into the marketplaces and homesteads and palaces of neighbouring countries. It raced down roads and rivers, touched every port on the peninsula's coastline, and out across the seas in the company of cotton, elephants, rice, women and spices. Too good a story to pass up, the details turned fanciful with each retelling: a comet; a curse; a jackal; a slighted guest... And then, typical of incidents of the kind, the Great Fire of 1237 was quickly outclassed by other calamities, both man-made and natural, leaving Cadambagiri alone at last to make sense of what had happened.

∼

On turning thirteen, the First Princess of Cadambagiri was wed
to the Crown Prince of Parijatapuri on the full moon of May
1237. The groom was fifteen. The wedding was held in the hilltop
palace which crowned the citadel.

Landlocked in the heart of Hind, Cadambagiri was a
peaceable little country, with only the fierceness of its summers
to contend with. Its boundaries, defined by token ditches and
thorn hedges, lay a hundred miles each way in the cardinal and
intermediate directions of the citadel, and were marked at those
points by lone watchtowers which weren't always manned. In the
latter part of the last century, the grandfather of the present Raja
had thrown a defensive stone wall around the palace, appended
by a gateway of considerable girth and height.

The wall and the gateway were frankly redundant: the former,
so shallow in parts as to be easily scaled; the latter, giving not
to the frontage of the palace but onto a grassland, dotted about
with ancient cadamba trees like silent green shrines. It was from
this flowering species that the name of the citadel, and indeed
the country, had derived.

Like his grandsire, the present Raja was given to ambitious
building schemes. He had marked his coronation, in 1232,
with an obligatory temple to Cadamba, the family's tutelary
goddess, which took him three years to complete and brought
the current total of the citadel's temples to twenty. The Raja's next
priority was to remove the architectural eyesores installed by his
forebear, for the wall (he rightly believed) occluded views from
afar of the palace, as well as views from it of the surrounding
lowland. Prospects aside, the dismantled masonry would serve
to reinforce the embankment of a tank (excavated by a different
forebear) outside the citadel. As for the gateway…why, the
Raja couldn't wait to smash the pointless thing to smithereens.
Regrettably, his long-cherished demolition project was aborted
a day before its appointed date, courtesy the visit of an itinerant
Oracle whom they hadn't seen in a while.

Floating into the palace uninvited and sliding into a trance, the Oracle claimed to speak for the Raja's long-dead grandparent, predicting the ruin of anyone who dared remove his architectural folly. A forward-looking man, the Raja had little time for such things as auguries and portents believing instead that everything (except natural phenomena) was a manifestation of one's thoughts and speech. Under ordinary circumstances, he might have humoured the old bat and done as he pleased. This time, he was persuaded by his Rani to desist lest some calamity visit her husband and render the good lady widowed in her prime. 'Women,' thought the Raja bitterly. And so it was that the wall and its forlorn appendage stayed.

The next time the Oracle visited, May 1236, it was to convey tidings from a different antecedent—the Raja's great-grandmother, no less.

'What now?' asked the Raja, warily.

'Delay not,' said the Oracle in trance, 'transform you must the large inner courtyard to a covered pavilion for the marriage of your first-born princess.'

'But the first born is not yet come of age,' the Raja said, 'nor have we received any suits for her hand.'

'Within the twelvemonth shall she be wed,' the Oracle said. 'Shall you the pavilion start then to prepare?'

'Shall it not become too hot inside?' the Raja said with characteristic foresight: Cadambagiri in May was hot as a brick kiln; the courtyard in question was enclosed by two levels of galleries and apartments which benefitted from the glorious light and cross-ventilation the atrium provided. To cover it with a roof seemed a crying waste.

'Rain it will that night,' the Oracle said. 'Begin work in haste or forever live to regret it.'

Had the Rani of Cadambagiri produced a prince instead of two princesses, there would have been no call for any wedding pavilion, for it was customary for the groom to wed in the bride's father's palace and to return with her to his father's palace. With little to be gained from rueing over what *could* have been, and with the Rani pressing him to heed the Oracle's forecast of rain, the Raja had little choice but to once again acquiesce. But this time was different. It was not for nothing that he was a practical man.

That the Oracle had marked the largest courtyard for conversion surely meant the wedding there would be a lavish affair…an indication also that any imminent son-in-law would hail from a country of considerable means. What better demonstration of Cadambagiri's own influence than an extravagant wedding-pavilion inside this old-fashioned shell? So it was that the courtyard's transformation commenced on an auspicious day following the rains…and before the Oracle could show up again with some new reason to complicate things.

Not surprisingly, the Raja derived immense pleasure from overseeing what he claimed was the fruit of his own wisdom and foresight: the pavilion, he had quickly surmised, would come in useful in due course for the nuptials also of his second princess. The new interior, therefore, was readied in nine months and without a hitch—no small achievement, given the materials and craftsmanship that went into it.

The tapered columns through two levels were whole teak-trees, imported from Pagan across the Kalingodhra Sea. Sandalwood for the roof beams and panels was purchased from Dwarasamudra in the southern countries. Ivory for the brackets and decorative inlay came from Kalinga: that Empire's elephants, alive or dead, were the best in all Hind. Fifty cartloads of Bengal seashells were burnt and ground with Cadamba river sand for replastering the walls of the enclosing apartments. Overlaid on these, miles of fine Bharukachchha muslin, steeped in limestone-slurry, were burnished with egg-shaped pebbles from the Ganges; the egg-shell-smooth walls were painted with mythological scenes in jewel-pigments from the foothills of the

Himalay. Lac from Lacadwipa in the Sea of Hind lent a mellow sheen to the old and new woodwork everywhere. The erstwhile courtyard's black flagstones were buffed until they gleamed. A square brick-and-plaster dais was positioned in the middle—and in its centre, an inset fire-pit—for the wedding ceremony. By the time the carved details of the pavilion were gilded and a gold cadamba-flower finial was affixed to the pyramidal roof-peak, the First Princess of Cadambagiri had not only come of age but was also spoken for by the Crown Prince of Parijatapuri.

∼

The Raja of Parijatapuri happened to be indisposed at the time and excused himself from the nuptials of his only son and heir. Officiating in his stead was Prince Narasimha Ganga—heir apparent of Kalinga and the groom's dearest childhood friend and confidant.

The wedding party from Parijatapuri arrived with a retinue of courtiers and priests and elephants which outnumbered the elephants, courtiers, priests, and kinsmen of the Cadambagiri clan. That the unequal alliance had at all been established owed no small a part to the closeness of the Oracle to the Raja of Parijatapuri. Like the Raja, the Oracle too absented himself from the wedding. Granted a generous brokerage, he was believed to have embarked on a Himalayan pilgrimage. The father of the bride was put out by the absence of the two worthies—he had particularly looked forward to impressing his Parijatapuri compeer—but quickly recovered upon hearing the awestruck gasps of his guests when the silver doors of the pavilion were opened wide.

An army of servants had worn their fingers thin from stringing miles of jasmine and oleander garlands, which spiralled up the teak columns to the ceiling, hung in swags from the enclosing galleries, graced the sides of the ceremonial plinth, adorned every guest and family member's neck and wrists, and filled the evening air—already heavy with incense—with their heady fragrance. Torches in wall-sconces caught the gilded details so that the air seemed to be adrift with fireflies. Suspended from the beams and pulled by ropes in the hands of hidden servants, lengths of glimmering brocade wafted gentle breezes overhead. The guests took their places around the ceremonial dais; smiling handmaids worked their way through the assemblage distributing raw rice to shower the bridal couple with at the climax of the ceremony. As for the hairdos, diadems, turbans and ornaments on display, the last time the Raja had seen anything like it was during his own wedding. 'How swiftly I have aged,' he thought, glancing to where his Rani was seated with his mother, the Dowager, and the womenfolk of the palace.

Something seemed amiss in that grouping. Just then, the priests began their readings even as the High Priest fed slivers of rare woods and spices and made libations of ghee and honey to the sacred-fire pit so the Raja returned his gaze to the bridal pair.

The youngsters (including the Kalinga prince) looked radiant as jewelled butterflies. Whether from the sight of his daughter the bride or the smoke from the fire-pit, the Raja's eyes welled with tears which would not go away no matter how hard he blinked. Swept away by the emotions of the moment, he quite simply forgot he was father also to the Second Princess.

～

Unbeknown to everyone, the seven-year-old sister of the bride had chosen to observe the proceedings from a latticed first-floor gallery, overlooking the great hall and in direct line of the dais.

The lights through the latticework cast a pattern of stars on the Second Princess's face. Had she known it, she might have brushed them away as though they were cobwebs but her eyes remained focussed through two stars in the screen. In all correctness, she knew, she ought to be downstairs with the rest but correctness was not her strongest point. No one, not even her grandmother the Dowager, was privy to the pain which burned and crackled inside her chest.

Ever since the Crown Prince of Parijatapuri had been deputed by his father six months previously to Observe Statecraft (whatever that meant) for a month in Cadambagiri, the Second Princess had become infatuated with the serious young man who had been assigned, between Observations, to supervise the two princesses' studies.

The Second Princess had been delighted by this development, for it provided not only respite from their regular tutor but also the opportunity to minutely study the object of her interest. Her sister the First Princess, in contrast, had been indifferent from the start to the prince. On the occasion of their first lesson with him, she had emptied her inkhorn over his dhoti. Another day, she'd placed a porcupine-quill hairpin in the backrest of his chair. She, more than once, had stuck a foot out, causing him to trip. She broke his silver-stemmed reed-pen. Such incidents hadn't ruffled the prince; that he was kindly and patient, generous in his attentions and encouraged both sisters equally, only caused the younger one to adore him more avidly. Until then, the word 'love' in her vocabulary had been reserved for her grandmother and a pet elephant. This new breathless, dizzying, smouldering sensation the accidental teacher inspired was not altogether unpleasant.

The time came for the prince to return home to Parijatapuri. It had, he said, been a most edifying month for him. Bidding farewell to the tearful Second Princess, he assured her that he was likely, within the twelvemonth, to revisit, and there was no reason for her to be disconsolate. He had kept his word—only in order to become her sister's husband. Had she learnt of it sooner, she would not have waited.

For what? She wasn't sure. For now, all she *could* do was hurl a string of expletives—bat piddle bullock-udder lizard dung stink insect—which she hoped would seep through the latticed screen and wreak its bad magic on that spineless anal pore of a rat.

Clearly the chants of the priests were more potent than the

child's heartbroken rant. The object of her fury was broadly smiling under a jewel-encrusted turban which seemed a size too big. His bride (who as a rule never smiled) had adjusted her features into a vague expression of bliss. The drummers had stirred and so too the players of the long snake-trumpets. At a sign from the High Priest and a jangling of bells to which the eunuchs in the shadows contributed their keening, the bridal pair got to their feet and exchanged garlands.

At that precise moment, something broke inside the Second Princess's chest. Tearing her fingers away from the screen, she spun around on her heels and ran through the dark, unpeopled passageways—gathering her skirts, kicking off her slippers, plucking the jewelled clips from her hair—and stopping only when she could run nowhere else.

The window she clung to opened onto a purple sky, suspended with a new moon encircled in auras of pearly pink and violet. From the emptiness below, the laughter of jackals flew up on a breeze. Hugging herself, the Second Princess turned and considered her surroundings.

The nuptial bed, crafted of chased silver and ivory, was dressed in silks and strewn with cadamba florets, its canopy fringed with seed-pearls and cadamba leaf-buds. The air in the chamber was light with the flowers' elusive fragrance. Everywhere, small oil-lamps flickered shadows onto the wall murals in which celestial nymphs flitted in the company of winged beasts. But the bed was soft, too soft, and the flowers tickled the Second Princess's shoulders and back. Climbing off, she stood gazing up at the canopy before her hand reached for the nearest oil-lamp.

A tremble through her arm caused the wick to gutter, sending up a little blue smoke tendril. But there was no shortage of lamps. When she touched a leaping flame to a tassel that dangled from the canopy, it was only to see what might happen.

The smell of burning silk was the exact smell of that time,

long ago, when she'd set her hair alight as an experiment. Another laugh from the jackals far away snapped her back to her senses. But too late. Stunned by the utter beauty of the blaze, she dropped the lamp and ran—this time stopping when she was far, far away downstairs.

The ceremony there had concluded. 'Father,' she said, locating him in the throng surrounding the bridal pair.

It took the Raja a moment to recognize the dishevelled urchin tugging at his hand. His next reaction was to want to tear to shreds whosoever had done this to his precious second child. But it wasn't that at all: she was babbling, something about having started a fire, they were all in danger, they must run outside, *quick*!

The Raja stared at her so she repeated the words as if he were a simple child. Then the frenzied screams began.

❧

As the months wore on, the main grouse of the local populace was that the culprit, or culprits, had not yet been identified. This telling detail provided the local gossip mills, already overworked, with more grist to keep them happily grinding. Ever since that ill-fated night, in any case, public opinion was perfectly split like the flickering tongues of a snake. Of course the Raja is in on it, murmured one faction: why else is a more thorough inquiry not conducted... A shooting star... All that lac and woodwork; a clever ploy to rebuild the old dump... A curse of the Oracle for not being invited... A jealous kinsman of the Parijatapuri clan... Shock and sorrow has struck our good Rani speechless... Have you heard, new taxes...?

Providentially, when the rains came, they were munificent so the dreaded taxes didn't pinch too much: a bumper harvest ensured that the royal treasury recovered enough to effect a complete transformation of the palace. In deference to the mood of the times, the 'new' palace consisted of the brick-and-stucco ground floor of the original—stripped of ornament inside and outside. A new jackwood roof smeared in pitch replaced the burnt floorboards of the original upper storey. The whole structure was limewashed white. The result was an austere low building, wholly invisible behind the old wall of its history. The restraint demonstrated in the undertaking helped restore some of the citizenry's faith in their Raja. Why, then, did he choose the first anniversary of the Great Fire to die by his own hand?

All it had involved was some datura-seed powder and scorpion venom mixed with honey. *The pressures of keeping silent in the face of knowledge were untenable,* the suicide admitted in a note found by his bed, and he must be excused: *no one was to be blamed for his cowardly act.*

Eleven days later, the mute Rani of Cadambagiri died of heartbreak. The orphaned Second Princess, all of eight summers of age, was installed on the throne with her grandmother the Dowager appointing herself Regent.

2

KATAKA

On a clear-skied morning of May 1244, Narasimha Ganga, Sovereign of Kalinga, surfaced with a head cold—his signature triads of sneezes flying down the hushed hallways of Kataka Palace.

Twenty-three, tall for his clan and built like the horses he liked to race, the Sovereign was blessed with fine eyes and keen senses, except at times like this when his head felt as though it had been danced upon by an elephant. He had galloped home last evening in an unseasonal downpour and thrown himself into bed without drying his hair. Rain or hail, he would ride out again today: he had recently acquired a spirited Persian mare.

From the age of four when he was placed in the saddle for the first time, Narasimha Ganga had become more enamoured of horses than of elephants. Unlike an elephant—which either plodded or bolted with no transitional pace—a horse was a more capricious entity, sensitive to the subtlest messages conveyed through its reins and rider's inner legs, knees and heels and soft tongue-clicks, which led it to walk, trot, canter, gallop, reverse, rear up, curvet, perform tight turns, or come to a quivering, snorting, wide-eyed standstill.

Heels down, back straight, Narasimha had quickly mastered the rudiments; and then there was no holding him back. 'A natural,' said everyone with knowing smiles. 'He *must* have been a royal steed in a past life; and see how the horses adore our little prince back.' Which was all very well; sadly, in the present life, Narasimha's favourite sport had exacted a cruel price.

A maternal great-uncle had remarked, quite early, that the inordinate time his great-nephew spent on horseback was sure to render the future sovereign of Kalinga acutely bow-legged. This is exactly what had happened. For all his youthful dash and daring, Narasimha was painfully conscious of his physical defect, which, he imagined, made him appear short and ungainly. In compensation he tended, not unconsciously, to walk with chest thrown out and head held unnaturally high and stiff. The effect was of a man perpetually moving through life as though he were wearing a sign, *Worship me: I am the original Man-Lion*. To those privy to the real reason, safely hidden in the folds of the royal dhoti, the strut was a harmless, even endearing, habit. Others were less charitable, branding the strutter unapproachable and insolent. Narasimha, cleverly, milked both opinions to his advantage.

Sneezing thrice in quick succession, he marched down the passage connecting his privy chamber to the Morning Office, as usual wondering why they had to come as these trumpeting triads instead of one or even two satisfying explosions like everyone else. Of course he had no answer: it was one of those things, like his bandy legs, which he'd learnt to live with. Three more sneezes. Pausing at a balcony, he observed, unnoticed, some ministers and their underlings hurrying to their offices in the ground floor of the opposite wing. In the courtyard garden separating the wings, a peacock was trying with little success to woo its hens. 'Stupid bird,' Narasimha muttered, moving on to the Morning Office.

Aside from the pigeons murmuring under the window eaves, the office was quiet. The business which occupied the mornings here was sifted the previous evening by other offices, with only such matters that required the Sovereign's personal attention sent up in a camphor-wood dispatch box, beautifully satinized by age. The box awaited on a long table. Grunting a greeting to his Scrivener and his First Secretary, Narasimha bade them to sit before taking the taller, silver-and-ivory chair at the head.

Two manservants had padded in meanwhile, one of them bearing a steaming goblet. Standing by their Sovereign, the bearer dribbled a few drops of a greenish mess onto the palm of the second servant, who promptly licked the stuff to prove it was safe. The taster, on such occasions, was randomly picked: there were people who routinely administered to themselves all manner of poisons, the better to render themselves immune to tests of this kind. Narasimha had little patience for these outmoded practices: if one's number was called up, one went and that was it. 'What horror is it this time?' he asked the servant who hadn't dropped dead.

'It is hard to tell, sire,' the man replied, pleased to have provided, and survived, the perilous service. He would be well recompensed. 'It is bitter but not unpleasant.'

'You have been requested, sire,' the bearer put in, 'to quaff it while it is steaming.'

He grimaced. It wasn't so much the draughts that made him balk but the idea of her, the Consort, dispatching them the moment she got wind that he was feeling poorly. Three more sneezes. He downed the goblet, pulled a face, and turned his attentions to the day's business.

Like the dispatch box, the Secretary and the Scrivener were inheritances from Narasimha's late father's time. The Secretary, seated to the left, seemed not to be formed of bones, blood and flesh but of black sculpting-wax. Horizontal caste marks adorned his forehead. A wisp of hair crowned his tonsured head. In his thirty-eight summers of age, he wasn't known to have smiled. Of similar vintage but diametrically opposite in every way, the Scrivener was a Sino-Persian polyglot with a penchant for poesy to all that he inscribed. A shapeless white robe revealed little of the underlying pale doughy frame. His straight blue-black hair fell to his shoulders and it was said he applied a heated iron to the ends. Except in the presence of the Sovereign, he sported a tarboosh of scarlet felt, worn at a slight tilt. Narasimha was fond of referring to his assistants as his Left Hand and Right Hand, much to the unspoken displeasure of the Secretary who, like anyone with a scrap of common sense, considered the left hand

unclean. Although they shared this table each morning—exactly
as they had with the late Sovereign—the Left Hand and the
Right never met in private: no matter how enervating, nothing
contained in the dispatch box was left in arrears for the next
morning. As its lid slid open under the Left Hand, Narasimha
hoped the morning's workload would be light. The Consort's
decoction had miraculously eased his congestion but his head
still felt like a clod of clay. He sat back and pressed shut his eyes.

'News from Chandrabhaga,' the Secretary began, unfolding a
palm leaf. 'The foreman informs you that the crowning stone of
the assembly hall is in place. Also, three blocks of Dwarasamudra
greenstone have arrived for the terrace shrine images. You might
wish to visit before the rains.'

At the behest of his late mother, Narasimha had marked his
coronation, in 1238, by breaking ground for a new temple on a
windswept beach of the Kalingodhra Sea. Six years on, the temple
was nowhere close to finished. The setting was significant. At
Chandrabhaga, where a creek of the same name drained into the
sea, Sambha, the youthful son of Krishna, the Eighth Incarnation
of Vishnu, had prayed to Surya the sun god for deliverance from
a curse—from his father, no less—which had struck Sambha
with leprosy. His prayers were answered and the episode was
celebrated in legend. To this day, legions of lepers thronged the
site to bathe in the waters and mud of the confluence.

'There is more, and this is more pressing,' the Secretary was
saying, 'He goes on to remind us that monies are still owed to
the garnetstone quarries. I've had the figures checked.'

Narasimha sighed. With each passing year, the privy treasury
steadily diminished, for the temple was deemed from the start
to be a private, not imperial, enterprise. He already had a name
for the edifice underway but was forbidden, by sacred decree,
to utter it aloud until the temple was dedicated. The rains next
month would again bring work to a standstill for close to eight
weeks; as always, there would be other, unforeseen delays…
'Have the payments released,' he said.

The Left Hand passed the document across the table to the Right Hand, who tendered the requisite signature seal from a trayful of seals.

An anonymous note, next. They hadn't seen one of these in some time. It begged to alert the Sovereign to a newly appointed Superintendent of Elephants' partiality to alcohol and young men. The writing appeared to be the handiwork of more than one hand—the Scrivener suggested the writer had simply alternated hands—and the wording too was carefully contrived.

Narasimha never understood what led some people to couple with their own gender. 'What do you suggest?' he said.

'The welfare of the elephants must be our priority,' said the Secretary, in preamble to a theme he would develop in a moment.

That moment was not to be, for Narasimha snorted and turned to the Right Hand. 'And your original thoughts?'

The Scrivener had learnt long ago not to be vocal on matters of governance. Because he was employed only to take dictation, he smiled a dimpled smile and went back to studying the tip of a stylus as if the fortunes of Kalinga were balanced on it.

'You are both useless,' Narasimha grumbled. 'Let's say for the moment that the...*thing* is his business. Any veracity to the drinking charge, have him dismissed, but not before a replacement is in place. And get to the source; I don't want anyone to imagine they can remain forever nameless.'

'If I may say this—'

'Good. Next.'

The Secretary reopened his mouth, only to shut it again. What was the point? The sovereign he had inherited was too impetuous, too much in a hurry to get things over and done with. Granted, he had demonstrated remarkable acuity last month in trouncing that perennial pest Tughan Khan, governor of the Bengal country. But military prowess wasn't everything; it was always the small vermin, right under one's nose, which led to the fall of kings and empires. Left to himself, he would subject the superintendent to a fine *and* public disgrace—tonsured and led through the citadel on a she-ass, no less, none of this summary dismissal and replacement. He had lost his moment, but only for a moment. Two other matters awaited; his opinion would be solicited again. Putting away the anonymous note, he reached into the dispatch box. 'A letter now from your Kiswahili compeer,' he said.

Narasimha's face lit up like a child. 'Now you tell me! Read it quick!'

The vellum scroll had travelled by sea from Kilwa off the east coast of Aphrike to Cambat on the west coast of Hind and thence overland across the subcontinent; the Scrivener had translated it from the Persian to Sanskrit last night. The writer, Sultan ibn Bone Suleiman and Narasimha had never met—that they ever would was unlikely—and yet the two were as soulmates in their correspondence.

The correspondence itself had been initiated by the Sultan in 1238. Paying tribute to the newly installed Kalinga sovereign, the Kiswahili emperor had expressed his desire to trade with Kalinga in bullion, olibanum, ivory and slaves for diamonds, women, tortoise shell, peacock feathers and blue dye. His letter had been presented at court together with the gift of a gold paper-knife in a carved ivory handle and sheath. Narasimha's Privy Council had advised restraint. The gift of a knife, they said, boded ill. Surely the Sultan was an ally of the Bengal potentate? Surely he was trading with Bengal in the same commodities? Surely he *was* the Bengal potentate?

Narasimha had thrown caution to the wind. And just as well: six years on, the friendship had not only survived but also proven the naysayers otherwise. Bone Soleiman's last missive had accompanied a live consignment, which had served the Kalingan army in its April victory. His latest closed with a renewed request for a batch of Kalingan milch cows to improve his native zebu bloodline. Narasimha would not keep him waiting. 'Let us reply forthwith,' he said. The Scrivener squared a sheet of paper and selecting a reed, held it in readiness over a silver-and-gaur's-hoof inkwell.

'Salutation friend,' Narasimha began, eyes shut, as though he were reading from a draft inside his head. 'The contents of your missive have been conveyed a moment ago to my eager ears. If I had my way, I would breach all restrictions of lineage and traverse two seas to deliver the promised cows to your doorstep. My tardiness in this matter shall be remedied in haste, now that the travails of war are behind me. Pray accept my gratitude once again for your timely shipment of warriors from Aphrike.'

He paused, collecting his thoughts. 'Those remaindered from their voyage to fight alongside my men, and whose numbers have sufficiently recovered from the campaign, are engaged nowadays with my labour gangs at the great temple, which is as yet incomplete. May it once again be said that their valour in battle and their strength and affability in their present employ has greatly endeared the Aphrikes to their Kalinga brethren. Regarding the cattle, my gift of thirty—' He paused, drumming the table with his fingertips. 'No, make that forty cows…and six stud bulls…together with handlers to ensure their safe passage and subsequent husbandry in your palace, shall board a vessel bound for your shores when the winds this year once again blow southwest. With this assurance, I remain your comrade… et cetera, et cetera.'

Dusting the paper with sandal-powder and funnelling back the blotting, the Scrivener passed the sheet over for Narasimha to feast his eyes over the crimson flourishes and curlicues.

'Beautiful. If only I could read it.' He handed the letter back. 'And what news of the ship?'

'It will be seaworthy in three months' time,' said the Secretary.

'Have the cows seen to immediately. Heifers, I should think, but not so young that they will not survive the voyage.'

The Secretary cleared his throat.

'Yes?'

'They will proliferate.'

'As they must.' He smiled. 'Unless we send him bullocks instead.'

Why is it that an argument, carefully prepared, becomes tongue-tied at the opportune moment? The Secretary had assumed the matter of the cows was a passing fancy, until last evening when he had checked and re-sequenced the box's contents. Everyone knew that the gift of a milch cow was the highest honour a ruler may bestow—generally upon a Brahmin, not some Muslim ruler of a faraway land. The idea of not one but *forty* heifers making a perilous sea crossing caused the Secretary a stab of pain, as though it were his own daughters who had been promised to exile. 'All I wish to say,' he began, only to have a gobbet of history spring from his lips, 'is that a gift of one thousand cows was shipped by one of your predecessors to the Brahmin settlers of the Camphor Island.'

'Ah, I don't aspire to eclipse the great Mujavarma's feat. Forty-six should suffice for Kilwa Island. Now, are we done here?'

The Secretary caught a look—something between condescension and glee—from his cross-breed colleague. 'There is one more matter,' he said quietly.

'Quick. I am tired.'

'You might prefer to read it for yourself.'

Most unusual. Narasimha eased open the birch-bark document. His eyebrows shot up taking in the signature seal: *Sovereign Cadambagiri*. With an incredulous laugh, he began to read:

> Salutation Sovereign | We offer felicitations on your routing of the Bengal threat and gratitude thereof for retarding his advance towards our country | A visitor at our court speaks of works commenced afresh upon your temple in Chandrabhaga-on-Sea | Our own fortunes as you may be aware have been imperilled since our installation to the throne

on the demise of our father and more so with the passing last
year of our grandmother the Regent | The past six-month
especially finds us engaged in a battle of wits against a section
of our kinsmen who are determined to unsettle our position
as sovereign | Towards this end these men have ingratiated
themselves to the crown prince of Parijatapuri | It is common
knowledge that the prince and you are childhood comrades
| We recall your presence at the marriage of this prince to
my sister the erstwhile First Princess of Cadambagiri | We
now seek your good influence to bear upon your compeer
to reconsider his affiliations with those of malefic intent |
Whether or not he pays heed is secondary | If nothing else
it will alert him that one more powered than he is privy to
his scheme | If he chooses to disregard your counsel we are
prepared for the consequences and so should he be | Our
decision to write to you is an impulsive one and may only
good come of it | From belated discovery that we have little
stationery at hand this late hour of night we needs must still
the workings of our mind | In honour and good faith…

He was not unaccustomed to appeals from women—the wives of
errant ministers, dispossessed courtesans, effusive young things
offering companionship and much else besides—but none had
closed her missive with *honour and good faith*. He set the letter
down carefully. As if suddenly self-conscious, it curled into itself.
He sat back with his fingers making a temple under his chin.

'What would she be now? Fourteen? Fifteen?'

The Secretary sniffed. 'Closer to fifty-one, methinks.'

Narasimha laughed. 'I promote you to court buffoon
forthwith. But yes; it is an archaic style.'

'She has benefited from the tutelage of the late Regent. They
say the elder's blood flows strong in her veins.'

'What else do they say?'

'The visitor she mentions is one of our men. The chance
observer may be forgiven for taking her for an adolescent prince.'

'What, an incipient moustache?'

'She sports the attire of a man, going so far as to gird her incipient breasts.'

'You have kept yourself informed! Proceed.'

'She is competent in the saddle, and equally so on elephant back. An instructor of archery has not yet fully recovered from an injury to an upper thigh some months back; her skills have improved since. She is as yet unwed. She is said to seek counsel of her ministers and then follow her own mind.'

'What would you do if I sought your counsel and then did as I pleased?'

'You do already, and yet I don't turn against the hand that protects.'

'You could try. But continue: what about her citizenry?'

'She is well liked. In the parkland behind the palace is a menagerie which commoners may visit for their edification and entertainment. Our observer has seen her in the company of a pet tigress…a cub, admittedly.'

'I trust his extremities are intact. Was he the bearer of this?'

'No, a runner is in attendance. Your response is awaited.'

'Your thoughts on the matter?'

'May I remind you that you were fortunate—' He stopped, frowning.

'Not to have been charred alive?' Narasimha completed. 'She was a child then. This is…different.'

'There is little to be gained from mending the ripped skin of a serpent.'

'I'll bear that in mind. However…' He turned to the Scrivener who was arranging and rearranging his reeds and nibs. 'Assure the lady that I shall grant due consideration of her request.'

The Secretary shook his head. 'But—'

'And one more thing. A gift of stationery might be appreciated. Some of the paper from Chin, perhaps, which we use so rarely?'

The Scrivener smiled. 'How much shall we send, Excellence?'

'Enough for it not to reach in shreds.' To the Secretary he said, 'Refresh my memory. I recall we travelled first to Parijatapuri and thence to Cadambagiri. That is correct?'

The Sovereign was always correct. 'That is correct.'

'Good. And we returned here directly after the…incident. How many days did we journey back?'

'Ten, I believe. The roads have been improved since.' He could see where this was leading. 'Her runner took seven with this.' He reached for the letter to put it away.

'No, leave that be. If we're done here now, I should like to be left alone awhile.'

∼

The Consort was not overtly surprised by a visit from her husband. It wasn't every day that the two met. The visits, unannounced, were his way of acknowledging her remedies and also her existence.

From the start, this former princess of Malwa and the prince to whom she was given in marriage had nothing in common—the true secret of marital bliss—by way of diversions and interests. Notwithstanding their ideal state, the marriage of four years was as yet unconsummated. Her cycle had begun the moment she'd entered the nuptial bed; it had scared him—enough to not return to it. Days turned to weeks, to months. She was happy to accept a co-wife, she told him one day, so long as she herself wasn't put out of doors or, worse, retained but shabbily treated.

He hadn't jumped at the suggestion. His initial disenchantment with his lot had turned to cool indifference. The production of an heir could wait; until then, he would live dangerously and continue to expand Kalinga's influence.

Under no pressure to curtail her own interests, and safe in the knowledge that some day, somehow, something would change, the Consort had immersed herself in a study of astronomy. The heavens, for all their dark distant mysteries, were a less complicated realm than that of humans with all their failings.

Celestial bodies, unlike earthbound beings, were reliable entities: ever watchful, omnipresent, unfailing in their abilities to enchant and intrigue, even when clouds conspired to obscure them from sight. Although the Consort followed every ritual prescribed by the palace priests, she had deduced quite early that shooting stars and eclipses were natural occurrences, not portents of famine, pestilence and earthquakes as they would have her believe. So too the moon's waxing and waning, which governed not only the Kushabhadra's tides and the germination of seeds but also the subtle workings of her body and mind. These views she prudently kept to herself, for it served little to propound them. Aside from keeping her occupied, astronomy, not astrology, provided the Consort a grip on her reality. Her observatory—she practically lived there—comprised an airy hall and its adjoining terraces in the uppermost storey of the palace.

The indigo-black ceiling was worked in silver-leaf as an accurate constellation map; along the cornices floated the Nine Planets in their chariots and the Guardians of the Eight Quarters on their cloud-elephants. The walls, where such existed between twelve tall window openings, were painted as an almanac and were repainted annually. At each window stood a sighting tube and a stand for a ledger and writing instruments. An enormous celestial-globe (the gift of an envoy of Zhào Yún) dominated the floor of the observatory. The Consort and her assistants were gathered around a table nearby, twittering and chattering over a new water-clock, when Narasimha arrived, unannounced, and paused outside the doorway.

The women were as yet unaware of his presence. The lone male figure among them, also twittering and chattering, was an orphaned cousin of the Consort who had fallen out of the sky some years ago…and stayed. The very sight of this timorous and studiedly unkempt young man unfailingly inspired in Narasimha a fierce loathing. Someone, presumably the youth himself, had crowned his wayward curls with a woodflower wreath. Oh, to strike that odious face, thought Narasimha, stepping inside.

The Consort's assistants took flight at the sight of him, only to resume their twittering the moment they exited from a different doorway; soon their voices faded to silence. Only the cousin, stuck mid-flight by some vestige of manliness, stood jittering from foot to foot like a drop of water on a hot skillet. Ignoring the Consort and him, Narasimha walked past the celestial-globe, giving it a twirl as he passed; it hummed to life like a giant bee. The Consort followed her husband with her eyes, at the same time gesturing to her cousin to make himself scarce.

An open arch at the far end gave onto a broad terrace, arranged with sundry contrivances of the Consort's hobby. The obsidian gnomon in a limestone sundial cut a sharp shadow between eleven and twelve. Narasimha's stomach growled; he turned and walked back inside.

The Consort didn't ask if his cold was gone: she could see it had. He didn't express gratitude: he never did. 'I came to ask,' he began, 'whether the stars and planets augur well. Any eclipses on the horizon that we must guard against?'

He was teasing her—her thoughts on astrology. She would indulge him. 'Extremely well,' she said. 'And not an eclipse in sight, lunar or solar, for the next twelvemonth. All the planets are calm and contented. You may rest easy.'

'Which is just as well, for I've asked Parijatapuri to visit. Let us lay on a fine treat for him.'

What opinion she had of his friend, she kept to herself. 'A fine treat involves effort and time. How many days have I?'

'Anticipate a fortnight; although he may well arrive any moment.'

'Has he nothing in Parijatapuri to keep him occupied?'

He laughed. 'And do let us try to be civil.'

'I am indifferent to him... As he is to me.'

'How does this work?' he asked, taking up the smallest of the nested copper bowls of the clepsydra and bouncing it from hand to hand. 'Light as a feather!'

'Mind you don't drop it. We fill the large one with water and float the small ones in it. Each has a hole in its base; the water gets drawn in.'

He held the little bowl up to the light. 'Ah, yes…I see it. What happens then?'

'It fills with water over a given length of time. And then it sinks.'

'Of course.' It made no sense. He replaced the bowl in its stack. To fill a small silence, he said, 'And…you are happy?'

'Happy?'

'Yes, happy. You are, are you not?'

'I do not understand.'

'A simple enough question. Yes, or no.'

'I could have been worse off I believe…' She stiffened. 'Why do you ask this? Is it the Turk again? Is it why you've asked Parijatapuri—'

He held up a hand. 'Still your imagination. It's nothing of the sort. My poor friend, I understand, is in sore need of entertainment. The least I can do is provide him some…*and* keep him out of mischief awhile. Ah, I *am* hungry; are you lunched as yet?'

'I shall, presently.'

'And do have his chambers prepared. He might bide with us longer this time.' With that, he walked to the doorway from which her assistants had taken flight, trying to remember where it led.

A long passage with windows all the way down the right side. The figure lurking there couldn't very well turn around and flee; it attempted instead to become one with the wall to the left.

'Slithering about as usual?' Narasimha said, affably. 'What *are* you? A gecko or a man?'

The cousin, a woodflower petal remaindered in his hair, simpered and batted his eyelashes: 'I was going in to ask if my cousin was desirous of anything.'

'*Desirous!*' He moved past with an exasperated snort but stopped and turned: 'Tell me…what *is* it that you do here, exactly?'

He simpered again. 'Nothing.'

Narasimha shuddered inwardly. But having started: 'Have you no better use for yourself than to while away your days in the company of women? Have you no male friends to sport or converse with?'

'Some have me for their comfort at night. By day, the ladies seek me for my wit. For everything else, I am quite useless.'

His frown deepened. 'It takes years of dedication to claim true uselessness. How much longer do you propose to hone your talent in the shelter of my palace?'

'You jest with me, cousin. You know I have nowhere else to go.'

'I shall temper my wit.' How must it feel to be so feckless? 'But tell me. Where do you see yourself a year hence? Two years? Ten?'

It was the first time anyone, much less the Sovereign, had posed such a thing of him. He shuffled his feet, found the broken petal in his hair and plucked it out of sight.

'Answer me. Have you no wish to better yourself? How old are you?'

'Seventeen, I believe.'

'*Seventeen!* At your age—' He stopped. It was the sort of thing his father would have said, and in that very tone of voice. 'Come now,' he said, 'you must have some desire to better yourself; everyone does, even the servants.'

He took a step forward. 'Since you ask, it is my greatest desire to see the world, which they say is a very large place. Alas, I am unqualified for any trade or craft.'

'You are lettered, are you not?'

'Alas, beyond the alphabet, I was denied an education by my orphaned circumstances. In compensation I possess a sweet singing voice which provides my ladies much delight. Also, a sentry of my acquaintance has presented me a flute upon which I play some melodies of my own composition. Would you like me to play for you or sing?'

'That will not be necessary.' Even the most useless of creatures had its uses. 'Go to the Second Secretary first thing in the morning. You have until then to bid farewell to your women.'

He let out a little wail. 'Am I to be *evicted*? Cousin, I assure you—'

'Cease your whinging. Given your way with the ladies, you should be well suited for what I have in mind. You'll receive your orders from the Second Secretary. Before submitting yourself to him, make sure you are bathed and correctly attired, none of your…' He made a circling gesture about his head. 'Go now, ask your cousin for some soap-oil and pomade.'

3

PARIJATAPURI

THE NIGHT-BLOOMING JASMINES WERE SHEDDING THEIR summer foliage on to the flagstones of a terrace. Moving crab-like on their haunches, two maidservants in yellow swept the leaves into mounds of brittle brown and grey. The *swish-swish* of their brooms drifted with the dust into an enclosing gallery. On a daybed there sat the Crown Princess of Parijatapuri, gravid for the third time, nursing a jade-green bowl of ice and pomegranate.

The first time round, she'd craved candied ginger with pomelo wedges; the second, raw mango and tamarind. The cravings this time were the most desperate, rendering her foul-mouthed and exhausted, until the Oracle had suggested ice to calm her fires. So it was that a quotidian supply made its way to the basement of the palace where it was stored and prepared for Her Radiance.

There lived, her father-in-law the Raja had said, a tribe of Himalayan men who moved without the ground ever touching their feet. Toiling by night, these men leapt about though the air, quarrying blocks of glacial ice, which other members of the tribe transported on their backs in tight coils of hay. Packed into the bottom of boats on the Ganges, the precious cargo made its way into warehouses downriver where it lay in beds of rice husk layered with crushed salt and more hay. From the warehouses to the markets, the blocks—only slightly diminished—travelled by night in special carriages. They were fortunate, the Raja said, that an agent of the trade had a cousin in the citadel. That Her Radiance devoured the cold miracle so avidly was doubtless a sign that she was laden this time with a hot-blooded man-child.

Himalayan ice, indeed. The stuff, one of her maidservants had let slip, came from a field less than a mile north of the citadel, where shallow earthenware pans of boiled water were set out in beds of wet straw to freeze overnight. But her father-in-law's fiction was the least of her worries. A month into the pregnancy, the Oracle had privately predicted another princess. Although she had little faith in the old wretch, she had purchased his silence with a jar of frankincense: if it indeed turned out to be another female, third time unlucky, she would be obliged to concede her title and accept a co-wife. Already, she had a plan in motion to forestall that execrable prospect.

If only, she wished (and not for the first time), the production of parasites were a less cumbersome thing. If only, from regulating how much or how little heat they received, she could ordain their gender without having to rely on fate. If only they could be reared in a bowl on dribbles of pap as though they were tadpoles and fry. Unlike her servants, she hadn't once miscarried. Yet the present pregnancy was the most trying. Her teeth had become yellow and pitted; she could scarcely wield a comb without uprooting her scalp in hanks; the backs of her calves had turned the colour and texture of monitor-lizard skin. She was constantly thirsty, and having drunk, needed to make water immediately. Her flesh felt as though it were broiling from the inside; the ice helped but—

A piercing squeal cut through the air. She looked up sharply.

Her two little princesses had been brought out to the terrace to be oil-bathed. Glistening brown scraps, it was a wonder their bones didn't snap under their nursemaids' hands. Another squeal, part-pleasure, part-pain. Piglets, she thought, narrowing her eyes: one day, you too will sit bloated like water-skins, waiting to discharge your ungrateful contents. She tried to lie back, but none of her parts seemed to behave. Her maidservant, crouched like a monkey by the daybed, adjusted a cushion under the small of her back; it felt like its silk-cotton stuffing had been replaced with wet sand. Thrusting it aside, she lay propped up on her elbows with the bowl balanced on the swell of her belly.

Watching the girls, she felt a wave of nausea which a piece of ice quickly assuaged. Much as she was loath to admit it, the first-born bore a chilling resemblance to her aunt in Cadambagiri. 'God's way of ensuring I will never forget,' she said to herself, grinding down the ice. When they were a little older, 'I too had a sister,' she would say, 'who was black as evil and ugly as filth. Jealous that your father chose me over her to marry, she set fire to my bridal chamber and thence to my father's palace. But fear not, her shade will never cross the threshold of this palace.'

The older child sensed she was being watched and tried to squirm free of her nursemaid. 'Hurry, there, you hags!' the Crown Princess shrilled. 'Do you wish them to shrivel in the sun like yourselves?' To the servant, hovering with a peacock-feather fan at the foot of the bed, 'Cool me, harlot! Can you not see I am burning?'

The bowl on her stomach rose and fell with her breath. She twiddled and pointed her toes, felt the tension drain from her calves and knees. The breeze from the fan balmed her feet. Playing her fingers through the fast-melting ice, she lay back and stared up at the ceiling.

A gecko was fused to a beam directly overhead. She hoped it would not come unstuck as geckos were wont to without warning. What was the associated ill-omen of having a gecko fall on one's face? On a pregnant stomach…? The gecko clicked cheerfully before darting forward and behind the beam. The Crown Princess shut her eyes.

She must have dozed off: the feathers of the fan were lightly, deliberately, tickling her feet. 'What are you doing?' she moaned, opening her eyes.

The servant had been replaced at some point by her husband. 'Do you wish me to stop?' the Crown Prince teased, trailing the feathers up her shin and lowering himself onto the edge of the bed. She reached for a scarf that was crushed under her back and pulled it across her breasts.

'Modesty becomes you,' the Crown Prince said, massaging her feet.

She propped herself up and studied him. Perhaps it was this light: he seemed to have added a new chin. His chest, once so firm and flat that she could drum her fingers on it, nowadays sagged. Your father, she thought, gets younger by the day and look at yourself.

The Crown Prince stopped massaging her feet and lifted the bowl off its perch. 'I've had an invitation from Narasimha to vacation awhile. With your permitting it, I could leave next week.'

'Was it not just the other day?'

'Closer to four months,' he said, adding with a wink, 'how could you forget?'

That mid-March night before the morning he had journeyed: that was the last time. He had returned to find she wouldn't have him again lest she miscarried. 'A month as always?' she said.

'Possibly so.' Helping himself to some pomegranate, he held the bowl out to her.

'No… Yes. Feed me.'

He scooped up what was left, shook away the water and held out his hand. How very like a small helpless animal she was: the dark unblinking eyes, the pointed wet tongue darting out and in, the lifeless hair and discoloured teeth. So when she bit, a quick sharp nip, it was to puncture the side of his hand. He snatched it back with a yelp, scattering the ruby arils.

She calmly picked off the most accessible ones, popping them one by one into her mouth. 'I suppose,' she said, 'your darling Narasimha is privy by now to the *other* thing?'

'You're insane!' he cried, staunching the blood on an edge of his dhoti. 'Why did you do this?'

'You tell him everything. And if you haven't already, that too will slip out in some fraternal moment of intimacy. Knowing him, he'll use it to advantage.'

He stared at her stupefied. All she did these days was plot ways to dislodge her sister from the throne of Cadambagiri. He was tired of being caught up in the affair; his own involvement had been to respond on her behalf to a muddled correspondence from a band of Cadambagirian courtiers who, clearly, had too much time on their hands. He could do with some respite from it; Narasimha's invitation couldn't have been better timed. 'He is my friend,' he said, inspecting the side of his palm which had begun to throb painfully.

'*He is my friend*,' she mocked him. 'Your friend can wait. I've done my bit, it's for you to strike before it's too late.'

He looked away.

Across the terrace, their oil-baths done, his daughters were being bundled into towels by their nursemaids. The idea of a massage was tempting but a servant was clearing away the oil jars and mats. 'Too late,' he mumbled and at once regretted it, for she rose off the bed and sent the bowl flying from his hands to the floor, where it sullenly broke into pale green shards.

'*Think!*' she said, stabbing a forefinger to his forehead. 'Everything is in place. Her men will put up no resistance...and you dare speak of vacationing? Is it *mud* you have for a brain? The one chance I have—' She broke off, snapping her fingers in the air.

'It is your urgency I fail to understand,' he said in a placatory way. From where she stood, she could easily render his manhood untold damage.

Her entire demeanour changed instantly and she dropped to her knees between his. 'Oh, my love, did it hurt very much?' she said, taking his hand and placing her mouth to the bite in a way that was at once tender yet troubling. 'I'm doing this for our security... You *must* trust me.'

'We are secure here, are we not?' he said carefully.

'Not if I bear a daughter again. You know what will be expected of you. Come what may, I will *not* let that happen.'

'But you said...'

'*If* it is a daughter.' Her voice hardened. 'I cannot see what is growing inside, can I? But leave that be; if it is true that my beloved sister is friendly with infidels, it cannot be without vested design. If she were to give herself to any one of them, my greatest concern is that Parijatapuri will be imperilled and not all of your father's troops will be any match for their cavalries. Now do you understand my anxiety?'

It finally dawned on him. She'd sooner kill herself than assume the role of a complaisant co-wife: her only alternative was Cadambagiri...but not while her sister occupied the throne there. But what if it were a boy? What if she miscarried? What if she were to die in childbed? Whatever the outcome, she seemed determined to claim Cadambagiri for herself.

She stayed kneeling, his hand in hers limp as a rag. 'Say something, my precious.'

A nerve had started to twitch in his left eyelid. Bad luck, they say. 'Why do you hate her so?' he said quietly.

'*Why*?' She seemed surprised. 'Because she is happy. That is why.'

'And how...what do you propose to...to do with her?'

'The dungeons I'm told are still fecund with porcupines.' She giggled. 'Do you remember that time I misplaced her in that labyrinth?'

He remembered the labyrinth. 'You *are* serious about this,' he said.

'We've been over it a hundred times,' she said in a wheedling voice. 'All you need is a loan of troops from Father; nothing extravagant, just enough to put on a show and with you in the lead. Can you not picture it?' Her eyes gleamed. 'There will be no casualties on our side, on that point I have her ministers' assurance. You will be victorious and Father will be overjoyed. Your first military campaign!'

He shook his head. 'He will never agree to it.'

'But you haven't asked him. Must I do that as well?'

'You know I cannot lie to him.'

She got back to her feet and sitting by his side, played with a curl of hair which had escaped his turban at the nape of his neck. 'Perhaps you must go to Kataka after all,' she said. 'Yes... perhaps it is for the best that you tell Narasimha everything.'

He stole a side glance. 'A moment ago you feared he'd use it to his advantage.'

'Not if you exercise invention and tact. That she consorts with Muslims may have reached him. If it hasn't, supply that detail and hence your urgency to safeguard your late father-in-law's country. That should get him suitably excited. You may add that she is unsound of mind...' She paused, biting a side of her lip. 'Yes... If you do this for me, I promise you the next one I carry will be prince. We shall make it as soon as I've anointed you Raja of Cadambagiri.'

At this, Parijatapuri felt a chill run through his being. It was bad enough having to inherit the title of Raja of Parijatapuri someday; he had no desire to compound his cares as Raja of Cadambagiri. All he wanted was to be left alone—to peruse the old tomes which filled the library, to pay the occasional visit to his Kataka kin, and to sire countless children for he adored the little beings and it mattered not a bit to him if they were girls or boys. That was the sum of his desires. The woman seated beside him thought very differently; he had heard the germ of madness lurked in all beings, waiting for the right conditions to come skittering to life like some monstrous centipede. He attempted to stand but she restrained him with a hand on his thigh. He stiffened, lest she turned violent again.

'That's settled, then,' she breathed, following some private train of thought. Her grip lightened. 'Now promise me. You will return before this *thing* comes bawling.'

He nodded. It was all he could do to keep her happy.

'I want to hear you say it.'

'I promise.'

A strange look flitted like a shadow across her face. 'My love,' she breathed, reaching into his dhoti.

Any other time, his loins might have responded with alacrity. She withdrew her hand. 'Go, then,' she said with a sneer, 'and send someone with more ice.'

~

Adopted at the age of twelve, the Crown Prince was the son of a Kalinga general and a courtesan attached to Kataka Palace. By privilege of birth, he was raised in the company of a true prince and other children of high rank. A year older than he, Narasimha had chosen him for his particular friend. Presenting the air that they were blood siblings, the boys had grown up sharing much by way of experiences: from a healthy rivalry in archery and horsemanship, to vying for the affections of their tutors of history, languages and the sciences; from comparing notes on pliant young ladies to charting their grandest aspirations for the future of mankind.

The demise of his father the general was the first upheaval in an otherwise halcyon adolescence. His mother, in the interests of herself and her boy, had quickly effected a move to have him adopted. Her most favoured candidate was a neighbouring ruler whose Rani had suffered a string of miscarriages before taking her own life.

The Raja of Parijatapuri had not remarried. Conveniently for him, the boy offered up for adoption was blessed with any number of admirable qualities. He was pleasing to the eye. Soft-spoken and biddable, he carried himself well. He was manly yet diffident. A bit more grooming and a suitable alliance in marriage, he'd make a fitting heir to the throne of Parijatapuri. All else aside, Parijatapuri owed Kalinga generations of allegiance; the adoption would serve to strengthen these ties. The Raja was only too happy to consider the Courtesan's scheme.

The transaction thereafter was quickly formalized, complete with the blessings of Kalinga Senior. But it was the break from Kalinga Junior which, for the second time in his life, shook the newly anointed Crown Prince's confidence. If separation from

his mother and his best friend weren't bad enough, the palace
of Parijatapuri was reputed to be haunted by unborn babies, and
the adoptive parent proved to be cold and distant. The adoptee
more than once tried ending his life, but each time realized how
his death would sadden the people he had left behind in Kataka.
As luck would have it, the adoption device permitted him to visit
Kataka twice annually for as long as his birth-mother was alive.
As part of the same device, the Courtesan had secured herself
a riverside palace, modest by Kataka standards, and from it
inducted new aspirants to her artistic lineage.

With Narasimha inheriting his father's empire in 1238,
Parijatapuri Junior had felt more secure in his own position
as a prince-by-proxy: it was common knowledge that the new
Sovereign of Kalinga and he remained close as bandits. Granted,
his visits to Kataka were less frequent ever since he'd got married;
but because Narasimha and he so regularly corresponded, the
revival of conversation was effortless when they met. If only, now,
he didn't feel this terrible foreboding from what his princess had
demanded of him.

Whereas a different man might have firmly bade his wife
to stop her nonsense, Parijatapuri Junior had repaired to his
apartments and remained there for the rest of the morning.
Contrary to routine, he did not lunch with his adoptive parent
and, claiming indigestion, twice refused the trays sent upstairs.
Nor did he spend the evening in the library, poring over a family
tree for a *History* he was penning of his adoptive clan. Hunger
gnawing at his insides, he lay now in darkness in his bed—unable
to sleep from the makings of a headache.

From his princess's apartments across the terrace, the
strains of a lute seeped through the clammy night—always the
same plangent melody, always the same garbling of notes in a
particular phrase. The music no doubt lulled his wife to sleep,
but its effect on him worked the opposite; there was no door
to seal out the hateful lament. If he had his way, he'd have the

player exiled—first amputated—but the lutanist, like the ice, was a gift. His head felt like it might split any moment like a coconut. Burying it in his pillow only aggravated the pain. Just when he thought he might actually die of it, the infernal playing ceased. He held his breath. A string twanged once, as the lute was put aside for the night.

In the ensuing black silence, Parijatapuri lay still, counting his heartbeats. At last sleep seemed to favour him…but only for an instant. In the image which floated unbidden under his eyelids, his princess and his father were seated on a swing, dandling an infant between them.

Parijatapuri had never claimed great intelligence, relying instead on a mystic other-sense which rarely failed him. Shooting out of bed with a throttled cry, he hastened to a small side chamber where his gods resided. A stock of stationery was always on hand here for the aphorisms which sometimes came to him in the course of worship. Tonight was different. In the flickering glow of a lamp, he composed a message which would make sense only to its intended recipient. His hand still smarted from the bite; the stylus barely grazed the palm-leaf. It was up to Narasimha to rub in some lampblack to reveal the writing: *crow is in cuckoo's nest | night-flowering jasmine bears datura seeds | when the moon starts to wane | lamb must rush to lion's side.*

Back in his bed chamber and working in darkness, he twisted the leaf into a tight cylinder and slid it into an old bamboo flute, plugging the end with a lump of beeswax. From an ivory box, next, he counted out some cowries. With the flute and the cowries, he crept out of his apartments and, keeping to the shadows, made his way down a dark stairway to a rear exit of the palace.

The sentries there, huddled over their hemp pipes, scrambled to their feet at the intrusion into their night, and then stood at ease on recognizing the prince's shape. He sent one of the men to fetch a runner. Pacing the galleries and trembling with anxiety, he almost changed his mind but the sentry returned almost at once with another man.

'To Kataka in haste,' Parijatapuri whispered, handing the runner the flute and the cowries—payment to six runners, beginning with this one, for the relay they must complete in as many days.

4

CADAMBAGIRI

A FORTNIGHT FOLLOWING HER LETTER TO NARASIMHA, THE Sovereign lady of Cadambagiri received a dispatch which she believed at first had been misdirected.

The square camphor-wood box was wide as her forearm and as deep. Stuck to the underside of the lid, a small palm-leaf engraving depicted a god riding an elephant. On closer inspection, a line of minuscule script revealed the personage to in fact represent the Kalinga Sovereign. Inside the box, a square of purple silk patterned in gold threads with winged serpents spewing flames enclosed a wad of blank paper squares. The buttery sheets wafted a fragrance of rice-water and dry jasmine. A separate pouch—black silk, silver dragonflies—spilled an assortment of writing reeds. The accompanying note assured the Sovereign of Narasimha's consideration of her request and begged her continue her correspondence by means of this gift of Chinese provenance.

All morning, the box sat on the Sovereign's desk with the lid propped up to display Narasimha's graven image. Waiting for a court artist to ready a reciprocal gift, the Sovereign practiced her writing. The shift from stylus on birch-bark to reed on paper was by no means easy. For one thing, she needed to temper the pressure of her hand. For another, her indigo ink tended to spread; a knife's-edge of cinnabar stabilized and turned it a satisfying mulberry-black.

The artist was ushered in. The small, circular painting showed a garlanded figure riding a tiger and holding an elephant-goad and a crucible of flames. The faces of the tiger and rider were rendered in profile yet both sets of eyes were shown (in the Cadambagiri style) as though the further ones had swum through the air to meet their respective pairs. The Sovereign asked for a runner to be on hand for an imminent dispatch:

Salutations king | Our grateful thanks for your missive and gracious gift which we now take delight in employing to this reply | We write with a poultice binding an ankle for we an accident did suffer this morning in the course of riding our favourite elephant | Arkasodhara by name and twenty summers of age the beast has remained our companion since our infancy | It is our habit to venture at dawn each day upon this elephant onto the parkland behind our palace for some moments of quiet | Our pleasant routine today was interrupted when our mount came to an inexplicable standstill and no coaxing would have him take a step forth or back | The reason for this mischief became clear when we leant forward over his head to espy in the grass at his feet the nest of a wild boar wherein the absent parent had secreted four piglets evenly small and striped | As we marvelled at our mount for stopping short of trampling the nest one of the piglets ventured forth to investigate the presence before it | At this our elephant emitted a sound more suited to a rat before backing two paces and then sideways and away at speed causing us to lose our place and drop from a great height | Only then did the wretch stop to retrieve us from whence we had cascaded | Unable to fully remount for the pain we were obliged to return to the palace borne upon his ivories | We recount to you this episode with the image of yourself on your own noble mount before our eyes | In reciprocation of that image pray accept one of ourself | With the assurance that we no longer employ fire to express our sentiments…

5

KATAKA

BECAUSE HE WAS RUNNING AWAY, PARIJATAPURI TRAVELLED
light this time, accompanied by two mounted servants and
a spare mount for himself. Rather than impose on sundry
collectors along the way, the party stopped in rude resthouses
where their plain appearance drew little notice. The week's
journey passed without incident. On the last afternoon, one of
the servants rode ahead.

The moon was high by the time Parijatapuri and the other
man arrived at the citadel gate. A file of travellers waited at it:
a new ruling required outsiders to furnish their credentials in
order to gain admittance. It wasn't a long file and it did appear
to be moving; nevertheless, Parijatapuri trotted to the head to
investigate, only to be sent back to the tail end. Peeved at being
denied preferential treatment, he made a mental note to bring
the matter to Narasimha's notice: while the intentions behind
the inconvenience were no doubt worthy, a more *practical*
mind would have assigned a separate checkpoint for visitors of
eminence such as himself.

He was still bristling when it was his turn at the gate. From
his saddle, he wordlessly held out his left hand, the little finger
of which flashed a gold signet ring. An inheritance from his
late father the general's estate, the ring was embossed with
the Kalinga ensign of a leaping lion over a couchant elephant.
The sentries took their time, turning the hand that wore it this
way and that while squinting and muttering. To compound
Parijatapuri's annoyance, he was allowed to pass without so much
as a bow of deference; his servant, waiting on the other side, had
been afforded more genial treatment. 'The working classes,' he
consoled himself. 'And so much for security: we could easily be
a footpad and his henchman who've waylaid a Kataka nobleman

and divested him of his horses and ring.' But, he reasoned in the same vein: what self-respecting footpad would ride into the citadel by way of the principal gate? More worryingly, had his other servant got past that officious set? Preoccupied now with the reception which may—or more likely not—await him, he followed a little way behind the spare mount and servant.

Sprawled east-west on the north bank of the Kushabhadra, Kataka's maze of streets fanned down to the river like a fishnet cast from the brick ramparts of the palace. The half-timbered houses lining the streets were asleep in the moonlight, not a glint from their windows to suggest they were occupied. Aside from three sets of hooves clip-clopping through the stillness, the only signs of life were sewer rats as large as cats and a drunk at a crossroads haranguing himself.

At long last they arrived at the gatehouse of a tree-filled estate, where a eunuchoid guardsman dragging an overweight leopard on a chain seemed more than a little put out at being roused from his sleep. Yes, His Eminence's servant had reached ahead of him; his own arrival was awaited.

In the forecourt of a small palace between the trees, six fillies at the hitching posts stood snorting softly into their fodder-bags. Persians, Parijatapuri noted, dismounting: their owners must be men of means. His own native geldings were led away by his servant. As he stood chafing his hands, a figure shielding a lantern hurried over from the dark hunk of the building. It was the second servant. A muted greeting; he followed the man down a shrub-lined path to the privies, first, and then into a rear courtyard. At the bathhouse there, an elderly eunuch helped him undress.

The scalding water, alternated with cold, shocked the aches out of Parijatapuri's joints. Shampooed and scrubbed, and then dried and laid down on a heated stone slab, he submitted himself to be stretched and pummelled—too pleasantly numbed to rise to the eunuch's arch observations on how he had aged. All too soon, he found himself wrapped in a fresh dhoti and shawl and released back into the night. At the rear door of the little palace, a different eunuch welcomed him with a jasmine garland and a dab of sandalwood paste to his forehead.

Upstairs, the chamber readied for Parijatapuri was perfumed with frankincense; the censer smouldering in a corner did little to repel the mosquitoes that whined and sang about his head. He removed the garland and sat at the edge of the bed.

Closing his eyes, Parijatapuri felt strangely comforted by a wave of melancholy. He let it wash over him; slowly lowering himself sideways, he drew his legs up and lay curled like a baby. A harsh crackle of laughter cut through the quiet from somewhere close by. He strained to listen—a snatch of conversation, a cry of distress—but the night had fallen silent again. Presently, a maidservant entered bearing a tray.

He would have preferred a bowl of curd and rice to the warm roundel of bread and tall tumbler of almond milk. But he was only a guest here and to fuss at this late hour would be unseemly. He ate quickly, using the bread to soak up the cloying sweetness. There was no danger here of ever being poisoned; nonetheless he finished the meal with a pod of cardamom from his personal supplies. He was about to turn in when the maidservant reappeared to say his mother desired to see the moon of his face before she retired.

All that Parijatapuri desired was to sink into a deep dreamless sleep. But better now than in the morning: he would lie in late before moving to Narasimha's palace. Collecting a small gold box from his things, he followed the girl down a warren of dimly-lit passages and stairways.

∼

The Hall of Enchantment was a confusion of lanterns and standard lamps, smouldering brass censers and gilded birdcages full of sleeping finches. A brocaded green silk fan creaked from the ceiling. A party of lutes, zithers and drums had collapsed like tired friends by a central platform where a dancer, or dancers, had shed crushed jasmines from garlands. The floor mattresses nearby still bore the impressions of a recent audience—a rowdy one, clearly, from the toppled wine cups and scattered platters of betel leaves. Perched on its stand in a corner, a dusty grey parrot slept with its head buried in its breast. To the left, on a couch piled with bolsters and cushions, Parijatapuri's mother sat cross-legged, staring vacantly into space. Two tall lamps on either side heightened the impression that one had wandered into the presence of a living goddess. Like offerings to a goddess, a tray of assorted sweetmeats gleamed wetly from a footstool in her reach.

The good life had settled about the Courtesan, rendering her appearance that of an outsized gourd with the face of a beautiful infant. Her hair was assembled as a mountainscape of tiered coils and ringlets from which had sprung a jewelled garden of clasps and pins. Two gold parakeets dangled from her ears. A large vermilion dot adorned her forehead. Her bright dark eyes, outlined and exaggerated to the sides with antimony, had a way of disappearing when she smiled. They disappeared now as she threw her arms out like a child asking to be picked. 'My lamb!' she trilled. 'Come sit, my sovereign!'

'You may have a long wait before you address me as sovereign,' Parijatapuri said gruffly, sliding down by her side and making a cushion of her shoulder for his head. But only for a moment, for her signature musk perfume barely concealed the underlying whiff of sweat and urine. He felt a twinge of guilt for having caught it. 'I see you are well?' he said, sitting away.

A playful shove. 'Not a word for three months and...*phat!* you show up when you please!'

'You love a surprise. Here...careful; it is full to the lip.'

The previous visit, he had brought her a basket of custard-apples—the first of that season from his personal orchard, picked at that particular stage of firmness so they may ripen to perfection as they journeyed. Tonight's gift was different—more precious than the gold of the box in which it nested.

She opened it, her eyes twinkling on him and then down at the contents. 'Ah, saffron! Bless you, my jewel! Enough to bathe myself in!'

'There is something else inside.'

She giggled, reaching a little finger through the stamens. It encountered hardness; she eased out a ruby the size of a pigeon's egg, spilling some of the saffron. Assessing the stone against the lamplight, she held it between her thumb and forefinger to her forehead. 'Like this?'

The effect was hideous. 'Perfect,' he replied.

'Mother is glad,' she said, returning the egg to its nest and tucking the box out of sight. 'I shall send for the jeweller first thing in the morning.' Reaching for his right hand, she began stroking it as though it were a small furry thing. Her own hands were soft, dimpled and sparkled with rings. She traced the lines of his palm with a painted fingernail and said, 'I hear your good wife is once again with child.'

Mother knew everything. He didn't respond at once and then only by way of a shrug and a sigh. She laughed, clapping her hand to his. 'So it *is* true what they say! My precious boy *has* been busy! And when is she due?'

He flinched. 'In five months, I believe.'

'Marvellous! I hear her little sister has been busy as well.'

He stiffened. 'What?'

'No, no! That's not what I mean. Although it might well come to *that* in time.' She leant forward conspiratorially: 'I hear your sister-by-marriage and Narasimha are engaged nowadays in an *intimate* correspondence.'

A blow to the chest couldn't have winded him more effectively. A sensation he couldn't control peeled his lips back in a rictus. 'No...how...? It cannot be...'

'Why ever not? My source is most reliable. As reliable as his stylus, as we like to say.'

It took a great effort of will to keep his voice level; it came out sharp and high, 'Your babbling makes no sense to me.'

'Hardly *babbling*. His clerk mentioned it the last time he visited.'

'His *clerk*? You mean his secretary?'

'No, no, the other one…the half-breed.'

'The scrivener?'

'One and the same thing, methinks. A shame we no longer see him as frequently; the girls are muchly enamoured of his silver tongue and smiles and uncapped tool of rare magnificence. Methinks he has acquired some regular comfort for it directly at the palace and little needs must venture our way. I'll have you know it—'

'*Enough*,' he cut her off sharply. 'This correspondence, if you please. I don't have all night to waste on this nonsense.'

'My, my!' she said, her eyebrows darting up in peaks. 'That tone of voice will elicit no more than I've said. If you don't wish to learn of the circumstances, so be it.'

He bit his lip. 'Forgive me, Mother; I did not mean to offend. Pray proceed.'

She reached for the platter of sweetmeats and selected a pinkish-brown spheroid, patchily glazed in crystalized syrup. 'Taste? They call these Monkey Nuts. My favourite.'

He declined; any other time, he might have done, even making a joke of it.

'Suit yourself.' She bit in and slowly masticated. 'Ah, divine. Now where were we? Yes… So, the half-breed appeared one evening to reclaim a scarf he had gifted one of his favourites. Saying he had to go in haste, he gave the girl a rope of pearls in its stead…Basra, no less, strung between gold seeds, mind, not glass beads. A most generous substitute, I thought at the time; he must have *really* needed it back.' A pause. 'Go on, indulge; we live but just once in this cruel realm.'

'The correspondence, Mother.'

'Patience! I am coming to it! Seeing as he was torn between a poke and having to hurry, we pressed him to tarry a while but he parried, claiming a prior engagement at which I jested, Ah, I knew it! another princess, whereupon he fell about in mirth, recovering enough to declare, Yes, yes! another princess, and none other than the *sister-in-law of your birth prince*. Imagine my astonishment! Whatever can you mean? I said, at which he cried, No, no! still your evil mind, he had only to dispatch to that sovereign lady a response from our Sovereign to her most curious epistle of that morning. With that, he took himself off, leaving his favourite dry that night.'

'That was all he said?'

She chucked him under the chin. 'That was all. But enough methinks.' A broad wink. 'I have it from a certain *other* source that your lady of Cadambagiri is as yet unmated. And of course, *our* good queen remains maiden still. A man has his needs, how much longer must *he* be kept waiting?'

His thoughts were racing. 'Would you perchance recall the date of this visit?'

She made a wet pout of her lips; like the rear end of a pig, he thought cruelly. 'Let me see,' she said at length. 'It has been a while. Hand me that ledger, if you will.'

He obliged. She took her time over the pages, running a finger up and down the figures and names. 'Here. I recall it well, for the previous evening we had the same olibanum merchants who are upstairs tonight. The half-breed paid his visit the following evening. I well recall this, for he remarked on these very sweetmeats the gentlemen upstairs brought us the last time as well.' She set the ledger aside and reached for a yellowish ovoid. 'I forget the name but heavenly…almond and date…oh, *of course*! Turds of Angels.'

He brushed away her hand when she tried feeding him. Popping it whole into her mouth, she licked her thumb and forefinger before commencing to dismantle her hair, placing each jewelled pin and clip in a slotted tray. She then shook out her tresses and, in a practiced flick, caused two thick hanks to settle upon her bosom like the wings of some giant insect.

Watching her, Parijatapuri was transported to a different time—of the two of them sitting just so, but in their apartments at the palace, helping her assemble herself for a formal evening of entertainment. Why did all that have to change?

'You are not fully present,' she said. 'Your mind is preoccupied. Do you wish to talk about it?'

If he opened the door to his fears, they would come stampeding like a herd of wild oxen so this pretence of impassiveness was preferable in all ways. She had once again taken up his hand. 'A bite, of course, but not *that* sort of bite,' she was saying, rubbing a barely perceptible mark on the side. 'A rat? The wife? Some other? Penalty for something you did… or did *not*, more likely?'

'I don't know what you mean,' he snapped, taking back his hand.

She smiled and shook her head. Men and their silly secrets. 'I have always admired your tact. You get that trait from your departed father. So we shall let the matter rest.' She stretched her legs. 'How many days will you bide here before repairing to the palace?'

A bead of sweat was making a cold trail down his side. 'I don't feel very well,' he began, trying to rise and finding his feet impaled by cramp. His vision blurred around the edges. 'With your permission, I must to bed.' He stood—only to reel to the floor in a dead faint.

～

The fever broke on the twelfth day.

He surfaced, drenched in perspiration, bare except for a cloth across his loins, in a strange bed, in a strange room, made stranger still by the clumps of leaves and roots hanging over the bed.

At first he believed he was dead, and not cremated but buried, in the manner of the Muslims, bones turned to sandstone, flesh to velvet, and this was the view from inside his grave. But, he reasoned through addled senses, you are neither Muslim nor dead and in place of earth and stone is this susurrus of pigeons and women…soft-fingered women who bathe your forehead with wet fragrant cloths now cold now hot and declare you are on the mend the worst is past the Sovereign has been informed you are awake but hush now you must…no, don't fight…*must* hold down this gruel—which meant he was alive, albeit woefully weak.

Later, three days later. They moved him to a different chamber where, more fully clothed, he lay in a bed with no canopy-forest of medicinal roots and leaves. Now he knew where he was, but had neither knowledge nor memory of all that had transpired between now and then.

He would never know that his mother had dispatched him in a litter to the palace when she could have attributed his collapse to fatigue and sent him upstairs. He would never know that Narasimha's physicians had worked day and night to ensure he didn't die on them. He would never know that maidservants had uncomplainingly held vessels to his orifices each time they discharged their putrid contents. He would never know that he had babbled unrestrained and someone had recorded his every delirious utterance. He would never know that a royal dispatch to the Sovereign of Cadambagiri had only stated that he was *out of mischief*. Nor would he know that neither Mother nor Narasimha had once visited his sickbed.

The air around him now was bright with blurred figures, flitting silently about like substances in dreams. He tried opening his eyes more fully, but his lashes felt as though they were caked in grit. He drifted back to sleep but the voice at his shoulder was sharp as a whip: 'Up.'

He tried to sit but slouched back. It was awful, the utter indignity of being seen like this. He felt himself being helped. Pillows to his back; a washcloth to his eyes; a sip of water; salve to his lips. He smiled weakly at the figure at the foot of the bed.

Narasimha passed the bowl in his hands to one of the maids.

The porridge of pulses and broken rice was flavoured with turmeric. He ate, almost biting away the maid's fingertips. When he was done, the girl wiped his mouth and chin and touched his lips with more salve. Shortly, it was just Narasimha and him and the cold white light.

Without preamble: 'Your flute conveyed the most curious melody. I was waiting to hear you sing the words but you got busy killing yourself.'

He swallowed hard: 'I apologize for any trouble I may have caused you…and everyone else.'

'I should like to say it has been a joy.' The tone was light. 'Your mother is a sensible woman; we have her to thank for your being alive. But refresh my memory. When did we last speak?'

'You were away at battle when I visited; which means we last met…oh, I don't know when. It seems like an eternity. I missed you. What date have we today?'

'The twentieth of July. Since your arrival, the rain showed its face and blew away. It will be a lean harvest.'

He looked away. 'Wherever I go, ill-luck follows like my shade. I will soon be on my way.'

'Oh. Were you on your way somewhere else?'

'This was all a mistake. The sooner I leave, the better for everybody.'

Narasimha laughed mirthlessly. 'You sought my protection from some terrible thing; now you have it, you speak of leaving. I cannot stop you but I suggest you recover more fully before going.'

'I feel quite recovered already, thank you,' he muttered, easing his legs over the side of the bed. His feet found the floor, and then his slippers. He took a step, tottered, and reached for a bedpost to steady himself.

Narasimha, not demonstrative, misunderstood and neatly side-stepped.

His arms dropped to his sides. 'You hate me, my frailty. I can see it in your eyes.'

Again that laugh. 'I have no time for this infantile prattle. There is much to be done; let's converse when I am back. I am most eager for all your news.' Was that a flicker of a smile? 'In your own words.'

'Will you be long?'

'I shall know that when I reach Chandrabhaga.'

Chandrabhaga. In all these years, Narasimha hadn't once invited him to the temple in progress. He sniffed. 'I trust it wasn't for my sake that you stayed behind.'

'Not at all.'

He could barely stand. 'I should like to go with you...if you can bear my company.'

Narasimha shrugged. 'Very well. Strengthen up, then.'

～

A long slow week of inactivity passed. With no further word about Chandrabhaga, the invalid feared he must have been left behind. On summoning up the courage to make enquiries of the servants, he was assured the Sovereign was very much in residence but otherwise occupied: the houseguest would be informed when they were set to travel.

More or less a prisoner now in this wing of the palace, Parijatapuri spent his waking hours resting and eating, with a regimen of meditation and light exercise to restore his energy and spirits. It was whilst standing on his head one morning that he set eyes, upside-down, on the white cat on the window seat.

The creature had materialized so unexpectedly that Parijatapuri almost lost his balance (which would have doubtless resulted in a broken neck) but managed to remain inverted. For one who didn't care very much for cats, he found himself entranced: unlike the sinister creatures which slunk about his own palace being hostile to humans and devouring rodents, the present example wore an agreeable, even erudite, expression on its slightly squashed face. Indeed, it seemed too elegant, too *refined* to have ever sniffed a rat, let alone hunted for prey.

Because its tail, hanging over the window seat, was so luxuriant, it was hard to tell if it was a girl or boy. From the thoroughness with which it sat washing its face, Parijatapuri surmised it must be female.

Its toilet done, the cat stretched its neck, revealing in the fur a narrow sky-blue tape from which dangled a shiny ornament. It then turned and contemplated the upside-down human.

To see what might happen, Parijatapuri twiddled his toes in the air. At this, the beauty leapt off the window seat and, tail held high, padded up to Parijatapuri and rubbed itself against him, the while making a sound like a rumbling tummy. Delighted by the strange development, Parijatapuri lowered himself so that he was now nose-to-nose with the cat.

The eyes staring back at him were a compelling blue-green—the right one bluer than the left. The ornament on the tape was a little silver bell, muffled by the surrounding lush whiteness. Parijatapuri ventured a finger to stroke it; the cat swatted his hand with its soft fat pads and opened its mouth in a soundless mewl, revealing needle-sharp teeth and a tongue the prettiest shade of pink. Parijatapuri could have gladly remained crouched like this, but the cat moved away to scar the leg of his bed. It then sauntered out of the door with its tail held high and lightly twitching.

Parijatapuri righted himself. Finding his slippers and grabbing a shawl, he followed after the cat—in time to see it dip round the end of the passage and disappear as a froth of white down a dark stairway. Convinced he was being led on some important quest, he felt a shiver of excitement as he took the steps down two at a time and was quite out of breath on reaching the lower level.

The corridor was lined with doors to the left and windows along the right. The cat was seated bolt upright in a slant of sunlight and staring up at a door as if willing it to open itself. Parijatapuri lifted the latch and nudged the door ajar—just

enough for the cat to slip inside. He hadn't meant to push it open
more fully but having done, checked himself from stepping in.

The light filtering into the chamber winked and glinted off
its cluttered appointments of pierced brass lanterns, curtains of
beads, urns of flowers, vases of peacock quills and unfamiliar
gilded objects. Carpets covered the floor and crawled up the
walls; cushions adorned a long low seat with couchant gold
lions for legs. The dark opening of a door to the right was
fronted by a black lacquered screen, inlaid with mother-of-pearl
birds and foliage. Two matching black chairs of similar inlay
sat at a table that was covered with folios, inkwells and jars of
assorted writing implements; a sheaf of papers lay fanned on
the floor underneath. Between the door and the table stood a
tripod of elephant tusks, supporting a large spherical object (of
indeterminate function) composed of greenish copper hoops
and rings. Had Parijatapuri taken a step through the door, he
would have spied an oblong wall-mirror framed in curlicues
of gilt; but because he didn't, he was spared a fright from his
own mottled and etiolated reflection. As it was, his chest was
pounding from a mix of fascination and dread: it was clear as
day that the chamber belonged to Narasimha's half-breed scribe.
It was just as well that he hadn't stepped inside, for heaven knew
what else lurked in its dissipated depths. No sooner did the
thought cross his mind, a draught shifted a bead curtain, setting
off a faint clicking. The white cat had reappeared (he'd forgotten
about it) and leapt onto the table where it arranged itself like
a luminous and vaguely sinister ornament. Lest the half-breed
sprang out next, Parijatapuri took a quick step back, at the same
time pulling the door to and sliding home the latch.

He was trembling. Breathing deeply to calm his nerves,
he recalled the conversation with his mother that night of
his collapse. There was nothing for it: the time had come to
tell Narasimha everything. *Everything*...from the half-breed's
indiscretions at his mother's, to his own desperate flight from

Parijatapuri. Inwardly thanking the cat for catalysing his plan, he set off purposefully but took a wrong turn into a narrow stairwell and thence into a dog-leg passage, and before too long was quite hopelessly lost in an eerily unpeopled wing of the palace.

The floors were thick with bat and bird droppings, the reek of abandonment suspended like dust motes in the brown air. In the shadows, clumps of weeds had struggled through the floorboards and died upon themselves. With the dirt scrunching horribly at every step, Parijatapuri permitted himself to imagine the worst—scorpions, snakes, other fanged vermin—for doing so invariably helped bolster his spirits at times like this when he felt at his most vulnerable and weak. *You'll be stuck here forever,* he told himself. *You won't be missed. You'll perish of thirst and starve to death. Your bones will be found a hundred years hence, when no one will know whose flesh had clothed them; you'll wander these hallways as a restless spirit with only the bats for company and other ghouls such as yourself.* To add to his woes he needed to make water urgently. Selecting a corner of a hallway he emptied himself noisily—ah! the few private pleasures remaining to men—the while studying some murals at eye-level.

The faded brushwork catalogued a variety of coital positions, hard to attempt except for a party of skinks. Under less fraught circumstances and better light, Parijatapuri might have studied the paintings closer; but a cold finger of fear ran down his spine for he knew, intuitively, that he was not alone in the hallway. His flow ran dry. Adjusting his dhoti, he gathered his hands in fists and spun around to confront the presence behind him.

The white cat sat washing its face on a window ledge.

'Oh, you *fearsome* beast!' cried Parijatapuri, laughing and hurrying across the hallway. But the cat was quicker and dove off the ledge. Albeit narrow, the window was not very high. Parijatapuri hitched himself onto the ledge and, squeezing through, let himself down into a sunny courtyard.

He smiled, recognizing a gnarled neem tree rising from a

circular plinth in the middle of the yard. As boys, Narasimha and he had spent many an afternoon in the tree's secret embrace, spying into the surrounding upper-storey apartments. Dappled in its shade, today, were a number of white heifers of the Vamshadhara breed—all of the same height and each sporting a red ear-tag.

The old galleries enclosing the yard, Parijatapuri noted with interest, had been converted to stables, and numbered in red on their lintels. More intriguingly, a length of whitewashed wall to one side was scrawled in charcoal with outsized letters of the Sanskrit alphabet. Half-expecting the yard to suddenly fill with reciting voices, he glanced around; but the heifers seemed disinclined to oblige. 'What whimsy,' he mused, shaking his head, 'to attempt to teach cows to read.'

As he stood there pondering the mystery of the alphabet, one of the heifers skipped over and nudged his hand. He turned to stroke her but was brought up short by a sharp voice: 'Mind, there! You may not touch my damsels!'

His peculiar choice of entrance had been observed by the dark figure in the shadow of the neem. The young man cradling the white cat had a flute tucked into his waistband. Pushing himself away from the tree, he stepped up to the edge of the plinth, smiling a smile which was neither unctuous nor insolent.

'Do you know who I am?' said Parijatapuri, frowning.

'Indeed,' the youth replied, stepping down so that they were both level. 'You are my Sovereign's brother prince. The poor man's been in a state over your health. I am happy to see you are well on the mend.'

What impudence, Parijatapuri thought. 'I don't believe we are acquainted for you to address me with such familiarity.'

'Oh, do forgive me, but we are acquainted. I am the Consort's cousin, which makes us all family. Surely you remember when, upon a previous visit, two years ago I believe, you suffered a small mishap, it was I who administered the balms to your...' He paused and flashed a smile, '...your injuries.'

Parijatapuri winced. An indelicate toss he had taken from one of Narasimha's mad mares had landed him on a small anthill which had, fortunately, contained neither termites nor snakes. The balm had stung his backside. Wretched boy for dredging up the memory. 'But of course,' he said brusquely. 'If I did not express thanks then, I thank you today. But you look…different.'

'It was a joy to be of assistance, so no gratitude is required. Since my appointment to the husbandry of these damsels, others too have remarked how transformed I am from my former self. For the better, would you agree?'

'I take it the cat belongs to you?' said Parijatapuri.

'Alas not. Pol belongs to my Sovereign's amanuensis.'

'What a big word. And what an armful is the amanuensis's cat. Is it a she?'

'He,' the youth replied, holding the cat up to display its sex. 'His name means *bridge* in the Persian language.'

'Yes. I possess a fair bit of Persian myself. And these… *damsels*?'

'They have no names, numbers only.'

'I see.' He looked around him. 'Not the amanuensis's as well?'

'Oh, no! They belong to my Sovereign. My work here is to keep an eye on the servants appointed to their upkeep… to inspect their stalls, ensure they are correctly groomed and watered and fed. Moreover, my Sovereign says music is beneficial to them and—'

'And you are also teaching them to read.' The possessive pronoun was beginning to grate.

The youth frowned uncomprehendingly and then, catching on, laughed happily. 'Your wit is *almost* comparable to that of my Sovereign. But no, the writing on the wall is for my own practice. Between my duties as Superintendent of the Gift, I've been educating myself.'

'The gift?'

'These ladies and six stud bulls in the yard behind are in

reserve as a gift from my Sovereign to a particular compeer of his.' He flicked a neem leaf off a milk-white back. 'That's why I stopped you from stroking her. But I *suppose* you may, given that you are his compeer.'

But Parijatapuri wasn't listening—or rather, listening only to his heart which had suddenly, unexpectedly, begun to sing. It made *complete* sense. Not unusual in itself, Narasimha's invitation to visit had seemed, on closer reading, to contain a subtext. And this was it: clearly, Kataka had had a surfeit of calves and he, Parijatapuri, had been chosen as beneficiary of nature's, and by extension Narasimha's, generosity. If his beloved soul brother were here, he would throw his arms about him and lift him in the air. Instead, it was just this odd young man, the white cat, and the Gift he may not pet (as yet). He tempered a smile which was in danger of overrunning his ears. 'Your Sovereign's *particular compeer* is a most fortunate man. Surely you must know who he is.'

'To that identity I am not privy. Nor am I aware how long these damsels must remain in my care.' He pulled a sad expression. 'Separation from loved ones is becoming a habit so I shall likely survive the imminent wrench.'

'Come now,' said Parijatapuri in a hearty way, 'it won't be so bad. You are welcome to visit whenever you wish.'

'Visit?'

'My palace…in Parijatapuri. Why, I might even appoint you our dairy superintendent. And in your leisure hours you can be my wife's flautist, spare me the torment of her talentless lutanist. I'll have a word with Narasimha—'

'Thank you most kindly, but I am not certain—'

'Nothing doing! I insist. But come… Give us a melody for my mood is greatly uplifted and I wish to prolong it. And I must ascertain the fluency of your playing. My princess is most exacting about her music.'

At this, the youth wordlessly handed the cat to Parijatapuri and drew the flute from his waistband. Clearing his throat, he arranged himself, one foot crossed over the other—rather like the Eighth Incarnation in the role he sometimes essayed as the cowherd-flautist. As the latter-day Krishna began to play, the heifers lifted their dark limpid eyes to him as lovers might. They weren't the only ones to come under the spell being wrought under the neem. Perched on the plinth with Pol on his lap, Parijatapuri believed himself to be the happiest man alive.

∾

It had fallen upon the Scrivener some weeks ago to tutor the Superintendent of the Gift in the intricacies of reading, grammar and penmanship.

The orders had come from the Sovereign, shortly after the Consort's wastrel cousin had proven himself in the husbandry of bovines. The Scrivener had, until then, little intercourse with the simpering youth who slunk about in the company of women and servants. Any misgivings he'd had about the teaching assignment—under pressure, moreover, to yield results before the heifers set sail—had been pleasantly dispelled. In the course of their first lesson, the candidate for instruction had demonstrated an extraordinary ability to correctly relate the marks in ink on paper to the spoken forms of the vowels and consonants. By the end of the week he was attempting simple sentences—*thou and I under the star-kissed sky* and such like nonsense—even if the manner in which he handled a reed had caused the Scrivener the nearest thing to physical pain.

But all that could be corrected with patience and practice. More thrillingly, who would have imagined a creature so easy on the eye would be capable of sustained interest in anything other than its own image—an image which had held its flesh and blood original in its thrall that first evening. Like most of the Scrivener's personal effects—the lacquered screen and chairs, the cat, the armillary sphere and silk carpets—the mirror was a gift from a Chinese envoy whose attentions the Scrivener had, over the years, discreetly cultivated. Catching sight of his own reflection behind the youth's, his heart had performed multiple somersaults of joy: praise be to the Sovereign, he had given inward thanks, for entrusting the beauty to his tutelage. For his part, the beauty had made a ritual of standing before the silvered glass for several moments and only afterwards settling down to his studies.

The Scrivener glanced up from a slim folio he was pretending to read.

The student sat hunched over the day's assignment, the tip of his tongue peeking from between his lips, the shadows of his eyelashes brushing his cheekbones like butterflies. Each evening, he sat thus—scrubbed and changed from his workaday wear and reeking of patchouli. His shawl had slipped slightly to reveal smooth firm skin which glowed like mustard-honey; the Scrivener imagined it must taste as bitter-sweet. He folded the folio over a finger and sat back with a sigh.

The past week and a half had been hard on him—not least for robbing him of these evenings with the student. Wrapped bandit-like in a headscarf so as not to inhale the fetid breath rasping up from Parijatapuri's sickbed, he had sat, at the Sovereign's bidding, reed at the ready, between dusk and midnight when the invalid tended to be at his garrulous best. The voice of delirium had yielded little more than themes of burning, biting rats, pits of ordure and appearing naked in public. On the sixth day of this tedium, the Scrivener had taken matters into his own hands.

All it had involved was a ripe breast here, a throbbing stander there, suggestions everywhere of libidinous intent towards a certain sovereign lady. The ruse had worked, whipping his own Sovereign into a delicious ferment. 'She is his *sister* by marriage!' Narasimha had raged, his eyes burning into the Scrivener's offerings. 'Wait till he recovers… He'll rue the day he set eyes on me… I will hurl him to an elephant…better still, back to Parijatapuri and his wife!'

All bluster of course, but the Scrivener knew how far he could go without jeopardizing his hands. As ample reward, he had returned to his chambers from that last night at the sickbay to find a stack of assignments, duly completed and left for correction by the personable creature he'd been obliged to neglect in the interest of intrigue. From wholly unlettered to *this* in under eight weeks! It was a miracle, and one that he could justly take credit for flowering. If only he could somehow, miraculously, extend a forefinger to that honeyed skin and retract it, as miraculously, to his lips…

'I said I am done, Master,' said the student.

The Scrivener slid his eyes away from the cup-like dip in the youth's neck. 'Ah! I was beginning to imagine you had fallen asleep. Let me have a look. There had better be no mistakes.'

The student pushed the sheets across the table and slumped back in his chair. They were conjugating verbs in the simple past tense. 'Before you begin, Master,' he said with a smile, 'do you not agree that in the unlikely event of my drowning, the likelihood of my reporting it in writing would be most unlikely? Besides, where would the opportunity present itself? Surely, not in my ladies' water-trough downstairs?'

'There are such things as oceans and seas,' said the Scrivener drily. 'Now see here… I *have* swum, not I *am* swum.'

'Very well, then; I *have* swum but I *am* drowned. How remarkable is this grammar thing.' He reached for the Scrivener's folio. 'Pray tell me; what is it that you read whilst I must only struggle with my reed?'

'Poetry… No! Keep your inky paws off it.'

'Whom by?'

'Yang Wan li.'

'Who is he?'

'A poet native to Chin.'

'And is he a friend? Like that envoy of Chin?'

The Scrivener sniffed delicately. 'Yang Wan li passed on seven years before my birthing. You could say he is my friend…' He tapped his chest, '…here, deep inside. Coming back to this, your writing is much improved but your spelling today! Horror upon horror!'

'Thank you, Master. In what tongue does your Wangyali compose his poems?'

'You could get the name correct. In Chin, of course.' He continued marking the exercises. 'I must give you a taste of it sometime.'

'I should like that so much, Master. Why not tonight?'

The Scrivener looked up. 'What?'

'The taste of it.'

'Ah. Because it is late.'

'Surely it will cost us no more than a moment of our lives.'

'You utter the most peculiar things.'

'Only to you, Master.'

In the ensuing silence, the Scrivener felt his ears turn red. His hands trembled a little as he set down his reed. They trembled again as he took up the folio and turned the pages. What *would* happen if he were to seduce the student? What *were* the penalties for bedding a relative of the Sovereign? Ah…to touch that sun-kissed skin… He'd risk anything…just once…to…to…

He looked up. The student smiled: 'Have you found what you are looking for, Master?'

I believe I have, the Scrivener said to himself. He could easily reach for a particular collection of Sanskrit couplets instead—far more suited to this reckless moment—but that would be taking the easy way. No, the polite poetics of Wan li would do for tonight. He read aloud without pause or inflexion from a random page. 'There!' he said. 'You've had a taste of it.'

'It is indeed a honeyed tongue, Master. But what did it say?'

'It said…he says,' the Scrivener said, diving back to the page and translating extempore: '"It is much better to close your eyes, sit in your study, lower the curtains, sweep the floor, burn incense… It is beautiful to listen to the wind, to the rain, to take a walk when you feel strong, and when you are tired…to go to sleep.'" He smiled. 'Admittedly, I do scant justice to the original. But it does give you a sense of our poet's…soul, if you will.'

'The poor soul. He walks when he feels strong and sleeps when he is tired.' He shrugged, the shawl slipped off his back. 'I too have several poems in my head… About cows and thunder and the mice that go chip-chip as I lie cold and alone in my bed at night… Other, *deeper* feelings which are secret. To write them all down would be a mountainous undertaking.'

'Which is why we must not get distracted. At the rate we're progressing, you shall soon be proficient enough to ink your poems for me…why! for the whole world to read.'

'Alas, Master. If only the Sovereign had presented me earlier to your care. I learned today that I am to soon quit my studies.'

'What?'

'Yes. The Crown Sorrow of Parijatapuri told me so this morning. Like your poet, he walks when he is strong and sleeps when he is tired, although in his case he seems more tired than strong each time he visits. I believe he is here to take away my damsels.'

'No, there's time yet for that.' He frowned. 'Wait, what did you just say?'

'The calves, Master. He's appointing me Master of Bovines in his palace *and* personal flautist to his wife… Oh yes, I too was astonished but for once I kept my tongue in check.' A dark look clouded his face. Laying a hand on the Scrivener's wrist, he continued: 'Master…pray place in our Sovereign's ears that I do not wish to leave Kataka. I would *die* if I were sent away… not now, not *ever*…not after I have found my happiness here, my *life*, not least from your loving kindness.'

The Scrivener was speechless for a long moment, his head aswirl with thoughts, not all of them to do with cattle and Kilwa and meddlesome princes. The hand on his wrist was warm and heavy and he rather liked the way it looked and felt there. He could quite easily tell the body attached to it everything— everything—but doing so would shatter this magical moment. But he would say this, for this too was the truth and for all his mischief, he prided himself in being a gentleman. 'Your visitor was woefully mistaken,' he began, 'for neither you nor your wards are going to Parijatapuri, but it's not for you to disabuse him. I suggest you put him out of your mind this instant and concentrate on your studies or you may only ever dream of writing your poems.'

'But he said he was here expressly for them! He said our Sovereign invited him—'

'No. Now listen to me. The trouble with your friend is that his entire life is a misery of uncertainties. He'll be enlightened soon enough to the newest disappointment in store for him but we mustn't concern ourselves with that certainty. Do you understand? If he ever broaches the subject again, say nothing.'

'If you say so, Master.' He shuddered. 'Such a colourless odourless man. And the way he walks with his eyes always to the ground as though he were shamed by the beauty of life. It so makes me want to lay about him with a stout stick.'

The Scrivener smiled. 'There's no call to be unkind. It comes from his being more yin than yang. Unlike our Sovereign, who is wholly yang.'

'You've lost me, Master.'

'Only compare. Have you seen two men more unlike the other? In deportment, as you so astutely pointed. In speech…? Temperament…? The very *essence* of manliness?'

'Is that what yang means? Manly?'

'Yes.'

He thought for a moment. 'There is one other I know who is more yang than the Sovereign.'

Oh, I love you so, thought the Scrivener, sitting up and touching his hair. 'Really? Who could that possibly be.'

'His brother-in-law the General, of course. Why, the very mention of his name...' He affected a dreamy roll of his eyes. 'Pa-ra-mar-di-de-va...*such* a mouthful of hard hairy manliness, unlike myself, so pliable and timid.'

'Timid you are not, my young simorgh,' the Scrivener said, with a little laugh. 'But enough gossip; we are here to cultivate your mind, not to discuss the Sovereign's kin.' He drew a fresh sheet of paper. 'Now. For tomorrow's assignment... '

'Tonight, Master, is for so many new words. What, pray, is your *young simorgh*?'

'I'll tell you another time. Concentrate.'

At this, the student leant forward, reading under his breath as the moving reed inscribed a new list: 'To dare...to venture... to touch...to hold...to embrace...to adore...to possess...to sleep...to dream...to *drown*? But I am already drowned, don't you remember?'

'Of course, foolish old me. Let me change that to...*rise*. Happy?'

A beaded curtain clicked. The white cat darted across room into the bedchamber behind the screen. The Scrivener stood. 'And now to bed must I as well,' he said, moving away. 'Pleasant night to you, my dear simorgh.'

'And to you, Master. May I stay and practice awhile? I shall be silent as a dream.'

'Don't work too late; snuff the lamps before you leave.'

'A moment, Master.'

He stopped by the armillary sphere and turned. 'Yes?'

'Pray tell me what a simorgh is, for I cannot, until I know, possibly concentrate.'

'A fabled bird with a gift for honeyed words.' Rather like yourself, he almost added. 'It appears everywhere in the legends and poems of Persia, my motherland.'

'Do you possess these legends and poems?'

'I carry one inside my head.'

'May I get a taste of it as well?'

'Persistent, are you not!'

'Only for that which I most deeply crave.'

The Scrivener's heart flipped over on itself. 'Well, then,' he said, walking back and improvising. 'It was late one moonless night in Chin that the simorgh first appeared to human sight...' He paused. Laying a hand on a warm shoulder, he applied the slightest pressure to it.

The student sprang out of the chair. Stumbling backwards, the Scrivener upset the armillary sphere, which fell and went gurgling across the carpets. Cursing himself for misreading the signs—it was so difficult these days to tell with the natives—the Scrivener scrambled for something witty to mitigate the moment. The student was quicker, and taller and stronger. Pushing the Scrivener against the door and taking his face in both hands, he pressed to his lips a hard lingering kiss.

6

CADAMBAGIRI

A CONTINGENT OF REGULARS DRAWN FROM THE INFANTRY HAD unloaded the ox-carts in a rear court of the palace. The slatted wooden crates were twice as tall as a man. In their brilliant white trousers and tunics and tall white headgear, the two Persians responsible for the delivery stood out like salt hills midst the swarthier figures milling everywhere. The women of the palace watched the proceedings from a balcony. A flurry of movement informed of the arrival of the Sovereign.

Her appearance at the balcony drew a hush over the gathering. The Persians stepped forward and bowed from the waist. The younger of the two men read from the scroll in his hands, pausing frequently for his colleague to translate: '*It is the order of His Excellence the Governor of Bharukachchha, may God keep him well, that we convey to Her Excellence the Sovereign lady of Cadambagiri, may God keep her well, this gift which may so delight Her Excellence as to grant these emissaries of Bharukachchha audience…*'

She shifted her gaze. The crates had begun to wobble and judder in a most alarming way. What curiosities, she wondered, did they contain this time? The Governor's gift last year of a clutch of droodroo from Dina Arobi were thriving in the menagerie; the birds' flesh was palatable as promised, but the eggs stank to the sky. In exchange for the birds, she had granted the Governor's boats toll-free passage down a tributary of the Padma which flowed through Cadambagiri. The request this time would be proportionate to the size of the crates; she would have to be prudent.

'…*between our countries for five years hence,*' the older envoy was saying; she had missed the crucial detail. '*And may it now please Her Excellence to accept these natives of Madagasikare, for her delight in such novelties is renowned far and wide.*'

The younger envoy had fixed the Sovereign in a frank stare. You seem to have a new admirer, she told herself. Quelling an urge to favour him with a smile, she made a vague gesture in the direction of the crates. The envoys bowed and proceeded to organize the throng pressing in on them into a wide circle away from the crates.

The regulars, unbiddable at the best of times, weren't good at taking orders...and certainly not from visiting grandees. Physically pushing a native man only made him more truculent; the Persians ought to have known it from their years in Hind. Just as the situation was close to getting out of hand—the junior envoy had raised a hand at a verbal jibe—one of the women in the balcony uttered a sharp word which immediately settled the obstreperous gang; another command was enough to dispose the men as a restive ring along the perimeter of the yard. When all was more or less under control in those ranks, the envoys went to the crates and threw open the door-flaps.

At first, the Sovereign imagined this to be an elaborate joke and the creatures that leapt out to each be a composite of two men—one perched on the other's shoulders and encased in plumage, with an arm and a hand held up like a neck and head. But no: although the lower extremities resembled the sinewy legs of men, these...*things*...were too monstrous, too *natural* in form and gait to be the work of human trickery. Rather, it was plain to see they were a class of giant birds that the Sovereign may never have believed could exist, but for the evidence, stamping their ugly three-toed feet and loudly snapping their spear-head-shaped beaks. Such was her astonishment that she brought her hands together like a child before some immense magic. At her example, the company at large erupted in cheering; the Persians exchanged a smile.

The creatures, meanwhile, had assessed their surroundings and finding themselves hemmed in, began to run confusedly in circles, shedding bits of red plumage. The din around them turned frenzied; the birds suddenly stopped running; the crowd fell silent. Blinking their enormous amber eyes, the pair threw back their necks and opened their beaks to the sky. Clearly they were thirsty.

Watching the display, the Sovereign felt a surge of affection and pity for the ungainly things, which were yet to be provided with a name. Even as she wondered what the Governor of Bharukachchha wished in exchange for them, the lighter-coloured bird scratched the flagstones with its scimitar toenails and hunkered to the ground with a loud hiss. Its mate, also hissing, strode over to its side.

Moments passed. The envoys stood conferring between themselves. Suddenly, the seated bird uttered a long low eruct like a dyspeptic bovine before lumbering to its feet and ruffing its hairs. A collective gasp flew around the yard, for everyone knew an auspicious sign when they saw it. The egg was as large as a man's head.

~

Salutation king | We recount for your diversion an incident of the morning | The Governor of Bharukachchha sent to us two wingless aves of rare height which vorompatra by name are native to the land of Madagasikare in the Sea of Hind | Their bodies have not plumage like other aves but are covered in reddish hairs not unlike the matted locks of mendicants | Unlike other aves the cock possesses a phallus such as that of a man | Its egg is a forearm in length and a forearm and a half in girth and white of shell | One sample of this type our hen did lay | Although fierce of countenance the vorompatra is but placid and possesses the cry of a cow in pain | In trade for these we have granted the Governor passage through our country for his caravans to and from the seaport of Vedapuri | His emissaries tell of a four-legged beast native to Aphrike which zarafa by name possesses the neck of a snake and legs like bamboo sticks and standing taller than an elephant is the tallest beast to walk upon land | The skin of this marvel

is said to be marked as the cracked earth of a riverbed | It
has for its diet a tree of thorns not unlike our babbula trees
| From talk of its strangeness of body and grace of gait and
mildness of temperament and sweetness of scent it is our
desire to possess a living example of its type | This wish the
envoys of Bharukachchha have vowed to fulfil…

~

The cadambas were in bloom following the rains; the air over
the hilltop danced with yellow butterflies. All morning, a stream
of visitors from the citadel wound their way through the old
gateway and thence to the menagerie in a corner of the parkland.

The vorompatrae had quickly settled into their new
surroundings. For all their graces and dark dancing eyes, the
emissaries of Bharukachchha had omitted a telling detail: the
birds had been reared from stock brought in years ago on an
Arab ship—not trapped in the dark wet forests of Madagasikare
as they would have the Sovereign believe. No wonder, then, that
the pair was not averse to people riding them.

Awaiting their turns, the children from the citadel had
invented a song—*elephant-bird run, elephant-bird jump,
elephant-bird try but cannot fly*—chanted to the birds' high-
stepping gait. The pairs of children already clinging on the
birds' backs squealed with delight (or fright) as two syces led
the birds on long leashes from collars round their necks. For the
less adventurous children, there were rides on a pony, a wobbly
camel and a cow-elephant. Vendors of candy, cane juice and
vorompatra-shaped wooden toys on wheels had set up little
stalls under the cadamba trees. There were acrobats, too, playing
at vorompatrae, and performing flips mid-air to swap places as
heads and legs.

If a carnival atmosphere prevailed at the menagerie, a small
cloud of discontent hung over a corner of the palace terrace.
From where they stood, the sextet of ministers had a view over
the cadambas of the excitement around the menagerie's newest

exhibits. The sight was wasted. The men hated their work; they hated their Sovereign. They could, quite easily, have quit her service, but the alternative was abhorrent: lettered and worldly, they had grown accustomed to certain privileges, the likes of which their peasant roots could have never provided. Their appointment by the Sovereign's sister as her stooges had come as timely validation of their existence and provided welcome diversion from their workaday routine. They were gathered this morning on the terrace to mull over unsettling news from the Crown Princess: with her husband called away to Kataka unexpectedly, there was an unforeseen delay in the planned siege upon Cadambagiri; her stooges must keep matters stirred at their own discretion, until further orders from Parijatapuri.

Given free rein, the best the ministers had come up with was woefully uninspired. 'A few handfuls of datura in the feed,' said the Minister of the Royal Household. 'The whole menagerie will be dead in a night.'

'With all due respect,' said the Minister of Temples, 'I suggest we eliminate only the newest wastes of space. It will be seen as an act of god for consorting with Muslims.'

'And entirely defeat the purpose,' said the Minister of Defence. 'The point *is* to rouse suspicion; it will lead to her doing something rash. That's when we move in.'

'True, but we must leave a message of warning,' said the Minister of Taxes. 'Anonymous, of course. It will give the witch sleepless nights.'

Yes-yes, they agreed: anonymity was good. But must she not suffer personally? Yes-yes, personal suffering was good. Her tiger cub next. Yes-yes, and then her personal elephant.

The Minister of the Treasury, deep in thought through the others' mumblings, came alive suddenly: '*Enough talk*. Who will perform the actual deed?'

'We cannot risk taking an outsider into confidence,' said Temples. 'It will have to be one of us. Or all six.'

Five pairs of eyes turned as one upon the Minister of Granaries.

A slip of a man, Granaries was preoccupied with graver concerns than the Sovereign's pets. Elsewhere in the palace, his infant son lay cramped (from a surfeit of jackfruit) with stomach pains. He started. 'What happened?'

'You are the *chosen one*, my friend,' said Defence. 'You may have a small deployment of my boys if you wish but it is your hand, really, that must perform the deed.'

'Deed?'

'The poisoned grain. Are you not attending?'

'I am...but no! I'll gladly provide the requisite—'

'No?' said Treasury, smoothly. 'Only recall the way you were slighted the other day in the presence of her Muslims. And for what reason? Simply because you were unable to provide figures of stocks the instant she asked for them? You fumbled, granted; but *that* manner of upbraiding? In your place I would have shown her right there and then who really runs this establishment.'

Royal Household was smiling at a more distant memory. 'And not for the first time, come to think of it,' he said. 'Do you recall...was it four years ago...? When the rats got in and how the Regent berated him?'

Everyone, including the ones who didn't, recalled the incident.

'Your humiliation that day, and again latterly, pained me to the core of my being.'

'And mine. You have every reason to feel humiliated.'

'Someone should stand up to her arrogance.'

'Any woman who spoke to me that way—'

'She needs firm handling by a man. A *real* man.'

'I will do it,' snapped Granaries.

'Good,' said Defence. 'You see, you are the youngest of our set and have a bright future in governance. We knew we could rely on your resourcefulness.'

'You have my personal assurance,' Treasury added, 'you shall be fittingly recompensed.'

In the ensuing lull, the men looked away towards the objects of their malefic intent. But only for a moment before stepping back from the parapet, lest the latest visitor to the menagerie catch sight of six turbaned figures who ought not to, at this hour, be idling on the terrace.

As the ministers watched from their new vantage points, the Sovereign trotted up alongside the vorompatrae and dismounted. She was accompanied by her aides—some on foot, others on horseback. One of them held open a cloth bag before the Sovereign. She dipped her hands in.

It made a charmed sight: the slight, straight figure, arms outstretched; the birds lowering their great glabrous heads to feed from her hands.

'Observe,' said Defence, 'the monsters are peaceable as lambs. That is the way to do it.'

∼

The birds had come with a month's supply of corn kernels to supplement their diet of molasses and boiled rice. The corn ration was brought under the ambit of the Granaries Department. A small bagful was spirited away to the private apartments of the Minister of Granaries.

The morning of the night marked for his assignment, Granaries visited the palace barber and had his beard and moustache shaved. A vow, he explained to everyone including his wife: he'd bartered his facial hair with the gods so they may hasten the recovery of his ailing boy.

So much for cosmetic treatment. The main accessory was a cloth bag with two compartments, rather like a saddle-bag, devised to be worn across Granaries' chest. Packed into each compartment were handfuls of corn kernels, coated and dried in a slurry of powdered datura seeds. All Granaries had to do was unfasten the bags and hold them up to the vorompatrae.

No sooner had his wife left for the sickbay to sit by their child, Granaries got busy. He braided his hair into two plaits, rimmed his eyes with antimony and changed the gold studs in his ears for his wife's earrings. Off with his dhoti, next, and into his wife's shift. The poison-corn breasts were tricky to fasten for want of an extra pair of hands; he undid and retied them to himself several times before adjusting the front to a satisfying effect. Throwing a shawl about his head and shoulders, he draped it across his new frontage. He then collected a skeleton key and a scrap of birch-bark, scrawled with the words *your tiger is next*. Tucking the note between his breasts, he slipped out of his apartments to a seldom-used servants' exit in the rear of the palace, and thence through the tree-shadowed parkland towards the menagerie. Unlikely as it was that he might be seen, he prayed that anyone noting his progress would take him for a she-ghost and not challenge him.

This too had been carefully planned. Some days previously, a visit to the menagerie had acquainted Granaries with its layout and possible setbacks. As expected, he was stopped at the guardhouse by two sentries. 'Our mistress dropped a jewelled armlet this evening near the big-birds' pen,' he shrilled, adding with a cackle: 'I have been sent to fetch it because I am too old for you boys to toy with.'

'Can't it wait till morning?' asked a sentry.

'No it cannot. You know how she gets if she doesn't have her way. Now let me through quick.'

The sentry approached. An ugly crone alright, and what an ear-splitting voice she packed. He lifted the drop gate into the menagerie. Granaries stepped through and quickened his pace.

'Take my flaming torch, Auntie!' called the other sentry.

'I have no use for it, nephew,' Granaries called back, 'with your Uncle Moon to light my way.' Whore's son, he added, under his breath.

The next bit was less fraught. The syces assigned to the

vorompatrae had retired to their barracks for the night. The birds' double-height stable, erected last week, was fronted by a tall batten-door with spikes. The iron padlock, shaped as a tiger with its mouth for the keyhole and tail for the shackle, was heavy and cold in the moonlight. Granaries' shawl hindered easy movement. He threw it off, the better to keep him sharp for the next step. Holding the key between his teeth, he hitched his shift up between his legs and tucked it into the waistband. He was trembling uncontrollably: this was the most daring thing he'd ever attempted; wait till he recounted it to his friends.

The skeleton key refused to oblige. Granaries swore under his breath as the key jumped out of his grasp. Cursing, he managed to retrieve it from the dirt at his feet. He would persist, or all his effort would be for naught and he would be the object of derision till the day he died. The prospect of failure filled him with renewed rage: towards the Sovereign; his life; this thankless undertaking. Shoving the key back in, he jiggled and twisted it this way and that, the while keeping the pressure on the tail. Just when he could bear it no more and was this close to tears, the shackle slid out with a dull click. Letting the two pieces fall, Granaries pushed open the door and stepped in.

Nothing had prepared him for the stench. It caused him to retch—enough reason to ruffle two forms which lifted like grey smoke in the blackness. Everything happened so quickly that he had no time to assign a sequence to events. The first kick shattered a shin. He crumpled to the ground and fell forward, slamming his face on an egg which smashed; the breast-bags caved into his chest, splintering a rib which punctured a lung; the beaks digging into his back were relentless as axe-heads. He still had it in him to scramble to a side, but the next kick took out an eye even as his head swivelled around on itself so the last sound he heard was a deafening crack.

～

Salutation king | At daybreak a most unsavoury sight awaited the servants of our vorompatrae for lying dead and covered in blood and excrement in their stable was our Minister of Granaries at first unrecognizable for the state of his carcase | From his attire and the appendages sported by him and from his behaviour and speech yesterday it was clear the wretch had sacrificed himself in exchange for the recovery of his ailing child | We have no patience for false belief and ordered the carcase to be cremated without ceremony for there is no salvation for those who wilfully cast away their life | The incident has fulsomely reinforced your counsel that the old order must change | The time has come to effect that change before the rot that has set into my palace renders further damage…

~

Some runners only ran; some horsemen only rode. Runners who also rode were rare and tended to guard their dual skills; it was their own limbs they preferred to keep well-oiled. It was one such talent that set out at daybreak from the palace.

His sling bag contained his midday meal. A water-gourd swung from his waistband. The Sovereign's scroll-case was attached to the end of a long wooden baton, its red-silk tapes dancing in the crisp air. As always, the runner stopped by a stream to eat. By dusk, he would reach the village of the next runner in the relay, rest up through the night and return to Cadambagiri tomorrow at a leisurely sprint.

Like all of his kind, the runner (who was also a rider) was firm and lithe. Not so the two mounted henchmen of the Minister of Defence, waiting in the forest along the route the runner would take. Their horses abreast, they stood blocking a bridle track that wound through the undergrowth and trees.

The runner saw them first. 'Make way,' he called, without breaking step, 'Move…!' And then he saw the clubs in their hands.

He'd been trained to anticipate every eventuality: rogue

elephants, snakes, brigands such as these. This was a first for him; he'd risk anything for the Sovereign's dispatch. With a bloodcurdling scream and flailing the scroll baton, he ran headlong at the horses, which predictably reared in alarm, throwing their mounts. Before the men could find their feet, the runner grabbed a horse by the bridle and launched himself onto its pair, whipping both animals into a canter—not forward, but back to Cadambagiri. Late that evening, the horses served as principal evidence of the attempted ambush.

～

The first intimation the Ministers of Taxes, Temples, the Treasury and Royal Hosehold had of the sort of day that stretched before them was the sight of their colleague, the Minister of Defence, being marched to the barber's by four women. Defence emerged, shorn of every last hair on his head, face and body. Onwards, then, into the labyrinth under the palace.

In a different wing of the labyrinth, two terrified farriers from the citadel—Defence's henchmen—had required little prodding to reveal the identity of their kingpin. Soon, Defence too would crack, spilling the real reason behind Granaries' visit to the vorompatrae.

Meanwhile in their offices, the four other ministers fretted. Had they been implicated by their imprisoned colleague? Would a summons come for them any moment? Would they be charged with treason and incarcerated? What recourse had they to preempt such ignominy? None whatsoever: they, more than anyone, knew it. Four lunches, sent over as usual by four dutiful wives, remained untouched, for fear is best for killing the appetite. By early afternoon, their fate was sealed.

The memos served to them were also pasted outside their respective departments. All four men were stripped of office with immediate effect. Appeals for clemency would not be entertained. Their salaries would be disbursed at the relevant cell before the end of the day. Their families and they had a week to vacate their apartments in the palace precincts.

For all their bluster of peremptory treatment and protestations of loyalty, Royal Household, Temples, Taxes and Treasury were, between themselves, a relieved set: they were free, no longer required to bow and scrape to the one they detested. That the freedom came with a windfall of cowries was, they convinced themselves, a twice-won victory.

The wives were the last to hear of their husbands' fall from grace. It could have been worse, the women said: a *lot* worse, knowing her... Knowing her, your replacements are doubtless already appointed and, knowing her, will be six women. It did little to bolster their menfolk's spirits.

That evening, the foursome once again convened. The venue was a public house in the citadel where it didn't matter that they might be recognized. The palm-toddy was heady and the service friendly. It was a short step from there to a popular brothel. The night was dense when the four tottered out, safe in the knowledge they had each other for comfort as well as a fresh plan: tomorrow, they would leave for Parijatapuri.

7

A CAMPSITE

THE SMOKE FROM THE COOK-FIRES DRIFTED LIKE COBWEBS TO the riverbank and out over the dark waters of the Kushabhadra. The royal retinue was camped on higher ground. A servant waving a censer hurried through the haze of horses and elephants.

The old stone tower, risen from an outcrop, served as a royal resthouse. In the viewing gallery upstairs, Narasimha and Parijatapuri were seated by a brazier, which was more smoke than fire, for the tinder was damp. The servant fumigated the gallery, arranged more kindling and repaired downstairs. Parijatapuri hugged himself and picked up where he had left off in the servant's presence: 'So yes. As I was saying, I fervently regret my inability to have been by your side when you sent Tughan Khan scurrying. I consoled myself that I was there with you in spirit.' He studied Narasimha's face. It was expressionless. Until now, the day's march from Kataka had presented little opportunity for conversation. On reaching Chandrabhaga tomorrow, Narasimha would have little time for him. This was his chance to unburden himself. 'These regrets,' he concluded, 'shall be my constant companions until my last breath.'

'Now, now,' Narasimha said, 'you mustn't distress yourself unduly with trivialities.'

'Trivialities? Do you not understand my helplessness? If you recall it, I was unable to attend the funeral of your father and your coronation due to the birthing of my first princess. And then your nuptials, due to our second princess. Each time I crave to be with you...' He made a feeble gesture. 'I could not bear it if you thought otherwise. As for your recent victory, perhaps it was just as well that I wasn't present on the battlefield. Had Father caught wind of what was on my mind, he'd never have permitted it lest…lest the purpose for which I was adopted were defeated.'

A joke now would be inappropriate. 'You might have been disappointed,' Narasimha said. 'There was no battlefield.'

'No?' He shifted a log in the brazier. It snuffed some of the struggling flames. 'Oh, see what I have done; hopeless as always…But the news travelled to us that it was a carnage?'

'That much is correct… Now leave that be…'

He let go of the log. 'I am sorry. Was there much bloodshed?'

'Ah, yes. Bloodshed.'

'Go on. Tell me.'

'What?'

'The campaign.'

He clicked his tongue impatiently. 'Where would you like me to begin? The beginning or just the climax?'

'Oh, wherever you wish. You know how I like it when you recount a story.'

'Only, this is no story but all fact. I'll take you directly to the sixteenth of April, the culmination of the first leg of the campaign. Tughan Khan had by then laid siege upon our fort of Katasimha, leaving half the guard dead and scattering the rest. Finding the place empty, he doubtless assumed our men had fled, abandoning our elephants, and set his troops to seize them as bounty. It was a ruse, of course. A hundred and fifty of our men with fifty elephants were waiting in the surrounding bamboo forest. When the Turk's men paused in their labours… let's say it was not a pleasant sight.'

'Oh marvellous. Pray do not stop.'

'Tughan Khan got away with his life. But more of his men fell to our troops, waiting at the ready all the way to Lakhnore, which outpost my brother-in-law then laid siege to and captured with little resistance.'

'Ah. Paramardideva the Valiant.'

'Speaking of whom—' Narasimha laughed, 'do you still

begrudge him taking my sister for his wife? I'll never forget your passion for her, how sick you made yourself the day they were wed.'

'Quit teasing, she is as an older sister to me as well. And I bear no grudges towards your invincible general. Who am I but a mere prince before that man among men?' He paused, biting his underlip. 'But let us not digress. You took the fort of Lakhnore. What then?'

'Despite its every exit being sealed, the Turk again gave the slip...an underground passage, we discovered belatedly. It isn't the last he has seen of me.' He stirred the embers with a stick, causing a fountain of sparks to fly. 'I have my eyes set on Lakshmanauti next. And thence further northeast. When the time is right, I'll launch another attack. Aggression, I've always said, is the best form of defence. My troops, happily, require little prompting. It helps that my warriors from Aphrike are of like spirit.'

'Warriors from Aphrike?'

'Did I not mention it? A particular compeer dispatched a vessel of warriors last year at my request. Katasimha and Lakhnore provided the perfect conditions for putting them to the test. For that spectacle alone, you ought to have been present.'

Parijatapuri gathered his shawl about himself. 'No one said anything about warriors from Aphrike. Where are these warriors?'

'You'll see them soon enough. Different from us, but altogether human.'

'And this compeer?'

'The Sultan ibn Bone Soleiman of Kiswahili. He rules from an island, Kilwa, in the Sea of Hind...' He trailed off, staring at Parijatapuri through the smoke. 'But of course,' he said slowly. 'Why did I not think of it?'

'Is something amiss?'

'No, a small matter of some cattle. You could take them with you—'

'Yes, *of course*! I shall do so gladly! A most generous gift!
Too generous—'

'Ah. So you've been in conversation with my Left Hand.'

'No. The consort's cousin said—' He stopped.

'Yes?'

What *had* the consort's cousin said? *A particular compeer.*
Nothing more. Nothing less. The smoke blew into his eyes.
He clenched and unclenched his fists. 'No, it is nothing…a
mistake… It is late; with your permission, I should like to turn in.'

'Already? I was hoping you'd tell me *your* story tonight.'

'There is no story.'

'Your fluted message suggested otherwise. Crows in doves'
nests, lambs bleating, hares fleeing. It sounded most alarming.'

'I wrote in haste.' He rose, managing a smile. 'I ought, instead,
to have conveyed other tidings. My princess is with child again.
It shall be a boy this time.'

Narasimha too had risen. 'My felicitations. When is the
birthing?'

'The middle of November, per my understanding.'

'I see,' said Narasimha. 'In which case I can hardly ask you
to go.'

'Go where?'

'To Kilwa, deliver the cows and come back. But no doubt
you cannot, not with another child on the way. It is no matter,
carry on downstairs. I shall do so presently.' He turned and leant
against the parapet, scanning the speckled sky for shooting stars.
There were none tonight.

PARIJATAPURI

'In the Himalay,' began her father-in-law the Raja, 'dwells a tribe which confines to certain caves those of its women who are due to birth during winter time. After it is delivered, the newborn is sewn into the skin of a lamb. In this way, the mother and baby must remain in the cave until the advent of spring.' The Raja was handsome in a ravaged sort of way—not a pinch of fat on his tall angular frame, his face cicatriced by the pox he had survived as a child. 'Are you not glad,' he added as an afterthought, 'that you are not of that tribe?'

She was in no mood for his pedantry tonight. She knew when not to respond but her tongue, perversely, acquired a mind of its own at times like this: 'Do they employ a fresh lamb skin?'

'It is skinned simultaneously so that the warmth is no different from the mother's inside.'

'What do they use for the sewing?'

'An iron needle this long,' he held up his little finger, 'and the gut of the lamb.'

'This would be the same tribe which quarried my ice?'

'No. A different tribe.'

'You possess such erudition on these tribes.'

'I do.' He was lost in thought for a moment. 'In the ocean of the east is an island populated by a certain tribe that dwells in trees. When one of their elders dies, the family partakes of the brain in a feast so that the wisdom contained therein remains with the clan.'

'Such savages,' she said. If only he would leave her be: it was late and she wanted to sleep. 'I shouldn't like my wisdom residing in someone else's head.'

'No head would be large enough to contain it.' He smiled wanly, shifting closer along the edge of her bed. 'Six more weeks?'

The hand which came to rest upon her belly was cold and moist. She felt the parasite twitch and draw inwards into itself. The first time, it was like a cat in a basket for she had felt it scratch. The second was a bird in a cage, pecking at her insides with its elbows and heels. This one, she likened to a fish in a pot of fluids from which it drew strength to turn and flip. Nowadays, there seemed to be more fish than fluid. A dark oily fish, waiting to slither out between her legs. She felt an intense need to make water, although she'd been twice before his visit. She removed his hand.

It seemed to sadden him. He rose from the bed, turning away as though he had something to hide. Moving to a window, he adjusted the slatted blinds through which the night was sending in cold slices of itself. 'No word as yet from your fool husband?'

'None at all,' she replied. The wisdom in her head told her to change the subject. 'It was remiss of me not to give thanks sooner for the new crib. It is most beautifully crafted, even more so than the previous pair.'

He turned. 'Nothing but the best for my coming prince.'

Go, she screamed inside her head, and said, 'I am unworthy of your kindness.'

'More than worthy,' he said, walking back with a thin smile. Her wish he'd leave was almost instantly granted.

There is a rule which proscribes servants from appearing unbidden in the presence of the master. The maidservant, little more than a child, stopped in her tracks and fell to her knees.

'What is it?' the Raja and she barked, she a beat ahead of him.

Without raising her head: 'There are four men, Worship, to see my lady.' The girl had never before addressed the master, much less been in such proximity of him. There were things they said about him downstairs.

'Men? Who be they?' His feet moved into the girl's line of sight.

Hairy feet, thick toenails. She shut her eyes tight. There is a saying that a cat shuts its eyes whilst lapping milk so that, the stupid creature believes, it won't be seen. 'From the country of Cadambagiri, Worship, they beg audience of my lady.'

'At this time of night?' He turned. 'Expecting visitors, are we?'

It did not augur well. 'I have no idea who they might be,' the Crown Princess replied, throwing a languid arm over her eyes. 'Vagabonds, doubtless. Send them away, my child.'

'No,' the Raja said, 'I had better go and see to it.'

After he had left, the girl scrambled forth on all fours to kneel by the side of the bed. 'What must I do, my lady?'

'You've done enough,' she spat, resisting the urge to strike the girl on her face; granted, her timing had spared her more attentions from him. 'The chamber-pot, you wretch. Quick!'

Not a moment sooner. And then this acrid jet of relief. The girl removed the pot to the privy latrine. Presently, the lutanist entered and picked up his instrument. The troublesome phrase of music got tangled as always. She usually had some imprecation or other for the talent, but tonight her mind was unquiet as a nestful of mice.

Part Two

9

CHANDRABHAGA

'SO THIS IS IT!' CRIED PARIJATAPURI.

He had never before seen the sea. It was with some trepidation that he had followed Narasimha up the brick-and-stone windbreak. They had walked from the royal lodge in an acacia thicket to the source of the roaring and moaning which had kept Parijatapuri awake through the night. So this was it: the bottomless Kalingodhra, filled, as legend had it, with as many sea-monsters as it was with divinities. A high wind from it nearly whisked him off his feet.

For a change, Narasimha did not move away—going so far as to throw an arm about his friend's shoulders as if claiming personal credit for the sun climbing the sky, the ominous black crags in the shoal to the right, the riggings of ill-fated vessels further out at sea. The tide was in ebb; the waves came galloping and crashing to the windbreak. Parijatapuri was compelled to shout to be heard over the din but his next utterance (on immensity) was drowned by the wind, the waves, the shrieks of the gulls wheeling and teetering overhead. The grip around his shoulders tightened; the next surge drenched them both to the skin.

Laughing and sputtering and still holding him, Narasimha turned so that their backs were to the sea. 'And there it is,' he said, with a sweep of a hand.

The leeward side of the windbreak sloped down to the mouth of a creek, its opposite bank rising as a flat headland. In centuries to come, the structure that squatted on the seafront will darken and tumble into disarray; the creek will shrink to a trickle and then leave no trace of having existed; the acacias will march from the thicket to colonize new dunes of sand; the windbreak will crumble and dissolve into the sea; the sea itself will ebb a mile

east. But later. Today, a landing stage on the opposite side was
crowded with men and women going about their ablutions in the
creek. Although they treaded water and some even attempted to
swim, their movements seemed laboured and clumsy.

Parijatapuri's stomach lurched. The outlines of the bathers in
the current bore the unmistakable taint of the blight which ate
away the extremities. Back home in Parijatapuri, such miseries
rarely emerged from their hovels outside the citadel. Yet here
was a whole tribe of their ilk—bathing in public. There were
no children to be seen, but a cruel trick of the mind impressed
the canker to the faces of Parijatapuri's little princesses. With a
stricken breath, he looked away.

Further upstream to the left, a low wooden bridge across
the creek was almost as busy as the landing stage, but with men
unloading iron billets off some longboats moored to its sides.
Parijatapuri squinted. No signs of disease and deformity there.
Yet between the unremarkable labour gangs were other men:
bare bodied, glistening with sweat, and in height, blackness and
build unlike any human he had seen.

'What *is* this place?' Parijatapuri gasped.

But of course. How could he, so well read and erudite, have
failed to associate Chandrabhaga with that old legend. Only
one as impetuous as Narasimha would contrive a temple in so
extreme a setting. And those had to be his brute warriors from
his *particular compeer*. He tried to phrase something appropriate
but the next wave almost tipped him over the edge. Roughly
releasing himself from Narasimha's grip he started back down
the windbreak—one eye on the Kalingodhra which seemed
intent on devouring him.

～

By midday, the sense of unease which had clung to Parijatapuri
like a bad smell lifted enough for him to partake of a light meal
of rice and broiled fish. There was only so much he could nap;
he had with him no fables or parables or even scriptures to read.

Restless, and with Narasimha away somewhere, he ventured out from the royal lodge in the thicket and thence, with a parasol-bearer for his guide, up the bridge that was now bereft of activity to the opposite bank that was the temple site.

There, overlooking the creek and the sea sprawled the partially complete complex, its farthest boundary abutting a stretch of black beach. The view at sunrise from the windbreak had been too brief for the true scale of the undertaking to impress itself upon Parijatapuri. This was different.

Gazing upon the works from a grassy embankment, he gauged the temple's plinth alone to be a good three hundred paces lengthwise, west to east, half that approximation in its width, and perhaps thrice the height of a man. A third of the terrace, to the seaward side, was occupied by an immense cuboid, its roof rising in diminishing tiers to a pyramidal profile. The remaining two-thirds, nearer to him, were ranged with towering stone piers supporting a complexity of iron beams. The plinth and the cuboid were as yet unadorned with carvings; in the surrounding ground stood stacks of dressed and numbered stone blocks awaiting assembly, overgrown by that particular sharpness of green which follows the rains.

Shielding his eyes against the glare from the sea, Parijatapuri found the rooflines of the cuboid swarming with the outlines of workmen, like an anthill. More figures were suspended in webs of scaffolding down the sides; everywhere, lines of ant-people passed blocks of masonry from the stacks to the terrace. Diminished by perspective to the size of beetles, a file of draught-elephants made slow progress up a ramp in the plinth: each dragged behind it a length of stone as long as itself; there was no dearth of Aphrikes assisting the elephants and native labour gangs.

Six years of intermittent building had brought the temple to this stage. From the scale of the works under way, it would probably take as many years to complete. Parijatapuri shook his head. If he lived to see that day, he would be a middle-aged Raja in his own right, but with no such monument to his name. He smiled morosely. It was enough that Narasimha had the wherewithal to indulge such extravagance. He, Parijatapuri, was quite happy to be a witness. It would make a fine story for his children and grandchildren someday. For now, he completed the temple in his mind's eye as if the whole of it were engraved with a stylus against the sky and the sea.

He sighed.

In the vision which shimmered before him, the edifice was adorned with carvings from base to tip. The assembly hall that was the cuboid had filled with pilgrims. The gold finial of the sanctuary-tower scraped the sky. Its splendour surpassed everything erected by Narasimha's forebears in the old capital Kalinganagara, in Ekamra, even the Great Temple of Charitrapura. None of those temples commanded so dramatic a setting; this one overwhelmed all who beheld it…even seafarers braving the Kalingodhra's fury. Attempting to hold still the image which superimposed the reality, Parijatapuri caught sight of some figures rounding a corner of the actual plinth.

The party advanced slowly, pausing every few paces for Narasimha—distinguished by his crimson turban—to inspect some feature, some structural element. The pyramidal rooflines held his attention for several moments. Some detail, next, at ground level. It was only now that Parijatapuri noticed the wheels that were leant at regular intervals against the plinth.

As he watched perplexed, a member of the retinue summoned forth a gang of Aphrikes standing nearby. To some brief from the man, the giants, working in pairs, effortlessly shifted the wheels, which were as tall as themselves, so that they were spaced differently along the plinth.

The new arrangement seemed not to please the Sovereign. The Aphrikes restored the wheels to their original places. Narasimha stepped up to inspect the spokes and hub of the nearest.

Parijatapuri gaped. Could it be that his friend had designs for the architecture to be mobile? Surely, even one as impractical as he was aware of the impracticability of any such scheme? The idea of the finished colossus rumbling forth like an ungovernable temple-car and plunging headlong into the sea caused an unseemly gurgle to escape Parijatapuri's lips. Quickly reassuming a demeanour of grace, he smiled smoothly at his guide and said, 'I dare say it will require more than an army of savages to budge it.'

'Not savages, sire,' the parasol-bearer replied, unsure if the guest prince had spoken in jest. 'It is but seven stallions that draw the Sun God's chariot.' He pointed into the distance. 'The septet is presently being readied in that there shed.'

Parijatapuri squinted. A number of brick-and-thatch buildings were grouped in a far corner of the site. He strained to listen: the breeze favoured him a faint rhythmic pecking of chisels and tapping of mallets. 'But of course...seven stallions,' he mumbled, and refrained from pressing the servant for details. After that muddle over those detestable heifers, he had resolved to keep all conversation with such people brief. But too late.

'And did you know it, sire? As the real sun floats in the sky, so must an iron image of the Sun God float in the sanctum air.' The man's voice had turned fawning, 'But for our sun-born Sovereign, who would have imagined such marvels could—'

'Oh, hush yourself,' Parijatapuri cut in, '*nothing* is a marvel nowadays.' If boatloads of iron could float down creeks, what was to prevent the same metal from lifting into the air. Or, for that matter, whole temples from cantering about on wheels. Knowing Narasimha, it would be sky-crafts, next, for the Nine Planets to whirl about the tower showering flowers on the terrace... anything for a vulgar display, those savages included. He felt a sudden, shameful stab of discontent towards his friend.

His thoughts must have travelled. Narasimha turned and shading his eyes, appeared to be frowning across the grounds at him.

'Regard, sire!' the servant said. 'Our Sovereign beckons. Come, we must not keep him.'

~

The draughtsmen, barely out of their teens, worked intently, inscribing the garnetstone blocks with figures entwined—full-frontal, right-profile, left-profile—in readiness for the sculptors in the neighbouring sheds.

The blocks ranged in size and shape from forearm-high rectangles to handspan squares. Whereas the drawings emerging on their surfaces depicted both sexes—bare, disporting as pairs, triads and larger groupings—the live models on the pedestals and benches were all men in scraps of cloth and string which scarcely covered their sex. And whereas the models were the more able-bodied members of the leper colony, the male and female figures they appeared as in the drawings were not only complete in all respects, but also gloriously exaggerated of phalli and breasts. The scenes occasionally included imaginary participants: a leering hermaphrodite here, a self-pleasuring dwarf there, the odd priapic simian, canine and equine.

As each inscribed block moved to the sculptors' sheds and was replaced by a new block for rendering, the models had a moment's respite to flex their limbs, crack a joke and check their bandages before assuming poses afresh. They had been briefed, on recruitment, to be as inventive as they pleased: this they obliged with sardonic smiles, for the intimacies they simulated were largely devoid of sensation and sentiment. When a draughtsman wished to suggest an adjustment—and because contact, verbal or physical, was neither desirable nor encouraged—a pointer with a padded tip was employed to nudge into place the drape of an arm, the bend of a leg or the tilt of a chin.

For their part, the models watched their efforts translate from raw line to three dimensions with cold detachment: that the panels modelled after them must in due course adorn the temple's sides mattered not so much to them as their wages—salt, oil and rice—at the close of each day. In time, they knew, their bodies would further rot and die and not all the mud and waters of the Chandrabhaga could reverse that plight. The old myth was just that: a myth. Only at night in their hutments—stomachs filled, stretched on their mats, in that brief crossing between wakefulness and sleep—did they permit themselves to believe they were human, *perfect*. If they seemed unusually animated today, it was because they had been alerted of the Sovereign's imminent visit.

∼

Parijatapuri's circuit of the temple's plinth had reassured him that the architecture under way was in no danger of going anywhere: the wheels were models in wood for replication in stone. But the walk had tired him and he could do with some refreshment. Following Narasimha into a shed from the sunlight, he was momentarily blinded. He blinked and looked around blearily, taking in the draughtsmen, the stone blocks and the entwined figures on the pedestals in pairs and groupings.

If he weren't repulsed enough to find the models were all male, he couldn't not notice the turmeric-stained dressings and cankered noses and ears. The expression of polite interest he'd sustained until now slid off his face like a gob of phlegm. Before he could turn and flee, his elbow was possessed by a firm cool hand.

'Behave,' said Narasimha softly, the while casting his easy smile around the company, 'there's no reason for fright; the blight does not transmit.'

It was not his style to gainsay his friend; but not today. 'Let go,' he said tersely, 'I shall not be teased in this way; let go of me before I embarrass myself and you in the bargain.'

Narasimha could tell he meant it. 'No, you are right. Wait for us in the studio ahead, you're likely to be more at ease there.'

The retinue—comprising the Secretary, the Foreman, the

Chief Architect, the Master Draughtsman and his deaf-mute brother, the Master Sculptor—stood a little away. Parijatapuri flounced past them without looking left or right. Shortly, the flurried entry of a scowling stranger instead of the Sovereign extracted a collective groan of disappointment from the models at work in the neighbouring shed.

But for one embracing pair, the women were individually posed as dancers in mid-step and as musicians holding drums, flutes, trumpets, cymbals and bells. Some gazed into phantom mirrors in their hands; others looked longingly into an imagined distance; another held a hand in the air, palm upturned, as though she were cheerfully bearing the weight of the heavens. Each woman was a prostitute by calling—in the best of health, in elaborate hairstyles, and adorned in copper jewellery which was theirs to keep. The blocks on which their likenesses took shape ranged from the discreet to the life-sized, for yielding as sculptures in the round as well as reliefs.

The presence of so many women quickly restored Parijatapuri's spirits. If only he had found them sooner instead of trailing behind Narasimha like an obliging sheep. Already, he could see where the arching of a foot, a hand on a waist, the slightest shift of gesture and gaze might greatly improve a rendering in progress. But it was not for him to proffer advice; so he moved around the pedestals, hands behind his back, bestowing the occasional nod and smile. Pausing by the draughtsman at work on the paired models—also the only ones to sport copper diadems—he looked from them to the block, and up again.

The taller of the two models had her companion's breast cupped in one hand. The shorter woman held a wooden dowel (the exact purpose of which eluded Parijatapuri) to her partner's midriff. The women had locked eyes. A delicious half-smile hung between them.

In the drawing in progress, the crowned heads of the

pair—purportedly of a king and his queen—were framed by the hoods of cobras with multiple heads. Having rendered the upper-quarters of the figures in fair detail, the draughtsman was occupied with detailing the lower extremities. The faint chalk outlines there emerged, in red-pigment, as the intertwined tails of snakes. The dowel in the short model's hand turned, under the artist's, into a splendid phallus.

Delighted by these tricks of the draughtsmen's trade, Parijatapuri stepped up to the pedestal on the pretext of admiring the models' ornaments. On the pretext of brushing away an imaginary speck of lint, he permitted a forefinger to stray—inspiring a bloom of gooseflesh up the model's leg. His touch seemed to have brought the figures alive. As he watched entranced, the hand cupping the breast began, ever so slowly, to caress it in circular movements; the shorter model worked the dowel in her hand; a thumb and forefinger tugged at a nipple; the dowel slipped between the legs...By the time the pair locked lips, their teasing had elicited the desired effect.

At first the draughtsmen pretended not to notice and then tried in vain to shush the ripples of mirth flying around the shed, even as the stranger in their midst attempted to collapse the wayward tent in his dhoti. Parijatapuri ought to have sported it with pride; but hurling a venomous look at the figures doubling over in laughter around him, he marched out, trailed by hoots and jeers. His cheeks were still burning when he entered an adjoining shed. It was empty—of people, at least.

Three giant blocks of a greyish-green stone were stood about in the middle like strangers who had recently met. There was something else behind them, draped in sacking. Parijatapuri walked up and peered under the drapes. Without any help from him, they cascaded to the floor with a rasp, revealing a life-sized horse of stuffed hide on a wooden base.

Forelegs tucked as if it were clearing a fence, the counterfeit was kitted in ceremonial tack—all scarlet tooled leather, scarlet silk tassels and braids, bells around the ankles and a beaten copper breastplate. The saddle, waxed to a dull polish, was of the high-pommelled kind reserved for the sovereign. A mounting-block stood nearby. Pushing it closer, Parijatapuri climbed onto the dummy.

It felt strange. He smiled. Gathering the reins and clicking his tongue twice, he pressed his heels to the unyielding hide belly; but one of the stirrups needed shortening. He freed his right foot and reached for the fastenings; the saddle slid sideways to the left with him in it so that he went sprawling to the floor on his back—his head narrowly missing the mounting block, his left foot stuck in the stirrup, his shin and knee pinioned by the inverted cantle and pommel.

Quickly recovering from the shock of it, Parijatapuri made to slither over the base and under the belly onto the other side, and in the process almost overbalanced the dummy onto himself. Using his free foot to brace it from toppling sent the pain shooting through his trapped leg from ankle to hip; he fell back with a plaintive wail. There was nothing for it but to lie very still. Sooner or later he would be missed, and then found and set right. To get his mind off his predicament, he tucked some of the sacking under his head and began counting the rhythmic chirruping of chisels somewhere in the vicinity.

He ought to have gone straight back to the lodge after his encounter with those wicked women. Instead, here he was stuck like a broken insect under a mock-steed. How unpleasant, he told himself, staring across the floor, if the infernal thing were to suddenly come alive. He would be torn to quarters…he would never again be able to ride…he would be crippled for life… bound forever to a throne on wheels… Feeling better for these thoughts, he shut his eyes. It was in such inelegant circumstances that he was found by Narasimha's retinue and restored to his feet; the saddle was righted and the girth tightened and double-checked, as though the welfare of the dummy outweighed that of the guest. Taking it all in without comment, Narasimha moved out of sight behind the stone blocks.

Left on the mounting block to chafe his ankle, Parijatapuri gathered, from snatches of conversation floating his way, that the monoliths were meant for three images, anticipated for three shrines due for the temple's terrace. A more involved exchange, pertaining to light to work by and failing eyesight, suggested the speaker was the Master Draughtsman. A laugh from Narasimha, and, '...have the walls dismantled...all the lights of day spilling in...'

The party moved into Parijatapuri's line of sight. To spare himself further embarrassment, he stood and turned away to subject a tassel in the dummy's saddle to intense scrutiny. Behind him, Narasimha hadn't stopped speaking: '...repositioned to benefit from the lights...Dawn! Noontide! Sunset!... How much time do you estimate?'

'Chiselwork included,' said the Master Draughtsman (speaking also for his sibling), 'a six-month each. It gives to our tools with ease, this stone from Dwarasamudra. With equal ease, it damages from haste. Finished and polished, it turns adamantine. My work alone will require no more than a week for each.'

'When do we begin?'

'It is your will, Magnificence.'

'At daybreak, then. I shall appear duly attired.'

Overhearing this, Parijatapuri deduced, with manifest distaste, that Narasimha intended the blocks to be carved into likenesses of himself. First the counterfeit chariot, and then those odious people pretending to be lovers and serpents and this here counterfeit equine. Was there no end to the deceptions on display? Unable any longer to quell his pique, he swivelled around on his heels. 'Am I to remain in attendance until this conceit is complete?'

His presence was acknowledged. 'Ah, my friend...I trust you are not muchly inconvenienced? Must you return, do feel free to leave anytime.'

10

KATAKA

'They are at it an inordinately long time,' said the Scrivener, pacing the Hall of Enchantment. 'I had better go investigate.'

'A fine clucking hen your winsome ward has made of Your Magnificence,' the Courtesan said, sipping her wine. 'He is safe, she's well versed with virgins. Do sit, you're making my head spin.'

'It's the drink.' He sat. 'It's not for him that I'm worried.'

'He couldn't do worse than that vulgar set of the other evening.' She shuddered. 'All those clots and bruises…I thought they'd gone pressing mulberries into my girls' withers and breasts.'

'Believe you me, he can be rough as a donkey.' He paused, '…Or so they say.'

'They?' She arched an eyebrow. 'You said he'd never been with a lady.'

'No, all I said was a strapping youth such as he must taste every pleasure at least once in his life. But leave that be; who were this *vulgar set* who dared mishandle your princesses?'

'Outsiders.'

'From?'

'The low countries, I hazard, from their mud colour and coarse speech. They claimed to be cloth merchants, not that I believed it. The conversation before they repaired upstairs ought to have forewarned me of their true intent.'

'Which was?' he said, tickling her knee.

'Stop that!' She swatted his hand. 'Methinks they were here at the bidding of a certain rival of mine. One of them was overtly interested in our monthly outlay on upkeep…another, if the girls were individually taxed. The third had the temerity to ask how I protected my assets.'

'Vulgarians indeed. In all these years not once have we probed one another's assets.'

'More to the point, not your everyday cloth merchants, I dare say. When I asked after their exact provenance, they hedged, claiming to be of no fixed address. When I asked to view their merchandise, they hedged again saying all that remained of their stock were odd scraps. So I let it pass and sent them upstairs. Afterwards, there was the matter of payment.'

'Oh…*those* types.'

'*Those* types indeed. What peasants, I sniped, to partake of hospitality and to then claim unpreparedness to recompense. Had they taken this for some charity? And no, I said, for I could see it coming, we extended no credit except to our most privileged set.'

'For which kindness some of us must remain beholden for life.'

'Yes. So. The servants meantime had alerted the guardsman… The sight so close of our spotted cat awakened their senses. After conferring among themselves, the most servile of the triad extracted a ring from his waist bag and offered it as surety. When I pointed that it would not suffice to feed a *common* cat, he produced an armlet—all this most reluctantly, mind—upon which one of the other two remarked that the items had belonged to a deceased friend, adding as a black joke that the gold could well be considered his last gift to them. Evidently, a fourth of their party had fallen into a drop-trap.'

'How unpleasant.'

'Yes. In some forest along the way. Not missing their fellow immediately, they'd taken the scream in the night for that of a pig. They found him at daybreak impaled on the stakes so they cremated him right there and covered the pit.'

'And not before divesting a dead man of his finery. Charming.'
'My thoughts exactly.'
'Of course they murdered him.'
She gave a little squeal. 'No! You're scaring me.'

'You ought to be *terrified*, what with consorting with lowlife… How much did you get on the surety?'

'It's barely been two days! What if they come back?'

'For a dead man's things?'

She reached under her cushions for a drawstring pouch of green velvet. 'See.'

The armlet was commonplace. Not so the ring. The carved chalcedony seal—a finely rouletted flower motif—was clogged with wax. Or dry ink. Or perhaps its wearer had clawed at the stakes as he lay dying. The reverse-lettering on the gold bezel was none too cleanly filed away, leaving some of the characters still distinct. Here a *da*… There a *ba*… A *ri*…

'I'd dispose of these, the sooner the better,' the Scrivener said evenly, returning the pieces to the pouch and handing it back. 'Nothing begets greater misfortune than gold off the dead or stolen from a pyre after the corpse is ash.'

'There was one other thing,' she said, tucking the pouch away. 'It seems the fellow who handled this matter quizzed the girl he'd had whether she or any of the others were daughters of mine. "We are all as daughters to our mother-lady," she claims to have replied. But he had persisted, pinching and biting, does not your mother-lady have a true son as well? Was he here recently? Where is he at present? As you well know, my girls and the servants are trained to be chary. So she speedily concluded her service and showed him downstairs.' She looked down with a frown, swirling the wine in her goblet. 'He seemed ill at ease that evening before his collapse. And then, not a word of farewell to me before they left.'

It took the Scrivener a moment to follow the shift in subject. He beamed. How felicitous to have chosen this evening for an outing. 'Come, you mustn't feel that way,' he said, patting her hand. 'Word from Chandrabhaga is that your vacationist prince is fully recovered midst all that sun and sea air in the care of his friend. Now, I *really* must see what our youngsters are at.'

❦

Back in his bed, the Scrivener rolled off the student and flopped on his back.

He hadn't been overtly surprised, earlier at the Courtesan's, to find the young man and the girl engaged in a game of riddling rhymes. Bursting upon the picture of innocence, he had dragged his startled ward to his feet and to their carriage and clattered back to the palace at unusual speed.

'Up,' he said, nudging the warm body beside him, 'there's work to finish.'

A groan, muffled by the pillows, and, 'Can it not wait until it is light?'

'Not,' he said, rising and whipping a sheet about himself, 'it'll take just a moment.'

'I am truly, utterly, achingly fatigued.'

'If you do this one little thing,' he purred, 'I promise you a treat you will never forget.'

The student wriggled and flipped over. 'Your last treat was a fair waste of time.'

The Scrivener found this new insolence exciting and at the same time worrying. Although they went to it every chance they had, something—he couldn't quite put a finger on it—had changed. 'On the contrary,' he said lightly, 'a most entertaining evening for me. You, on the other hand, must be shattered by your inability to pleasure a lady.'

At this, the youth lunged from the bed and, making a feint at the Scrivener, strode out into the study where he threw himself into his chair and gathered Pol onto his lap.

'That's more like it,' said the Scrivener, placing a stylus and a rectangle of palm-leaf before him. 'Keep it legible, but not too refined.'

'Why not paper and reed?'

'No questions. Consider this a lesson in composing a minatory missive; the learning will hold you in good stead someday. Begin.' He stood behind the chair, his fingers lightly

drumming the backrest. 'Your most honourable exalted highness
Parijatapuri… One concerned for your safety begs you to pay
heed…' He paused, expecting some protest; there was none
forthcoming. He continued: 'Some men of Cadambagiri are in
the capital making enquiries of your bearings… Their motives
are deathly… Your life is in peril… Destroy this and make
yourself scarce… A well-wisher.' He smiled, chafing his hands
and cupping his ears. 'That will suffice. Rub in some ink.'

'Why would anyone care to harm the Crown Misery?'

'Never you mind.'

'He will know it is I who wrote this.'

'Not unless you intend to deliver it personally and claim
authorship.' He scanned the blackened lettering. 'Well done.
Come morning, this shall travel in the Sovereign's dispatch
box along with a note from me…and we needn't care of the
consequences.'

'A note?'

He pointed to the ceiling with a wink and a smile. 'To say it
was found upstairs'

'You are insane! He will know it is I—'

'Oh don't be silly. Come.'

'Where?'

'Back inside. Your treat awaits.'

'*I don't want it*,' he shouted, rising and thrusting Pol into the
Scrivener's hands. Gathering his things from where they had
flung them about in their urgency, he moved to the mirror to
inspect a purplish mark on his neck before wrapping his dhoti.

The Scrivener stared at the smooth long back. Ah, my cruel
simorgh: someday you too will be spurned by someone of like
beauty and conceit as yourself…only then shall you remember
how you torment me with your tricks…

So thinking, he stepped up and trailed a soft-padded cat's-
paw down the bare back.

In less than eight weeks, everything would change. Had he

planned it himself, he couldn't have picked a better time. 'By the way,' he breathed, lightly squeezing the paw in his hand so that its claws would unsheathe, 'come the full moon of November, your damsels and you are to embark on a very long journey.'

~

In a different wing of the palace, the Consort was seated at the Sovereign's desk, composing a personal, not official, letter to Cadambagiri.

It was only when her husband was away that the good lady ventured upstairs to his apartments, a battalion of maidservants in tow, to launch an attack on weeks and months of manly untidiness. The regular manservants appointed to the wing were only too happy to be divested of their long-brooms and short-brooms and mops and pails—the while protesting how well they tended to the master's needs. This morning, the women's foray into their domain had coincided with the delivery from the sorting-offices downstairs of a parcel from Cadambagiri for the Sovereign; it was not unusual for dispatches of a personal nature to await his attention on his desk.

Under ordinary circumstances, the Consort might have given the delivery a cursory glance and gone back to supervising her women. But its size and provenance had whetted her curiosity. After ignoring it unsuccessfully for much of the morning, she went back to it. It wasn't particularly heavy. Ripping away the travel-soiled cloth wrappings, she rested her hands on the cubic wooden box for a moment before unhasping the lid.

It was packed with sandalwood shavings. At first, she took the object inside for a pottery artefact, finished in a creamy and lightly pitted glaze. The accompanying note dismissed the premise: a vorompatra (whatever that was) had produced the thing… An *egg*! The sender closed with *your faithful compeer's wish that you too find as much delight in holding and beholding this natural marvel as we do each time our hen furnishes an example of its type*. It had led the Consort to an identical box under the

Sovereign's bed—and in the box, a pile of correspondence on identical stationery and in the same hand.

Leaving her maidservants to get on with their chores, the Consort had perused the letters—from the last-but-one to the earliest (on birch bark), in the process chancing also upon a painting of the writer in the attitude of a goddess on tiger-back. From the frequency of the dispatches, one might imagine her runners were possessed of wings on their heels. Beyond an early reference to Narasimha's portrait, to a gift of stationery from him, to Chandrabhaga, and sundry allusions to matters of statecraft, it was impossible to tell whether the recipient had responded with equal regularity.

Fairly soon in her reading—how *oddly* the writer expressed herself—the Consort was nonplussed to find the letters conveyed no illicit intent towards her husband. Nor was there any hint of debauch between the lines; nothing that seemed remotely coded; no poesy. Rather, an impassioned heart seemed to have sought refuge in the written word from her worldly cares and found in Kataka a sympathetic eye. Reading the first letter again, the Consort couldn't help but wonder how one as enervated as the Junior Parijatapuri had it in him to plot anarchy. Was this the reason Narasimha had invited him to vacation with them? What was it that he had said about keeping his friend *out of mischief*? What, then, was she to make of Parijatapuri's feverish admissions to her, not too long ago, as he lay abed in the sickbay? None of it made any sense; it vexed her to even try. As for the oft-repeated greeting in the letters to *your noble consort whose acquaintance we hope to some day make*, she was not a little bit piqued that Narasimha hadn't once cared to convey the writer's sentiment. Sitadevi had never considered herself a *noble consort*. That she might be viewed as such was faintly amusing. Noble consorts don't pry in their husband's affairs, she said to herself, returning the letters to the box in chronological sequence. She then stood softly drumming her fingers on the lid, an idea taking shape in her mind.

There was little to lose in initiating an independent correspondence with this Sovereign of Cadambagiri. Doing so might well earn her a friend for life: only her water-clocks and sundials knew how much she craved a confidante, more so since Narasimha had banished her cousin to the cowsheds. There are no coincidences, she convinced herself: this egg was destined to be delivered to my hands.

After her maidservants had left with their baskets of laundry and rubbish, the Consort helped herself to Narasimha's stationery and spent the rest of the evening at his desk. All that remained to be done was a fair copy:

> Fond sister-sovereign | With joy the Consort Kalinga opens this missive which must be the first of many to quicken the distance between ourselves | We have long wished to make your acquaintance | May the written word until we speak enable an exchange of our deepest thoughts and feelings | On the subject of feelings we feel bound to relay a matter of import to your eyes | As he lay recovering from a fever some weeks ago in our care your brother-by-marriage bade us sit by his side one night of rare lucidity before he sank once again to his ocean of nightmares | On that occasion he spoke at length of your beauty and courage and intelligence and wit and his times of laughter and friendship in Cadambagiri until the cruel hand of fate had intervened | He greatly regrets being wed to one who has made a cat's-paw of him and rendered him a fugitive from his own palace | It was never his desire to usurp upon your inheritance | Quite the contrary he seeks your pardon for the misdeeds of his princess | He is sojourning nowadays in Chandrabhaga with our husband and poses no threat to your throne and country | This matter we thought prudent to bring to your knowledge...

She paused, sucking in her cheeks. She had done well in her decision to write. Setting down her reed pen, she carefully lifted the giant ovoid from the box by her side.

The thing was opaque against the lamp. She placed her eye to the manmade orifice at the base. A fathomless, faintly glowing void. It smelt of sandalwood…and raw egg; she wrinkled her nose and drew her head back from it. The sound of its emptiness, next, was unlike any other silence: a heavy humming stillness, as though her ears were sealed. She returned the egg to its nest of wood shavings, trying to imagine the monstrosity that had laid it.

From what she had gathered from the letters: a type of bird capable of bearing two children on its back. One capable of killing a man. One being reared for its unpredictability…an avian cavalry.

The Consort felt a surge of affection for her new-found friend. *Do furnish us in haste* (she concluded) *a portrait of yourself riding upon your marvellous egg-laying giant…*

~

On the terrace of a safe house overlooking the Kushabhadra, the former ministers of Cadambagiri shouted for refills. They were dining on turtle stew and rice dumplings. The safe house was owned by a blue-eyed tow-bearded yavana gone native. Downstairs, a brawl had erupted—the third that night—and was cheered on in strange tongues when it spilled to the street.

'It is for such a life that we were made,' said Royal Household. 'I feel more youthful tonight than I have in weeks.'

'Uncertainty has that effect,' slurred Taxes, sucking the stew from under his fingernails.

'Thank me for our decision to quit Cadambagiri,' Treasury put in, slapping Taxes' back. 'Had I not insisted, we would still be rotting in that cesspit.'

'Let us entirely the past forget!' cried Taxes, coughing and hacking.

'Forget! Forget!'

'Servant! More drink here, and hurry!'

And so they slurped their dinner, downed the toddy, and sat back to belch. If they hadn't a great mission to accomplish, it would take little to keep them in Kataka for the rest of their days.

The bravado which had fuelled the original foursome's flight from Cadambagiri had lost none of its sheen in the intervening weeks. Arriving in Parijatapuri, they had claimed cousinship to the Crown Princess; in response, the fearsome Raja had consigned them to a room in the servants' quarters unceremoniously. Just as they were beginning to fear they had been forgotten, they were granted audience with the Crown Princess.

They had last seen her that ill-starred night of her wedding. Heavy now with child and altered beyond belief, she seemed not to have lost her fighting spirit. The audience was brief. She asked them to forget Cadambagiri for the present and go to Kataka and eliminate her husband.

The promise of a principality each was enough for the quartet to put aside any doubts they may have had on their ability to fulfil the new brief. For readily accepting to carry out her bidding, they each received a new horse, a fresh set of clothing, and a purse for personal expenses. Before they set out, they were given a wicker cage of pigeons and the addresses in Kataka of their quarry's birth-mother and a safe house in the citadel.

Temples' death in a drop-trap had come as an untimely, albeit felicitous setback: his mount fetched a tidy sum in Kataka's stock market; his personal effects provided for the occasional indulgence. Selling their own horses not only swelled their purses but also drew less attention to themselves in this disreputable riverside enclave. After a week of mingling with the thriving local and Arab, Chinese, Suvarnadwipan and assorted yavana populace of smugglers, soldiers of fortune, fraudsters, panders and prostitutes, the so-called cloth merchants from the southern countries experienced a thrilling surge in their confidence, enough to embolden a visit to Kataka Palace.

In this outing, the party (led by Royal Household) had met

more success than it had at the Courtesan's palace (under the leadership of Treasury). The Sovereign, they learned at the Petitions Department, had cancelled public audience for some weeks; if they so desired, petitioners could deposit their appeals in the petitions box by the entrance and await word from the office.

The visitors, in this instance, had not so desired. Instead, for the discreet gift of a red cowry, a clerk had supplied the relevant detail. The Sovereign was sojourning at Chandrabhaga-on-Sea. Two yellow cowries purchased a more relevant detail: the royal retinue had indeed included the Crown Prince of Parijatapuri; they were not due back for another month at the least.

Delighted with this breakthrough, the threesome had hurried back to the safe house and enlisted the services of the yavana innkeeper to chart their forward journey. 'For to go to Chandrabhaga,' he had lisped, tracing a yellowed thumbnail on the table along an imaginary map, 'take a boat down the river to Khalakatapatna. A boat north from there will take you to Chandrabhaga which is not far away; there will be many taking iron for a new temple there. Take care, for those boats are the private property of the king. Clear?'

Clear, they had nodded.

Their belongings readied for the morrow's journey, the threesome had one more errand to complete before turning in for the night. In the cramped quarters they shared, Treasury plucked a pigeon from the cage and to a wing-feather attached a pellet of paper with a horsehair. Come dawn, the courier would fly homeward to Parijatapuri bearing the message: *Quarry in Chandrabhaga | Your faithful servants follow to eliminate.*

11

PARIJATAPURI

A MONTH BEFORE THE BIRTHING WAS DUE, THE CROWN
Princess was delivered of a prince—the first to the palace born
in some four decades. It was a difficult birthing. The princess's
screams could be heard all the way down at the palace gates.
Purportedly premature, the newborn was large, fully formed,
and covered in black hairs. Within moments of emerging, he
opened his small eyes and expressed himself in tones which
rent the mid-October midnight to ribands. Rejected by the
mother on sight, the unprepossessing mite was cast to a milk
mother—kept in preparedness in the event the Crown Princess
died in childbed.

At daybreak, the normally reclusive Raja made a special
appearance at the drum-pavilion over the palace gates to
announce the birth of his male grand-heir and declared a four-
day public holiday. No sooner had the town criers transmitted
the dual glad tidings in the market squares, the sweet merchants
got in on the act, distributing their dripping delights to the
citizenry and outsiders and untouchables alike. To the jangling
of bells and wafting of incense, every temple and roadside shrine
sent up special prayers to grant the newborn fame, fortune and
everlasting life. A number of midwives induced labour so that
other Parijatapuri babies might share a birth date with their
new prince. In the main market, a luthier, an unguentary and
a saddler renamed their respective works *New Prince* and then
quarrelled over first rights over the name.

Meantime in the palace, the court astrologers were done
casting the newborn's horoscope and began the complicated
process of selecting a name and middle name and last name
for him. The court bard composed a commemorative poem
(comprising a hundred-and-eight different words for 'Valiant')

which the court musicians set to drums, strings and voices. Between arranging a dance drama to enliven the imminent naming ceremony, the principal courtesan relayed, through voice-courier, a coded message (*grandfather has squeezed gold from his mango*) to Kataka to her mother-courtesan there. For accurately predicting the birth of a prince, the Oracle was gifted four maiden acolytes. Every servant and sentry in the palace received a silver coin as an increment. All in all, life in Parijatapuri might have turned quite different had the Crown Princess produced another princess. The gods have favoured her finally, said everyone: third time blessed. And speaking of princesses, no one was more pleased than the siblings of the Heir Apparent.

The First Princess and Second Princess—whose births, six and four years ago, had merited little joy—were permitted to visit the nursery on the fourth morning of their brother's life, during the brief interval the milk mother had to nurse her own baby.

Pressed shoulder to shoulder, the sisters peered into the silver-and-mirror-panelled crib in which the object of their curiosity lay softly snoring under a brocaded coverlet. A trail of milky spittle glistened on his chins.

'He looks exactly like a rat,' whispered the First Princess not inaccurately, running a light fingertip down a furred cheek.

'Don't call him that,' the Second Princess whispered back, brushing away her sister's hand. 'Grandfather says he is…*special*.'

'How so?'

'I'll show you,' said the Second Princess, lifting the coverlet. 'See?'

The girls stared solemnly at the grey-red stump in the middle of the belly.

'What *is* it?' ventured the First Princess, not wanting to know, really.

'That's where he was plucked from a special tree,' said the Second Princess. 'Now look here.' She lifted the coverlet more fully to reveal a fatty blob of dark flesh between the legs. 'We don't have that and *that* is what makes him a special baby.'

The baby twitched his nostrils but continued to sleep.

'A special baby rat,' said the First Princess slowly.

'No. A baby *man*!'

'A baby rat man.'

'You are just…*jealous*,' said the Second Princess who was growing up to be quite the little lady. 'When brother becomes Raja, he shall make you…our *servant*.'

'What shall you be?'

The Second Princess thought for a moment. 'The Rani,' she said firmly. 'I shall pluck many babies from my trees.'

'That will be nice. I shall feed them to my cats.'

At this, the Second Princess pinched the First Princess under her upper arm and twisted the flesh. 'I shall tell Grandfather you called him a rat,' she shrilled, causing the Heir Apparent to wake up, fix the faces above him with his small eyes and emit a continuum of ear-splitting shrieks.

'Enough, you two,' called the milk mother from her window seat, setting aside her baby and huffing to her feet. Their little disagreement thus quelled, the sisters exited the nursery—the younger a step ahead as always.

$\sim$

The night-blooming jasmines, fallen from their high arching branches before daybreak, were wilting in the sun beating down on the terrace. Two servants on their haunches swept the flowers into mounds of crinkled vermilion and white; the swishing of their brooms drifted with the bruised fragrance into the galleries.

'It is said in the scriptures,' said the Raja with an amicable smile, holding out a yellowed curl of paper to the Crown Princess, 'that there is no greater crime that a wife may commit than to connive in eliminating her husband.'

Written evidence of said intent had winged home some days ago and—with its intended recipient in confinement—fluttered into the wrong hands.

The Crown Princess smiled, reaching for the thing; the Raja drew his hand away, and teasingly forth and back a few times. She snatched the scrap and in a glance read the contents. Her smile stayed in place. 'A crime greater than consorting with the father of her husband?'

'Father only in name to the husband.'

'Therefore daughter-in-law only in name.' Making a tight ball of the paper, she flicked it between thumb and middle-finger to the terrace. 'But who be this sinner who wishes to eliminate her husband?'

'The mother of my grandson in name.'

She laughed. 'Had it been another granddaughter instead?'

'Irrelevant in the present.' He sat. 'Enough. No more of your games. Why this extreme step?'

She knew when not to deny all knowledge. 'His avarice knows no limits,' she said, sitting up and pulling a shawl across herself. 'He has conspired with a section of my sister's kinsmen to usurp upon Cadambagiri. I cannot permit it, not after my cousins travelled all this way on her behalf to seek my advice. They have proof of his correspondence with the rebels... If you doubt me, I have only to send for it.'

'You thought it fit to keep so grave a matter from me?'

'Only in order not to trouble you with my cares. My entreaties to him fell on deaf ears.'

'But to *eliminate* him...? Surely—'

'On the pretence of vacationing, your son in-name has travelled to Kataka to garner forces from his best-beloved there. The throne of my dear departed father today; tomorrow, it will be your throne he will eye with complete disregard for honour, loyalty...for all you have given him, a courtesan's illegitimate. Speaking of whom, who knows what wiles she indulges him; beneath his placid exterior lurks *her* dark treachery. But leave them be; my deepest concern is for my sister's life. The cousins inform me the poor child is on the brink of madness from fear of what might happen.' She moved closer to him. 'How can I, safe in your care, permit such an outrage? Would you permit it if she were a daughter of your loins?'

'Those cousins of yours—'

'They risked their lives coming to me. I cannot betray their faith in my abilities. In their mission to render the rebels headless, I've cautioned them to make it seem like an accident. Once this dark period is behind me, I shall invite Sister to consider her throne and country a protectorate of Parijatapuri. With your acquiescence, needless to say.' She looked down at her hands. 'I pray the years have treated her kindly; she was always more beautiful than I.'

'I find that hard to believe,' he said, brushing a curl off her forehead. She remained silent. He continued, almost to himself: 'What a waste. He could not have been a satisfactory husband, not with spawning only females.'

She shrugged her shoulders. 'My servants are happier with their men.'

There was a long pause. 'Who is the better? I or he?'

'Who do you think?' she replied.

'Good.' He ran a spatulate forefinger down her cheek. 'Granted this second chance, I shall personally groom the child from the beginning.'

'Our son could wish for no better inheritance.'

'In the other matter,' he said, rising, 'if any assistance be required, you have only to ask it of me. I wager your cousins are incapable of eliminating anything, let alone the disappointment.'

'If needs be, I will seek your aid.'

'There was one other thing.' He touched an unexpressed breast. She almost screamed from the pain. 'You do aver he is mine?'

Her eyes welled. 'How *could* you doubt me?' she gasped. 'Who *else* is there?'

'The Oracle seemed to think otherwise,' he replied. He might have done more had her daughters not chosen that instant to burst in on them.

'Grandfather! She called you a rat!'

'No, Grandfather, I did not!'

'*She did, she did!*'

'It is untrue!'

'*She said she'll feed you to her cat!*'

'Ah, such calumny at so tender an age!' the Raja said with a laugh, pulling the girls close to his sides and then propelling them before him across the terrace: 'Come, let us go pay your noble brother our respects whilst your mother lady restores her beauty.'

~

Mastered in the healing sciences, the acolytes worked in silence, anointing the Oracle's supine form with warm medicinal oils.

His hair gathered in a top-knot and his beard in a tight braid, he dared not flinch or open his eyes lest he destroy the sensations in which he was drowning.

The simultaneous workings of four pairs of hands felt as if a great octopus had taken possession of him, its sole object to transport his pleasure to unexplored heights. Never before had he felt so…appreciated as a man. He stifled a giggle, willing his mind to go blank. As one pair of hands stroked his right leg upwards from ankle to hip, so the pair diagonally across did the same for his left arm from palm to armpit. As the other pair worked on his left leg from ankle to hip, so the pair diagonally across did the same for his right arm from palm to armpit.

Suddenly, the hands began sweeping like waves across his chest and abdomen—right to left, left to right, fingertips to toes, toes to fingertips, driving the body which was no longer his into a frenzy of not knowing which side was which and what part was where. In one swift move he was turned over and laid down on his front even as the hands continued their workings up and down and across his back and the backs of his arms and legs and his soles and toes and between his toes and his fingers until one of the acolytes straddled his hips and slipping her hands under his armpits lifted his chest while another held down his legs and the third made him lick a palmful of honey and the fourth drew an obsidian blade across his tongue causing more than the tip of it to fall cleanly away.

The Oracle felt not a thing—neither then nor later—for the oils had permeated his skin and a lump of alum quickly clotted the surgery. He awoke to a new day to find himself a little bit numb and pain-free and quite effectively speechless.

12

CHANDRABHAGA

WITH TWO OF THE THREE GREENSTONE BLOCKS MOVED TO THE Master Sculptor's shed, Narasimha was to be found these days in the saddle of the counterfeit, sitting for the third of the Sun God's images.

For the first two standing figures, anticipated for the south- and west-facing terrace-shrines, they had posed him in horsehide boots, like those the Sun God purportedly wore day and night. The dowels in his hands were transformed into the stalks of two full-blown lotuses, flanking his face. When the boots came off at the close of each sitting, his feet felt and smelt vile. Will posterity ever guess, he had asked himself then, what pains I've endured in the interest of myth *and* history? Will posterity ever know that I am in fact moustached and bow-legged?

And what will they say when they gaze upon this, he mused today, eyes shut, smiling, the reins of the dummy horse light in his hands. He was a drowsy god now, leaping the invisible bridge between daytime and darkness at the close of a long day of traversing the heavens. Already, in the drawing taking shape on the greenstone, the careering horse, eyelids heavy, drooping head, echoed its rider's dreamy countenance.

A familiar footfall sounded nearby. It was that hour of the afternoon when they dealt with matters of state. 'Ready when you are, my dear Left Hand,' Narasimha said.

'Word from Khalakatapatna,' the Secretary began, 'is that Your Excellence's vessel is seaworthy. They seek word if you wish to inspect it.'

'How much longer for these sittings?'

The Secretary indicated, with a slight movement of his head, to the Master Draughtsman to furnish a reply.

'I should be done in four days, Magnificence.'

'And then I shall be delivered of your company to do as I please?'

'For the present, Magnificence. We shall require you again when my brother commences work on the faces… That will be some months hence.'

'To Khalakatapatna, then,' Narasimha said, opening his eyes, 'and onwards from there to the capital. Our guest might appreciate the diversion from a road journey.'

A clearing of the throat. 'We've received another message for him.'

'What a popular man!' Seeing how free from cares Parijatapuri seemed these days, Narasimha had withheld a delivery for him last week, instead appointing to his side one of the warriors from Aphrike. 'And what delight is it this time? Yet another nameless warning?'

'A letter from his mother. I thought it prudent to inform you before reaching it to him.'

'Have you not read it?'

'I would not presume to do so without your leave.'

'Rightly so. Go on, read it.'

A struggle with the scroll-case. 'She writes,' the Secretary began, stepping up to the counterfeit and lowering his voice, 'my precious lamb—is how she addresses him—a most reliable source has conveyed news of the birth of a large and…*complete*… boy-child to a certain wife a month before she was due to be confined. Word is that the father of the child is its grandparent. My heart…*bleeds*…for the cuckold, for only now do I fully comprehend his turmoil that night of the…*saffron*…? Bid him seek counsel from his…*most trusted compeer*…for it is well-nigh impossible for him to return to that heinous pit of *entanglements* without further imperilling his life. With her constant prayers for his eternal safety, your own mother beloved…'

'Astonishing. Her precious lamb will be most discountenanced to learn we have pried.'

'The same fate as the other missive?'

'No, no,' Narasimha said. For one so harmless, his friend certainly inspired extreme feelings. 'There is no call to protect him from *everything*. He might even appreciate the brutality. Seek him out and—' he shook his head, 'No. I suppose we must extend whatever assistance we can.'

～

These past weeks of sojourning by the sea, Parijatapuri had conquered his fear of the Aphrikes—enough to accept one of them as his chaperone at Narasimha's insistence. He still kept his distance from the sheds of lepers and those wicked women, preferring to observe progress on the stallions for the chariot, the basement mouldings, the pilasters and cornices...and advancement, too, on the Sun God's images.

As for his own advancement, a daily constitutional on the beach had put a spring in his step, even as the sun and salt air bleached his hair in a not unattractive way. His skin glowed with a coppery tan. He ate with relish and slept untroubled by dreams. His smile reached his eyes.

A kerchief across his face to filter the stone dust clogging the air, he was seated in the junior sculptors' shed. They were busy these days with friezes of trappers in pursuit of a herd of forest elephants. How adroitly the figures leapt to life under their delicate chisels and mallets! There was even an elephant-birthing scene... A long shadow fell across the floor before him. He turned.

The chaperone—a cheek wound from the Katasimha skirmish worn as a permanent grin—wordlessly held out a scroll case. Easing out the contents, Parijatapuri recognized his mother's spidery hand. A dense silence seemed to take him in its embrace, muting the chisels and mallets, the murmur of workmen, a crow's cawing, the distant waves. Abruptly, the sensation released him. The chaperone and he shared no language, yet, 'Would you believe it,' he said, removing the kerchief, 'my mother has written to alert me that my wife and her father-in-law, who is not my real father, have a bastard begat. Which finds me asking myself: what is the child to me?'

He began to laugh—so hard that the tears streaked his stone-dust covered cheeks. Recovering, he reached for the chaperone's hand and pulled himself to his feet. 'This,' he beamed, waving the letter, 'is a *most* happy development. Lead me to the Sovereign!'

$\sim$

'There you are,' Narasimha began from the saddle before Parijatapuri could say a thing, 'I have been thinking. Of the old days…of how we used to say of what use kingship if one did not employ it to the benefit of one's kin, the welfare of one's allies… for the Empire's well-being? I've given it considered thought these past days. I truly wish to appoint you my envoy to Kilwa, to the court of Bone Soleiman. We spoke briefly of the cows; I have none more trusted than you to deliver them to him. Granted, you mentioned a child due sometime but—'

'A great honour, Narasimha. When must I leave?"

He had expected some sobbing protest. 'Did you hear what I said?'

'You'd like me to take the cows to Kilwa. Yes.'

'It is a considerable distance away.'

'I am well aware of where Kilwa is.'

He frowned. 'More lives are lost on the high seas than we care to enumerate. In accepting, you do so in the knowledge that you may not survive the journey.'

'I believe I am aware of the hazards,' Parijatapuri said, handing his mother's letter to him. 'Read this. Under the circumstances, I have nothing to lose from accepting your embassy. No kingdom…no family…not even a *true* royal lineage to fall foul of by crossing the seas.'

What utter hell, thought Narasimha (pretending to read) it must be to be cuckolded. 'My commiserations,' he said. 'You must wish to reconsider in the light of…this?'

'Thank you. There is nothing to reconsider.'

He handed the letter back. Parijatapuri crumbled the birch-bark between his hands, the while smiling brightly even as the pieces fell to the floor about his feet.

'I find it hard to believe you feel no rancour,' Narasimha said.

'How *can* I? Do you not see? They have unwittingly rendered me a service; I am indifferent to the...the bastard child. Of course,' he added, not unkindly, 'you would not understand, from not being a parent. Remember well: before you become a father, consider the legacy you bequeath your progeny. Oftentimes they won't thank you for it. Although in your case, it will be different—' Suddenly awkward, he looked away, 'Only glory, not shame. So. When would you have me leave? For Kilwa, I mean. To the palace of your *particular compeer*.'

Narasimha gave him a worried look. 'The ides of November, in three weeks.'

13

KHALAKATAPATNA

THE SHIP-BUILDING ENCLAVE, WHERE THE KUSHABHADRA SINKS her rotting gums into the Kalingodhra, is a rough unwholesome unsightly place. Unlike the port of the same name a mile upriver, the shipyard boasts neither waterfront parks nor marketplaces where one may stroll taking in the life and merchandise from near and faraway lands; there are no women to be seen or trees for shade, instead there are droves of flies. Except during the rain (when all works cease) the air is so thick you can stir it with a stick; it stinks of burning caulk, fish oil and rotting fish. There is little relief from the clangour of metal, the deafening crack of timbers and falling planks and the occasional, inexplicable boom which must surely issue from some unearthly thing.

The principal shipyard has long since outgrown its grids of wet- and dry-docks and breakwaters to become this blur of factories, smithies and furnaces. At any given time, up to a hundred vessels may be seen in various states of repair or readiness. Most belong to the Sovereign; the rest are of Arab and Eastern ownership. At low tide, the piers teem with rats, blue crabs the size of rats, and packs of pyes which prey off the rats and crabs. Come dusk, swirls of mosquitoes rise from the sewers abutting the tenements of the shipwrights. The men (and boys) at their hereditary trade speak a harsh guttural dialect and at the top of their voices, for nearly all of them are deaf. Each year, their numbers fall to tuphos, ball-rot, elephant-leg, neck-swell, leprosy and dropsy. It is rumoured that the Sovereign will make the port city of Khalakatapatna his new capital once his temple in Chandrabhaga is dedicated. Conditions in this hellhole, then, will surely change. For the present, the Sovereign's newest ship is berthed in the main dock, close to the exit conduits.

Fifteen months in the building, the *Arkaja* is eighty cubits in length, forty cubits at its widest, and forty-two cubits at the mast-tips. Twelve days since the vessel was lowered into its element, the ironwood-and-teak hull has not revealed a single leak. It sits low and deep, completely still, lime-white to the waterline and pitch-black beneath. Four tapering ladder masts await rigging: this will be done after the Sovereign has placed his seal of approval and leaves. The portholes are framed in ochre and red; two circular windows in the prow are rendered as the irises of two painted 'eyes'. The figurehead is a springing lion, twice life-size, carved from the bole of a mango tree and covered in gold leaf and lac. In anticipation of the seas it must brave, the lion's mane is windswept about its ears into waves ending in shell-coils; its goggle-eyes are set on a sightless vanishing point. Chains of copper, silver and onyx amulets are strung from its gaping ivory fangs; these catch the tawny afternoon light and tinkle in the rancid air. The couchant elephant of the Kalinga ensign, also gilded, is a meek footstool for the lunging feline. The name *Arkaja*—Born of the Sun—is carved and gilded on either side of the figurehead.

A riverboat drew up under the figurehead. It rocked as it was towed to its moorings and juddered on touching the jetty. Steadying himself, Parijatapuri hitched his dhoti and stepped nimbly after Narasimha onto firm ground first, and immediately up a gangplank into the ship.

How *motionless* it felt.

The vast wooden deck, newly waxed, was hemmed by a waist-high and generously curved parapet. An airy pavilion, accessed by a short flight of steps graced the prow end. To the left, mid-deck, stood a square hut flanked by wide passages; the pit of a stairwell in the middle ground was guarded on three sides by a railing. Beyond the hut, a shed with a humped roof—its eaves following the curving sides of the deck—seemed to extend to the stern end. Squinting up at the crow's-nest in the mast second from aft, Parijatapuri felt a wave of dizziness. 'What hell have

I got myself into?' he asked himself. With a little ingenuity, he might yet extricate himself from this predicament. He needed to *think*. 'Narasimha…' he called. 'Pray where are the privies?'

Narasimha, in a huddle with the Secretary and the shipwrights, turned. 'Privies?'

He nodded.

'Ah, the *privies*. You simply sit on the side and evacuate. To make water is easy—'

He could no longer hold it back. 'I cannot, Narasimha!'

'What? Make water?'

'Your embassy. I cannot go.'

Narasimha stepped away from the men and walked up with a smile. 'Did I hear you right?'

'Don't be angry, please. I'm afraid—'

'You gave me your word.'

'I wasn't thinking clearly. You cannot—'

'You were thinking all too clearly.' He pointed to the Secretary. 'He was witness to your declaration of willingness. I cautioned you of the hazards; you agreed—'

'No, Narasimha! Let us pretend otherwise! You, for whom greater men will gladly give their lives, should have no trouble finding another in my stead. Your general, a champion among men… Or that boy, the one with the cows…a fine young man, *he'll* make the perfect envoy—'

'If I am in need of your advice, I'll ask for it. As for the fine young man, he is going. You *and* he. You can oversee his chronicle of the voyage—'

'Do you not hear me? *I am afraid!* I *beg* you to relieve me. If you force me against my will, only sorrow can come of it. My left eye's been fluttering nonstop lately, you *know* what it means!'

'Too late, stop your fluttering.'

'Oh, how you must abhor me! Tell me so plainly and I shall jump into the sea and that will be the end of our friendship. Have you no appreciation for my abject dread? I am ill-suited for an embassy of such import as this!'

'*Import*?' He laughed. 'Ferrying a herd of cattle, an embassy of *import*? The truth is, I am saving you from yourself, from making a fool of yourself and from what you had planned against your sister-by-marriage.'

He exhaled violently. 'You know of *that*? But how could you? All this while, all these days and weeks… Ah…! So it *is* true what Mother said about your scribe—'

'My scribe?'

'Nothing. Forget I said anything. I wouldn't wish to cause more trouble.'

'No, no, my friend, not so quick… What did she say?'

'She?'

'Your mother. It is common knowledge that my Right Hand visits her, *that* is of scant interest; a different matter, however, if he's been wagging his tongue about matters of state. Out with it.'

'Only that you were engaged in personal correspondence with our lady of Cadambagiri. Pray do not take him to task—'

'What else did she say?'

'That's all I recollect. And then I lost consciousness.'

'A pity, when you could have been usurping upon Cadambagiri instead.'

'No! You must believe me! It was not *at all* that way. I am the *victim* in that mess—'

'As always. And it appears you have some men after your life. The choice is yours. Stay dry and confront your enemies, or…' He waved expansively towards the sea, '…sail off to Kilwa, forget your cares a while. By the time you return, ten months hence—'

'*Ten months*!'

'Give or take, anything can happen. It is, you realize, our maiden attempt into the Sea of Hind.' He looked away with a grimace. 'What I would give to captain this palace.'

'Knowing my accursed fate, I might never return alive.'

'It's a risk we take as men, but do try. That this great vessel sailed to Kilwa during my reign will be written in history…and with you aboard as my trusted envoy. We'll record the event on the temple's sides; there are provisions for it already. Can you not *see* them?'

'See whom?'

'The friezes, you fool. On my temple. This very ship, making her stately way west...the cows peering over the sides...these masts, sailcloths billowing. We'll have you in the pavilion there, pointing to the horizon, out over the figurehead. Can you not see it?'

Parijatapuri attempted a slow smile, biting his upper lip. 'May I say something?'

'Anything, except release from your embassy.'

'No, I only wished to say...I do fancy a panel to myself. On the temple, I mean.' He spread his hands, thumbs touching, 'A small one, this wide, will suffice...'

'Provided you promise to come back.' Narasimha laughed and clapped him on the back. '*Of course* I grant you a panel to yourself, must you even ask it? That settles that, then. Come, I must inspect the facilities downstairs... But first the privies.'

∽

By some unspoken decree, Treasury had appointed himself head of the mercenary triad. 'Has either of you,' he said, 'killed a man with your bare hands?'

The question elicited a nervous titter from Royal Household and Taxes. They were seated on the steps leading down to the principal pier, a pot of roasted chickpeas between them. For a small toll at the dock-gates, one could loiter away a whole day on the piers, watching the vessels crowding the port like outlandish insects.

Since their arrival in Khalakatapatna, the threesome had made little progress in their onward journey to Chandrabhaga, and not for want of trying: the few crafts sailing there were imperial property and flatly refused custom, not even for the promise of white cowries. They hadn't become disconsolate.

Rather, the impasse presented a welcome interlude to their wanderings. Here were yavana women with scarlet lips who brazenly trod the waterfronts with their skirts trailing in the filth. Here strutted white men and yellow men who went fully clothed and spoke in cawing tongues and behaved as though they owned the place. Here were game-fights between men of all shades inside cages and pits, cockfights and dogfights, and unequal fights to the death between leopards and hyenas, lions and bears. Here, one gambled for high stakes and emerged the richer in skills, even if poorer of cowries or teeth. In the markets, gemstones sold like ducks' eggs, slaves like poultry and virgin girls and boys as if they were sheep. Many of the waterfront lodges had comfort-rooms in the back where both clientele and trade stayed tireless day and night. And it was just as well that the three friends were stranded: it was rumoured that the Sovereign of Kalinga had sailed from Chandrabhaga to the shipyard downstream, and was due to make his way to Kataka through the port today. What the trio hoped to achieve from this knowledge from the pier remained to be seen.

In the waning light of the day, the steps of the landing stages were disappearing one by one in the rising tide. A short distance from the men, a lifeless dog had spilled its innards for a commotion of crows to unravel. 'The reason I ask,' said Treasury, returning to the subject of killing, 'is because it takes skill to accomplish cleanly. Any fool can make a mess of it like a dog's entrails.'

'Have you,' asked Taxes, waving off a wayward fly, 'killed cleanly?'

'I certainly have,' he replied, 'but a long time ago, before we became acquainted.'

Royal Household frowned. Treasury and he had grown up together in a nameless Cadambagiri village. The braggart, if memory served, hadn't killed a thing. If anything, Treasury had been a timid frail boy who played with dolls and a nuisance of female kin—one of whom Royal Household had gone on to wed. The unbidden thought of his wife prompted a wrench of longing—for her touch, her cooking, their children's voices, his own bedclothes and bed. He'd had enough of this misadventure: enough of flea-ridden whores and brothels, the messes that passed for food and burned his bowels; enough of this company. '*Enough*,' he said...and having started, 'I have been meaning to say this for sometime. I am going home.'

Treasury and Taxes regarded the speaker as if he were something crawled from a dog's intestines. 'Home?' said Treasury with a curl of his lip.

'Yes, *home*,' Royal Household said, thrusting the pot of chickpeas into Taxes' hands and getting to his feet as though he intended to march off to Cadambagiri directly. 'To my old life and my family. There is nothing but trouble to be had from this foolery; it was all a mistake, I shan't have any more of it. We had a *life* there. I was mad to have followed you...but no further. My mind is made, try stopping me.'

'An impressive delivery,' said Treasury lightly. 'But do reconsider, for not only are great rewards in reach, there is also your word of honour to our mistress—'

'*Your* word of honour,' Royal Household shouted, turning upon Treasury with unexpected spleen. '*You* spoke on our behalf. I have no desire for *your* mistress's rewards. I had a bad dream last night. What happens after...whatever the consequences—'

'But bad dreams are but dreams,' said Treasury. 'This is *life*. Reality! Come—'

'Not this foolishness, no! *Do you not understand?* I am going!'

'Don't act in haste,' said Taxes. 'The quarry is near...' he pointed downriver, '...somewhere there, even as we speak. Don't forsake our company now, not after all we have endured in the cause of justice. Only think of our other brother languishing in the labyrinth, of the other two and their unavenged ends. Only think how your talk weakens *our* spirit.' He might have added more, but for a restraining hand.

'No, let him be,' said Treasury. 'If his mind is made, who are we to change it?' He picked his teeth with a fingernail before continuing, 'Listen, my friend, go back with us to Kataka and thence homeward if you so need. But let's make a fine farewell of it, part as friends, for who knows when and where we must meet again. Say yes, and we shall speak no more of this fight nor bear any ill will. And pray sit down—I am getting a crick in my neck.'

Royal Household shrugged by way of response and sat sullenly, a little away. The dead dog got submerged, the crows took wing. Presently, a drum-boat appeared on the Kushabhadra, clearing a channel through the water traffic. A barge followed in the slipstream, its deck a-flutter with bunting and pennants. A band of drummers in the aft were making a merry din; it was hard to tell who was who in the open pavilion, mid-deck, behind the oarsmen. The threesome on the pier remained seated in silence long after the barge had progressed upriver and vanished from sight.

As darkness fell, small lanterns flickered and moved midst the bat-wing sails of the Chinese ships, midst the lateens of the Arab dhows, and on the small country boats darting between them like hungry water rats. More lights appeared on the opposite bank and under the footbridges where the scavengers lived. Presently, the pier inspectors began clearing the steps of loiterers and pimps.

That night, in an alley behind the old customs house, Treasury and Taxes taught themselves to kill cleanly. Having done, they divested Royal Household of purse and ornament and sat him against a wall as though he were a drunk who had choked on his vomit.

14

KATAKA

THEY WERE BACK AT WORK IN THE MORNING OFFICE. Unusually today, the table was set with a fourth chair. The pigeons under the window eaves were silent; somewhere in earshot, a conference of sparrows was in progress; from the terrace gardens, other small birds with big voices were regaling the morning with ascending *tu-weets*.

Waiting for Parijatapuri to join them, Narasimha and the Secretary and Scrivener sipped their turmeric-teas in silence. He appeared at long last. His hair, damp from a bath, hung about his face in tangled tendrils, but he was dressed with studied care in crisp new whites—the very model of an envoy on the brink of an uncertain assignment. A large ceremonial medallion flashed on his chest from a gold-beaded necklace. Touching the ornament with a jewelled ring-finger, he addressed a mock bow to the empty chair, 'My apologies—I awoke late,' and sitting, tasted his tea, gone cold, and grimaced.

'Your timing is perfect,' said Narasimha, reaching for a letter he had drafted. 'I should like you to be privy to the contents; you'll be presenting it to the Sultan upon your first audience of him so attend to it closely.' To the Scrivener, 'The usual salutation…and,' with a slight inflexion of voice, 'The esteemed bearer of this missive and gift of bovines is a prince in his own right, the Crown Prince, no less, of our ally country Parijatapuri, and one whom I consider my blood sibling.'

He glanced across the table; the recipient of the rare compliment inclined his head sideways and smiled at the new signature-seal ring on his right thumb.

'It is my fervent belief,' Narasimha continued, 'that His Eminence Parijatapuri and the bovines in his care are in your gracious presence, neither discomfited nor in any manner damaged from the rigours of their voyage. In attendance on the animals are their handlers and physician, all well trained, and also a superintendent who will prove to be a lifelong asset to your livestock yards.' He stopped, and looking up at the Scrivener said, 'Better you than the Consort or I to inform her cousin he is to remain there. He wished to see the world and should have little reason to complain. Assuage his fears and any tears that may spring.'

The Scrivener had dreaded the moment he would be called upon to ink his lover's imminent fate. Having done, his hand had turned to lead. And now this. He could feel the Secretary's lizard-eyes on him. Willing his voice not to betray him, he said, 'I shall do so, Excellence.'

'Good.' He turned back to the draft: 'To mark this maiden circuit of my new ship, it is my desire to acquire a beast native to Aphrike and known variously as kilin and zarafa. A living specimen may be entrusted to His Eminence Parijatapuri, with due instructions for its husbandry aboard ship and its subsequent care and stabling. With prayers for the health, longevity and increment of the cattle delivered herewith and for the enduring strength of our kinship, I close this missive with my fondest and most respectful et cetera et cetera.'

'What manner of beast is a kilin?' asked Parijatapuri, toying with his new ring.

'From a diagram by him,' said Narasimha, indicating the Scrivener, 'and a description from a certain other hand, a type of camel with pelt marked like a dry river bed.' He held up his forefingers to the sides of his head and then touched the middle of his forehead. 'And not just two but three horns, am I right?'

'That is correct, Excellence,' the Scrivener said. He was a fool to have dived off the safe island of lust into the murky waters of love; he had only himself to blame for the misery that awaited. He had grown accustomed to the boy's company, his teasing ways, his taste—knowing full well that it must one day end.

He'd be hard pressed to find a replacement. 'And of what use is this oddity?' the Crown Misery of Parijatapuri was saying, apparently addressing him. 'Little aside from the ornamental, *Your Eminence*,' he replied, and inwardly: *rather like yourself*. Checking the note of impertinence in his voice, he added: 'In Chin, the land of my father, where they are not native, kilins are considered harbingers of fortune and serenity.'

'Plenty of which we could do with,' Parijatapuri said, 'so long as your harbinger does not butt or bite.' He rose, rearranging his fine wool shawl so that the medallion on his chest was still visible but not too flashily. 'Now I *must* take your leave. I've pledged Mother my company the next two days.'

Narasimha performed a parody of a slow regal wave. 'Try not to become sick,' he said, and, after Parijatapuri had left, 'call for more tea.' After the Secretary dispatched a servant on the errand, he said: 'I have been meaning to ask. Any progress on the source of that minatory missive that you so kindly forwarded?'

'None whatsoever, Excellence,' the Scrivener replied, a beat too quick, taking up a scroll-case in which his lover's fate must be sealed.

'A pity,' Narasimha said, 'I had expected the hand behind it to have by now confessed.' He traced the grain of the table with a fingertip. 'I wager the talipot leaf on which it was writ was from the same stock we employed for a charter to Simhala last May. They were notched at the edge.'

The Scrivener set down the scroll-case. Could he have possibly been *so* careless? He swallowed. 'It was I who wrote it, Excellence,' he said quietly.

'And overreached yourself?' said Narasimha. His tone was affable, almost kind.

'I apologise, Excellence. But it was true that His Eminence's life was in peril.'

'Did you *truly* believe I would have inflicted it upon one already beset by cares? Why?'

'An error of judgement in a moment of madness. It will not happen again.'

'No. It will not. Compose a reference in any language of your preference and I shall gladly append my signature to it. You may leave after your ward has departed.'

At first he did not understand. And then he did. The chair grated to the floorboards behind him. 'Excellence—' he began.

'Alas,' Narasimha cut in, 'where trust is lost there can be little left to salvage.'

He stared at the speaker in the ivory chair. There were rulers who severed the writing hands of errant scribes. His own hands, he realized, had become clenched to his chest; he dropped them to his sides. The blood surged to his fingertips as though it were some viscous ink which might, any moment, spurt from under his fingernails. Before the anguish he felt could fully muddle his senses, he bowed from the waist, took a step sideways and back and made his exit. The servant returned and, gauging the air, set the tea-tray on the table and made himself scarce.

In the ensuing silence, Narasimha stared out of the windows to his right. A speck of a kite was inscribing wide loops on the cloudless sky. The kite was joined by another speck. 'You are thinking I have been impetuous,' he said, following the birds' airy transit.

'On the contrary,' said the Secretary.

The birds drifted out of sight; his eyes shifted to the adjacent rectangles of sky. Nothing. 'Find a replacement!' he yelled, thumping the table. The scroll-case jumped, the tea goblets splashed.

'Your father treasured me not only for my counsel,' said the Secretary after a moment.

'Meaning what?'

'I served also as his scrivener until the cross-breed courted his favour.'

Narasimha narrowed his eyes; he had never regarded the Right Hand as a cross-breed. 'Really?'

'How were you to know it, occupied as you were with your equines? My Persian has long lain dormant, yet may be effectively revived. Admittedly, I am unlettered in Chin or any of the yavana languages.'

'Those can wait.' As if he were loath to touch the letter to Kilwa, he moved it across the table with the end of the scroll-case. 'Begin with this... As many times as it takes for an *exact* copy. You have under two days to prove yourself.'

~

The Consort had been obliged, the past few weeks, to oversee goings-on in the pharmacy.

A long table was overrun by jars large and small, labelled in red on their stomachs and lids. Checklist in hand, the Consort opened a box. It contained a year's supply of neem tooth-sticks. 'The nit-combs,' she muttered, 'I don't see them. Have you them there?'

A duplicate checklist in hand, her cousin rummaged through a box at the other end of the table. 'Here,' he said, holding up the combs.

'There should be two sets.'

'There are. I hope I won't be expected to check *his* head for lice.'

'You can serve as his consort for the duration of your voyage.'

'Your husband,' he said, laughing, 'has gifted him a chaperone to render that service. A big black chaperone, dazzling of teeth and fists like maces to reduce to pulp anyone who causes him grief. I hear there are people out to snuff his life.'

'You mustn't believe every word of gossip,' she said brightly, crossing tooth-sticks and combs off her list. 'Is the eyeliner there as well?'

He fished out two greenish-black glass phials with ivory stoppers which doubled as applicators.

'Yes. Don't forget it every morning or the glare from the water will ruin your eyes in under a week.' She winked. 'And make sure *he* does. A blind envoy is as good as none. Toothpicks, next.'

'Here.' He held up a cylindrical lacquered box. 'The chaperone's teeth are forever on display.'

'Enough about the chaperone,' she said. 'Let's go over everything together. Begin here… Six jars of coconut hair oil.'

'Checked,' he said, following his list.

'Sesame body oil, six.'

'Checked.'

'Soapnut bath powder, six.'

'Eight.'

'You can't have too much. Come…you count, I'll check; it'll be quicker.'

'Patchouli pomade, twelve…*twelve*? Is it to a brothel that we are going?'

'You can never smell too sweet.'

'Sandalwood powder. Liniment bandages. Peacock-fat unguent. Basil pills. Arrowroot pills. Mint digestive. Marigold ointment. Lime poultice. Saltpetre. Lip salve. Alum. Limes in brine… One a day each, mind, against scurvy…'

A knock on the pharmacy door, and: 'A moment, Your Excellence.' It was the Scrivener. He looked, the Consort felt, a little pinched—somehow curved into himself like a broiled shrimp. 'Forgive the intrusion,' he said, entering, 'but a word in private, if I may?'

'What is it?' she said, moving around the table.

His eyes were bloodshot, as if he had been drinking. Or crying. Or both. 'Say nothing please,' he said in an undertone, giving her a sealed square of paper. She frowned, seeing to whom it was addressed. 'Might it be possible,' he went on, 'for one of your assistants to courier it in haste? I would have gone myself but,' he pointed with his chin towards the table, 'there is much to be done before they leave. Moreover, I have a crocodile of a headache… Might there be something here to deliver me of it?'

'Where does it pain?'

He touched his temples delicately. 'And down the back of my

neck…and here…' He rubbed the middle of his chest, 'A burning sensation; I fear it might be my spleen.'

'Are you breakfasted?'

'Alas, I have no appetite.'

She moved away with an exasperated sigh. Selecting a small jar from a shelf, she shook out some brownish stamens into a small copper dish: 'An infusion in warm water should ease both head and bowels,' she said. 'Was there anything else?'

'Thank you, my lady,' he said, 'only the missive, it *must* reach today. But pray do not send *him* on the errand.' Without once meeting his lover's eyes, he left the pharmacy.

∼

Evening. They were seated side by side on a bench in a rear garden of the palace. Behind the towering silk-cottons lining the river's edge, the Kushabhadra glided past like a swathe of liquid tiger-stripes. The day after, the lover would leave for Khalakatapatna to board the *Arkaja*; already, the calves had been dispatched down the river and loaded on to the ship.

'Is it not remarkable,' said the Scrivener, watching a troupe of monkeys in the trees' leafless crowns, 'that ours is the only species graced with the ability to read and write?' He had kicked off his slippers to twiddle his toes in the dewy grass. In the trees, the monkeys were causing the roosting parakeets to screech.

'Really?' said the lover absently. The world, they said, was a very large place, and he was on the threshold of verifying the claim.

'Think about it,' said the Scrivener. 'When was the last time you saw a monkey read or write?'

'You read and write all the time.'

'Ah, such rare wit,' the Scrivener said with a dry laugh. Their doings, earlier, had had an element of wretchedness, the things he must say hanging over them like a dead bat. He had decided to delay the telling; it was for that he'd brought themselves for an airing. 'The Sovereign,' he went on, 'ought to keep you back as court jester instead of wasting you on his Kilwan friend.'

'I will certainly keep the Kilwans entertained. In what language do they speak?'

'I believe we've been over this a thousand times.'

'Tell me again.'

'Kiswahili. Also Persian and Arabic. Greek, other yavana languages. Given your talents, you'll get accustomed to their tongues in no time.'

'No Sanskrit.'

'Not very much, I'm afraid.'

'How then am I supposed to express my needs? How must I tell the Sultan Splendid that I crave musk melons drizzled with honey, a softer bed and a hard chaperone in it?'

'The Sultan should be so lucky for such sparkling chat.'

'Indeed! But really…what a waste of my studies if I am unable to converse with him.'

'An education never goes to waste. We invested in yours so that posterity may declare, ah, look what a faithful chronicler of that voyage the Sovereign's selfless Right Hand did make of that callow boy. Try not to fail this hand, for it has groomed you well in the months we've had.' He paused. 'At first, leave all conversation to your Misery. His Persian is more than adequate.'

'It is?'

'I was called to put it to the test the other day. Clearly, one of them was paying more attention to his studies when they were boys.'

'Persian notwithstanding, the Misery had better not consider me his personal servant, for I shall protest.' He shot him a side glance. 'For what was it that you came to the pharmacy?'

'I did?'

'And pretended I did not exist.'

'Oh, that… I was suffering from the gripes. I needed something for it.'

'That was afterwards. I saw you giving her something. A message.'

'You'll cut yourself one of these days. It was a note to a friend.'

'A man friend?'

'Is this an inquisition?' Wretchedness was making him trenchant. 'If you *must* know, a *lady* friend. Your Misery's mother, as a matter of fact. Satisfied?'

'Will you visit her again?'

'The moment you have quit my sight.'

'Will you think of me? After I've quit your sight?'

'I might. If I remember.'

He laughed gaily. 'I imagine I should be quite changed by the time I'm back. You'd better memorize every little part of me.'

The Scrivener smiled a tight smile, swallowed hard and looked at his feet. He should say it now. He took a deep breath. The moment passed. The boy leant against his shoulder and nudged him lightly. 'I *so* wish it were you rather than he going with me.'

'I too wish it were so,' he murmured, shifting away slightly.

'Do you mean it?' He sprang to his feet: 'Why don't you! Tell the Sovereign that your company will greatly benefit the…the Empire! Tell him—'

'That is out of the question,' he said sharply, and then with sudden tenderness, reached for his lover's hand and pulled him down by his side. 'Think. If I were to go with you, who will take care of the Empire's correspondence? The Secretary is incapable of rendering that service.'

'The Secretary,' he spat. 'I wager he was behind His Eminent Emptiness coming with me.'

'No, quite the contrary. Do you recall the note I made you write, that horrible evening when Pol drew blood, and that other letter from his mother? They had the desired effect, removing the poor man out of harm's way.' He paused. 'Hopefully, by the time he returns, the fuss around him will have blown over completely.'

'What *is* the fuss, really?'

'He is an impediment to his wife…to her wish to be rid her

sister the Sovereign of Cadambagiri so that she may lay claim to that country as her birth-right, all to herself. She therefore wishes to get rid of him, the Misery, as well. And there appears to be a child of dubious seed. I wouldn't be surprised if she did away with it, too.'

'It is all most confusing.'

'It is all most uninspired. Wickedness often is.'

'So let's leave that be! Quit being the Sovereign's amanuensis. Tell him you must return to your motherland…anything, so that we may never be parted!'

He smiled. 'Thank you. I am moved beyond belief. But you're mistaken, Kilwa is *not* my motherland. As for Persia…' He frowned. A dimly lit barge was cutting downriver behind the silk-cotton trees; he followed it until it slid away. 'No… I will never go back.'

'Do you realize, in these many months, you haven't once mentioned your earlier life. Yet you know more about me than I know myself.'

'Only because I am a good listener.'

He laughed and took hold of the Scrivener's hands, clutching them to his chest. 'Will you tell me today, for who knows when we shall be alone again.'

If ever, the Scrivener almost added. 'What would you like to know?'

'Everything.'

'Everything? I so wish I had it in me.'

'But you can! You *must*… Where you were born and how you came to be here and…and *everything*!'

'It's a long story.'

'It's not as though I'm going anywhere tonight!'

'Very well,' he said, reclaiming his hands. The other thing could wait. 'Don't blame me if your hair has greyed by the time I've finished.' He took a deep breath. 'Ready?'

'Yes!'

'So... I was born in the seaport of Siraf on the Bahar Faris in the year twelve hundred and twelve. My mother was a prostitute and my father a Chinese shipmate on whom, as it so happened, I never set eyes. I was an exceptionally forward child with an ear for languages that I picked up with ease from my mother's guests; she only spoke Farsi. Seeing how silver-tongued her little mongrel was turning, she arranged for lessons from a professor of linguistics who lived four streets away. "Words, not coin," this worthy was fond of declaring, "are the currency of the truly rich." "Words, not paints, are the hues of the mind" and "He who weaves words needs no silks", "Calligraphy is the music of the eye", and "He who reads needs neither women nor wine"— which, in my case, didn't wholly apply, for I was as yet disdainful of drink. And so, for six summers until the age of twelve, I spent two turns of an hourglass at the professor's thrice a week, immersed in Old Farsi and New Farsi, Latin, Greek, Chinese and Sanskrit, becoming proficient also in Persian, Chinese and Devanagari penmanship. No small wonder, then, that I even *dreamt* in languages, conducting whole conversations with simorghs and dragons and kings and mendicants, in familiar and other tongues which—in the contrary way of dreams—are intelligible during the dreaming but on waking turn to pure gibberish. In reality, meantime, I had developed a confusing affection for the professor—to call it an *attraction* would be too great a thing, a sort of calf love, you could say—which I wisely kept unexpressed.'

'Like my calf love for you?'

'Possibly. Now, if the duration of an hour be measured by the funnel of fine sand which grows as a hill in the lower half of an hourglass, the one at the professor's surely contained an extra handful of sand. Having taken me through my lessons the first hour, he would invert the device and, leaving me, repair to the market on his quotidian errands, returning within the hour to check my progress and then set my assignments for the next time.

It was not unusual for him to become held up sometimes—he was well respected in the quarter and people sought his counsel on sundry cares—but one cold December afternoon he was unusually delayed. Staring at the hill of sand, I was possessed by a forceful sense that something was amiss and that I must go home in haste. And so I did. Imagine my astonishment upon finding the professor's slippers and walking cane and market basket placed outside the curtain through which my mother received her clients. I parted the curtain and stepped inside. I had never seen the professor undressed but there was no mistaking the bald pate, the long pale back in which the vertebrae protruded like a zither's frets. His flaccid buttocks and shrivelled shanks were jogging fitfully between my mother's legs. She for her part was half-sitting against her pillows with her head at an unnatural tilt and staring—at the professor's tarboosh and robe which hung like a spectre from the wall by her bed. A great confusion of emotions led me to grab a brass plate and strike it with all my strength against the professor's head, from which it recoiled with a bright clang. Giving a violent twitch, his body went still. His face buried itself into my mother's neck. I expected her to scream and push him away but she stayed unmoving and blankly staring. I stood perplexed for a moment before reaching over to prod her shoulder, upon which she fell sideways to her right, causing the professor—still plugged into her—to fall to his right. A thick worm of blood from his nostrils was seeping through his whiskers and spreading like wine into the pillows and sheets; my only thought was how I was going to get them clean again.'

'You killed a man with a *plate*?'

'The native sailors of Hind only ate off these heavy brass plates, for they believed that eating off anything else would render them unclean. They often asked to be fed after they had finished. We owned a dozen—the utensils, I mean. So I dropped the plate and ran outside and did not stop until I reached the docks where I jumped into the first dhow I saw and hid under some sacking, shaking with rage and revulsion at what I had done and seen. The dhow's rocking must have stilled my senses and lulled me to sleep for when I threw aside the sacking, the sky had turned into a sieve of starlight and the movement of the vessel felt different. In the light of some lanterns swinging in the riggings, I espied the forms of men working the lateen. It was too late to jump out unless I wished to drown—I shall have you know that I cannot swim—so I dove back under the sacking and thence into the longest night of my life. Discovering a stowaway in their midst at daybreak, the Arab master of the craft said I was lucky not to have picked a Chinese vessel, for then I surely would have been eaten alive. "My father is an important Chinese seaman," I replied and asked if he would kindly take me to Chin. At this, the Arab laughed long and hard, recovering enough to say it was to al-Hind that they were bound and back to Siraf in three months; I could earn my keep for the circuit by working as a deckhand and lying with him. Thus, after thirty-four days in a brisk northeastern and with six stops along the way for sweet water and trade, we made landfall at the port of Kulam on the Malabar country of southwestern Hind.

'It was by now January. I had had sufficient time in the interim to realize my mother, poor wretch, had been paying for my scholarship in kind, not coin, and had expired in the course of settling her dues that frightful day. Certain stoning to death for killing a man aside, I had nothing and no one in Siraf to await me, anxiously or otherwise. So I told the master upon landfall that I would find my own way to Chin onwards from the Malabar and made myself scarce before he could entice me back, and that was the last I saw of him, his dhow and his men. As luck would have it, I spent a good twelvemonth in Kulam, working in one of the pepper factories as a bookkeeper's apprentice and in that time witnessed the world and its many types and creeds pass before my eyes. That was the same year I attained manhood, sprouting some hairs on my upper lip and chin and also bedding with many a native woman and man. But restlessness had begun to

champ at my heels so I quit Kulam and for the next eight years
wandered about Hind, earning my keep as an itinerant writer of
letters for the unlettered, translator of charters and decrees for
tradesmen and governors and, upon one long hot summer, as
a teller of stories from behind a fragrant wet vetiver screen to a
sad raja's dying rani. It is no idle boast that I've fathered more
than a few mongrels during those years of rough living. Then,
in the February of twelve-thirty-three, I fell in with a party of
elders from Chin who were performing a journey of knowledge
before returning to Canton by way of the Kalingodhra Sea. It
was with them that I arrived in Kataka and set eyes for the first
time on this palace which, even those days, had the guard of
three hundred elephants and women sentries. My companions
opined that it would be an education for us to attend the sitting
king's public audience and so we did. When it was our turn
to present ourselves before the late Sovereign, may God keep
his soul, I expressed a desire to serve in his offices as a scribe.
Bemused by my confidence yet finding me refined of elocution
and deportment and indeed as well lettered as I claimed to be,
His Majesty appointed me his personal scrivener—which, as
you can imagine, was of manifest displeasure to the Secretary.
And thus, here I am, full twelve years in the service of Empire
and two Sovereigns. I recall vividly the day you appeared in
our midst, the summer of twelve-forty, and I said to myself, ah!
who might *this* mischief be?' He paused. The monologue had
made him lightheaded. 'So now you have it. My life story. The
day after tomorrow, you and I shall be parted and then I must
plan my next journey.'

'Next journey?'

'Oh, a figure of speech.'

'No. I know you too well. I believe you're keeping something
from me.'

'I have spoken unfettered of events I have shared with none
other.' He looked up at the sky. 'Look…a lone star; ill luck for
the one who first sees it. I must go in.'

'Because of a stupid lone star?'

He stood and held out a hand. 'No, because of a stupid thing which awaits my attention at the Sovereign's decree.'

They crossed the gloaming in silence and stopped at an archway into a dark stairwell. A rambling jasmine overhead had bloomed a myriad perfumed white stars. A tentative arm curved around the Scrivener's waist. 'Do you want me upstairs, Master?' After months of disuse, the honorific had slipped unbidden from his lips.

'Not tonight, my young simorgh,' he said, pushing him away. 'Go now! Sleep well.'

～

A short while later, the Scrivener sat on the edge of his rumpled bed, hugging Pol to his chest and rocking forth and back. Dismissed. Dispossessed. Tossed like a shop-soiled tarboosh to a rubbish heap. Still clutching the cat, he rolled slowly backwards and curled onto his side—shutting out the mewls of a peacock on some terrace, the footfalls in the Crown Prince's chamber directly overhead, the creaks of the palace as it shrank into itself for the night. The cat struggled out of his embrace and dove off the cold bed.

For a fleeting moment the Scrivener considered killing himself—a handful of datura would do quite well; or drowning in the river; a silken cord from a beam—but the prospect of being found bloated and inelegant, nibbled by fish or swinging over his excrement, was enough to send the choices scurrying out of his head. No, of all the mortifications bestowed to mankind, a life bereaved of love was by far the cruellest. Only from continuing to live would he honour these past seven glorious, bittersweet months of his life. With a muffled cry he buried his face in a pillow…but only for a moment. Scrambling to his elbows and knees he began to root through the bedclothes like a fevered pig—grunting and snivelling and committing the traces of happier times to olfactory memory.

15

CADAMBAGIRI

BOTH LETTERS ARRIVED THE SAME MORNING. THE SAME PAPER stock and similar inks, one scrawled in a familiar hand; the other, in letterforms rounded and clean as the ears of mice.

> Salutations friend | By the time you read this your relative shall have set sail across the seas to discharge an embassy I have vested in him | It shall be ten months before the winds restore him to our presence | This matter I convey for your peace of mind | Kalinga Ganga

~

> Fond sister sovereign | Thrice erewhile have we begun this epistle and thrice set it aside for mundane affairs conspire each time to interrupt our newfound joy in missives | Now those chores are complete and we may once again resume our communion of minds | The image of yourself—for which artistry we give thanks—rests by our side so that we may gaze upon your countenance and imagine your presence and laughter and manner of speech | From the same image it seems to me that the gait of your mount must greatly differ from that of a four-legged beast | Perchance your hen shall achieve better success in brooding her eggs for this missive accompanies a quantity of medicament a handful of which in her feed for four weeks will fortify the shells of her eggs | You enquired in your missive after our progeny | Suffice it to say the closest we have to maternal feelings is for a cousin who is presently readied to embark upon a sea journey at the bidding of our sovereign | At the approach of his departure we feel as a mother might when a son must leave for battle and may never be seen again | These feelings we durst not voice to our men for fear of sneers about them as an abject failing of the womanly heart and mind | Yet our hearts and minds you will agree are stronger by far than those of men in their tolerance to pain | Stronger also in their capacity to inflict

pain | But we digress | Voyaging as well to the island of Kilwa
in the Sea of Hind is your brother by marriage to reach a gift
of bovines from our sovereign to a goodly potentate of that
country | The journey must provide your relative much respite
from his cares of the past months not the least of which was
the ailment from which he has since recovered fully | These
days he moves as if of some love draught he has sipped | When
we jested that he will doubtless return with a new princess he
turned most serious and declared nay he proposes upon his
return to beg audience of a certain princess whose heart he
did betray and seek her forgiveness first and favour second
| What if she were to spurn your fancy we posed of him
whereupon he avowed to wander the land as an ash-covered
mendicant singing praise of that personage until she learnt
of his plight and opened her heart to him | Then you have
faint acuity of our sex we jested for warbling mendicants are
at best provender for hungry tigers and of scant interest to
women whereas a manful advance with some token of troth
might perchance stand him in better stead in the eyes of his
flame | What manner of token he fretted | That is not for me
to say we replied not helpfully | Upon the departure of your
relative and ours in two days hence we shall have occasion
for more leisured correspondence | With this assurance we
close this missive | Sitadevi

Part Three

16

THE *ARKAJA*

ON THIS THE SEVENTH DAY OF OUR EMBARKATION (THE Superintendent of the Gift in his secondary role as Chronicler of the Voyage wrote) my newest attempt to describe this sea journey promises better success for I recalled your words to write as though I were speaking to one particular of my choice. Until today each prior effort to commit my thoughts to paper and ink seemed wanting in some way so I cast those mutterings to the waves. The breeze one moment calm the next wild conspired to steal these pages for I would forget to place the finished page in the second box by my side. This has been remedied since the appointment as my assistant the toothsome chaperone whose services His Eminence claims to no longer need. With this pleasing giant bearing a glass lantern over me I may pen at ease for an hour before daybreak when the rest of the day comes cawing onto the deck. Here I close my first noting.

∿

Let us turn our gaze today upon my company. As our Sovereign to our empire so our shipmaster to this water palace. This one-eyed personage of mixed native and Arab line has forty-three summers of age and claims he can master any vessel blindfolded if needs be from having traversed this sea route more times than he can call up to mind. The living eye is a most curious hue of green. Its bearer comes to his post from steering other vessels for other owners and was taken from the previous one for a release price of twelve ivories. It is said that younger shipmasters go for twenty but those are less trusty and given to much vice. Under his command are various types and ranks of men. The first numbering four are his deputy and their two servants and a lookout boy who is not a boy but a dwarf of middle age. Next are forty men to work the anchors and masts and sails. Then are twelve men appointed to the kitchens and the water bins and six attendants each to the granary and pantry. Forty soldiers next are archers and fire-throwers who have thus far had no call to show their skills. Then there are four men appointed to the shore-sighting crows and messenger pigeons and the cats which keep the palace clean of rats. Beneath these are eighteen cleaners and night-soil servants evenly divided between the decks. All these are the crewmen. Of the remaining company are twelve handlers and one physician of our forty-six bovines. Lastly the toothsome giant and one servant each of His Eminence and myself. Save for His Eminence and I and the shipmaster each man is known not by name but by given number and that number must remain his for the duration of his company on sea. Not counting His Eminence and myself there are one hundred and thirty-four men upon our ship and the shipmaster is first by virtue of rank. It is crowded but we shall be lighter of livestock for the return journey. Here I conclude this note on numbers and ranks.

~

Today let us to visit the quarters and arrangements of His Eminence and myself. The pavilion in which I write is a climb of eight rungs to this elevated stage directly behind the figurehead. From here I gaze upon the full length of a hundred and eighty paces of the deck. Evenly spaced fore to aft are four masts fashioned as ladders each one broad of base and narrowing on high and to each is tied numerous oilcloths of white by means of ropes through copper not iron rings. At work day and night in these are crewmen like monkeys who sing and it is always the same songs but the words are strange and it is only the tune that I can imitate upon my pipe. His Eminence declared the first day that the sight of these men made him giddy and how much more giddy they must feel on high to which the shipmaster declared that such men feel no giddiness or they would be plying some lowly trade on dry land. The living chambers of His Eminence and myself are directly below this elevated stage and made as two

chambers of equal size with a wall between. A round window
in each is decorated from without as an eye. A shutter within
serves as the eyelid. I have found by chance that our ship like
its master is rendered one-eyed for His Eminence in the right
side chamber claims the sea wind and light hinders his sleep.
Our beds are of string and suspended as cradles of babies for
beds on legs do not serve well on a ship. A most refreshing sleep
may be had in it but one must perforce lie singly or else become
snared therein like a bird or fish. In each chamber is a chest the
lid of which serves as a seat. Inside are our cloths and ornaments
and in my chest also my boxes of papers and writing things. In
the antechamber are kept our shared needs in the care of our
servants. I have been diligent in the application of antimony and
bathe once in two days whereas His Eminence bathes twice a
day and uses no antimony for he claims it stings his eyes. His
Eminence and I climb to this stage to partake of our meals and
are waited upon by our servants. Upon eating His Eminence
performs two circuits of the deck with head bent and repairs
into his chamber whereas I proceed to my duties in the cattle
shed. The shed is commodious and clean and my wards are thus
far faring well. My work done there I tarry awhile to converse
with the shipmaster who yesterday gave to me a glimpse of his
missing eye. There was naught to be seen under the eyelid. Here
I conclude on quarters and habits.

~

Let me speak now of some rules by which the crewmen must
conduct themselves. Because there are in all one hundred and
thirty-six mouths to feed it is the lowest rank who eat first and
then the others and the shipmaster lastly. Likewise the sleeping
order among those ranks. While one or other party beds inside
the lowermost desk another must remain wakeful and working.
The sleeping quarters are most crowded. Every man has a
bedding shelf and his belongings in a sack are hung over it. It is
common for these types to engage in fight over some missing

thing or wrongfully taken shelf but such fights are quickly quelled. No man may smoke of the leaf below deck for a fire there would be unfortunate but this rule is much disobeyed. On the subject of fire a pot of embers is tended at all times inside the hut of the shipmaster and this is deemed most precious for it is from these embers that the cook fires are daily kindled afresh. All aboard our water palace perform their duties with care. There are various types of punishment and the most feared is the body cage.

~

Yesterday our nineteenth day on sea it came to light that two porters from Khalakatapatna had tired of loading our palace and gone to sleep in the fodder store and failed to disembark with their fellow porters of hay. Upon waking and finding themselves at sea the pair had taken fright and stayed hidden midst the bales until they were uncovered by the servants given to feeding the bovines. The unfortunates survived these past many days on stolen water and raw rice. Finding them unskilled for anything the deputy has cast them to the lowermost rank to assist the night-soil servants.

~

We are not at any time of day or night lacking of company upon the sea for we are surrounded at all times by a number of vessels bound for Simhala and the Camphor Islands. Then there are some vessels of Chin and the oilcloths of these are ribbed with bamboo and cane and appear to my eyes as the wings of bats. There are other crafts also which ply at great speed but with oars not sails. These are native to the Bengal country and keep their distance from our water palace. All this I have learned from our shipmaster who is a most handsome man behind his animal countenance. As we keep our southward course it is with land always in sight to our right and thus shall it remain until our advent into the western sea whereupon all will be different. So the shipmaster has said.

~

A type of boat made as a wooden utensil with a lid draws up by our side once a week at a mirror signal from our deck. To these types are let down our buckets as one might into a well and drawn up again and the sweet water thus collected is poured into our water bins. One thousand buckets are taken each week and for this service the boatmasters are given coin not cowries. This manner of watering will change the shipmaster said upon the western sea which is the Sea of Hind. I must prepare for many changes there he said with a wink of his living eye.

≈

We are one man less on this our twenty-sixth day at sea. One of the porters of Khalakatapatna has gained his freedom by leading the shipmaster to a purse he had hid midst the fodder bales. It must have been a rich exchange for the shipmaster let the man down to a water boat from the port of Vedapuri. Upon learning his fellow had through cunning given slip the remaining man had wept and claiming the purse was common property begged that he too be relieved of our company. In response the shipmaster led the fellow by the nose to the lower deck and bade him to retrieve his own stash from midst the hay but there was naught to be found and so the wretch was proven to have been truly betrayed. Upon hearing the sorry tale His Eminence sent for the shipmaster for a conversation in private. The stowaway has since been delivered of cleaning night soil and taken instead as a foot servant of His Eminence. The ways of the powerful as I am learning are truly inconstant.

≈

Today we espied a stretch of coast most densely grown with brownish trees not unlike our toddy palm trees. That palm His Eminence said in his knowledgeable way is not the toddy but the talipot from which type is harvested the best of writing leaves. Those plantations said the shipmaster are the property of a king of a southern country and the leaf is most prized for its smoothness of grain and long life in storage and for this reason the plantations are guarded by ferocious dogs the size of asses. Some fronds of this palm had washed in the waves close to our side and one of these His Eminence instructed his new servant to draw up by means of a hooked pole. The seawater and sun had turned the leaves evenly black but these dried to red and I smiled at the memory of a note I was put to write a certain night upon one such leaf. I shall write again in two days' time when we are due to enter the waters of the Simhala country.

17

KATAKA

A LITTLE OVER A MONTH OF THEIR MOVE FROM THE PALACE, the Scrivener's cat succumbed to their altered circumstances.

With no Morning Office to attend, no love toy to pamper and teach, the Scrivener had taken to rising late, treating himself to a leisurely breakfast and bath, and then doing little of consequence until it was time to repair downstairs to the Hall of Enchantment. Humans, with our infinite capacity to adapt and survive, frequently benefit—even bloom, as the Scrivener did—from a change of residence and pace of life; but not so creatures of habit such as cats who have become beholden to us for their every comfort and need.

Confined day and night to a cage—lest he wander about and aggravate the Courtesan's purported allergy to cat-hair; or fall prey to the leopard at her gates; or, worse, try finding his way back to the palace—the beauteous Pol had rapidly lost his mind, hissing and spitting and turning like a wild cat upon the hand that fed. Soon, his mewling protests were replaced by a sullen, shut-eyed silence. His blue-white luminescence turned brown-grey as though he had wandered through some cobwebbed passage. His favourite treat of fish brains barely elicited a sniff. It ought to have been clear to the Scrivener that his pet was starving himself; but intent on healing himself, he turned a blind eye to the signs. The end came one cold December night. The Scrivener returned to his rooms from the Hall of Enchantment to a piteous sight. In a valiant attempt at escape, Pol had strangulated his neck between the bars of the cage.

With trembling hands, the Scrivener folded the thin weightless body in some silk and, at daybreak, cremated it in a corner of the garden on a pyre of sandal twigs. Collecting the ashes in a silver goblet, he made his way to a landing stage on the

Kushabhadra, whence he sprinkled the meagre remains to the current, saying, 'Farewell, fond friend. You were a good cat.' He then went back to the Courtesan's, burnt the funeral robe, took a hot bath, and for the next three days stayed upstairs, receiving no commiserations and eating nothing.

He had lived long enough among the natives to observe their mourning practices. Having never before mourned anyone or anything, he used the occasion to do so wisely—mourning also the loss, years ago, of his mother and homeland. The experience afforded him a prescient vision of the sort of life that lay ahead. It terrified him. On the fourth morning, he emerged feeling lighter than he had in a decade of indolent living. Bathed and dressed and clear of eye and intent, he went downstairs to seek out his hostess.

～

In the Hall of Enchantment, a novice with a sweetly imbecile face was practicing her steps in a fitful way to the somnolent drumbeat of a eunuchoid hag. As though it had always resided there, the Scrivener's screen with its nacreous birds and foliage was angled as a backdrop to the Courtesan's seat; the screen's matching chairs stood by like mute attendants, each bearing a tray of drinking cups and wine jars across their armrests. Seemingly diminished by its over-bright setting, the oblong mirror reflected its old companion the armillary sphere; and inside the sphere dozed the Courtesan's grey parrot. The Scrivener's trove of cushions and carpets graced the lumpy floor mattresses. All this, towards pleasures partaken and present tenancy; only the appurtenances of his calling remained in his keep, untouched and unseen in the boxes they had travelled in from the palace. The time had come to effect their release before they too went the way of his cat.

An eye trained on the graceless novice, the Courtesan was having her hair done by a flock of servants. At the Scrivener's entrance, she brushed the girls aside, at the same time attempting to climb out of her couch and sinking back with a little squeak. 'My beloved!' she cried, throwing her arms out to him, 'I have been worried sick! They tell me you've been starving and lamenting but I was chary of coming to see for myself. Come sit, my darling! I've made enquiries about a replacement for your cat—'

'That will not be necessary,' he cut in, 'I have a matter of urgency—'

'Why! So have I! Only last night I was saying how comforting it is to have a man under my roof in permanent residence. As you are well aware, it has long been my desire to pen my life story. Your perfumed words…the life I have led…the work will be our contribution to posterity!'

He frowned, his eyes tracing a meandering vine of blue grapes in the carpet's weave. What was it about these natives, so desperate to immortalize themselves in stone, paint and ink?

'I have it all inside my head,' she was saying, 'and all that remains is to set it down in rhyming couplets… A love epic, if you will, in the old style, commencing with my lofty birth in Dwarasamudra, my abduction to Machalipatna and sale to a brothel, the general's *glorious* courtship and rescue of me, his untimely demise, my present parlous circumstances, the arrival at my portals of a silver-tongued worthy and for the conclusion… *the grand festivities of our marriage!*'

He looked up, dumbfounded.

Her girls were done fussing with her hair. The braids and ringlets framing her spherical face heightened the impression she gave of an outsized and latently mad child. 'I refer, of course, to the worthy before me,' she said, clapping her dimpled hands. 'It is fated, do you not think, that he and I must sooner than later become betrothed?'

On the platform, the novice had stopped twirling while the drummer tightened his drum skins. The Scrivener turned; the girl flashed him a demented smile. He attempted to quell the laughter gurgling inside him but it issued from his pursed lips like a wetly sputtered breaking of wind. The more he tried to contain himself, the harder it became; he doubled over on a mattress, laughing so hard the back of his scalp contracted in pain. 'Forgive me,' he managed at last, gasping and struggling to his feet, 'I am unworthy of your hospitality…unworthy mainly of your noble hand. I came only to give thanks for your kindnesses and to bid farewell.'

'*What*…!' She opened and shut her mouth stupidly. '*Farewell*? What do you mean?'

'Yes, I leave today.'

'But that is impossible!' she said, her eyes flashing. 'What will you do? On what will you *live*?' Her voice rose a pitch: 'Who will…cook and care for you as we have, what will you *eat*, where will you sleep? Oh—!' She gasped, pressing a jewelled hand to a breast and the other to a flushed cheek. '*I knew it*! Another *woman*! Who is the harlot? I demand to know, I will pinch out her eyes! Oh, wait—! Is it that…that *girl*, your favourite?'

The Scrivener was not by nature superstitious but was suddenly loath to air a plan for fear of tempting the evil eye. 'The truth is,' he said, 'my father in Chin has sent for me. I set sail for Champa today and thence to…Chin.'

'Your *father*? How did *that* happen? You told me he was *dead*.'

'I did not know it then,' he said, warming to the lie, 'but now I do, that he is indeed alive, and only for a short while. He needs me by his deathbed.'

'Why is it that each time—' she broke off, looking away with a loud sniff. 'Oh, so be it, then!' She continued bitterly, 'It is *all* a lie and I know it. But bear this in mind: if you needs must come back…my doors are forever, *forever* open wide—' There was a catch in her voice. The next moment she began to rock forth and back and side to side, at the same time plucking at her braids and ringlets. He took a step forward; she at once set up a hideous keening as though she were in physical pain. Her servants dashed forth with little cries and threw a protective cage of arms about her quivering body. Not to be left out of the excitement, the drummer gathered his drum into a galloping beat; the novice spun faster, flinging her arms this way and that like a disjointed puppet. '*Begone arse face!*' squawked the parrot, coming alive in its globe of tarnished hoops and rings. Before the exhibition about him went completely out of hand, the Scrivener bowed to the heaving couch of women and hurried out of the Hall of Enchantment.

18

PARIJATAPURI

'In the kingdom...of Zabag,' the Raja said, his voice emerging in muffled spurts, 'stretches a shallow lake...between the royal palace...and the sea...and to this lake each morning... the Raja throws...a small *gold brick*... When he dies...these will be gathered and...and divided justly between...his family... and...servants and army and...*ah*! ...the poor of his land... Does that not...a most noble ruler make?'

Ever since the Crown Princess's milk had dried, the Raja had taken to coming to her at any time of night or day. A far cry from the first rushed affair which had spawned the Heir Apparent, their couplings nowadays were unhurried. It pleased him if she put up a fight: scratching and biting and buffeting his chest, and then turning meek and biddable as a child. Another trick she had was to lie rigid and unresponsive as a dead body, coming alive without warning and bringing him to his climax. 'Whereas in the country of Simhala...' he went on sputtering into her neck, 'the practice...of that Raja...' That he spoke nonstop was his method for delaying his moment.

Seeing as this would be her lot for the rest of her days, the Crown Princess had consulted a senior handmaid for something to render herself barren permanently. The prescription—seven cups of elephant-dung-water and honey, three doses of silk-cotton-seed-powder in ghee—were more commonplace among prostitutes than with princesses in their prime. Vile though the stuffs tasted, she didn't for a moment regret safeguarding herself: not for her those unreliable pessaries of rock-salt and sesame oil; not for her yet another parasite.

For his part, the Raja came to her with the right-shoulder-blade of a black cat tied at his waist, the curving right-tush of a wild boar worn as a bracelet on his right wrist. The first time she saw these, she feared they would counter her secret prophylactics and attempted to divest him of them. Surely one as virile as you, she had said, has scant need for such playthings for boys? Any harder and stronger, you will rip me asunder from here to here…

'Ah, my sweet innocent,' he had replied, 'with these talismans to render my seed sterile, we may sport without fear of burdening you with child again,' adding with characteristic pedantry: 'Even the scriptures laud him who sires one worthy son than a houseful of wastrels. Having done, all I wish is to make a true prince of our godsend.'

Their godsend. At four months of age, the Heir Apparent showed no signs of losing his birth-pelt. If anything, the hairs seemed coarser and darker with each passing day. Perhaps the ice the mother had craved so avidly had caused the embryo to sprout a warm coat for itself and now the parasite had no way of shedding it. The Crown Princess hoped it would, come summertime, for the hirsute thing in its mirrored crib was the ugliest baby she had ever seen. Surely the speed at which it was growing had something to do with the milk-mother's milk? Such women were much given to tricks to hasten the weaning of charges to pap. Loath as she was to enter the nursery, sooner or later, she would have to investigate… Her daughters' voices on the terrace outside brought her back to the moment.

'…and for such people there can…' the Raja was grunting moistly, 'there can only…be…be—' Enough. Throwing her legs about his waist, she thrust a heel between his rear. '…death!' he screamed, as if a knife had been plunged into his back. For a long moment they lay still. 'Where did you learn that?' he mumbled, rolling sideways.

I teach myself, she laughed inwardly, snuggling backwards against him. Outside, on the terrace, the chatter and laughter of the little princesses drifted and receded and soon became one with the afternoon quiet.

∾

A speechless oracle is a worthless oracle. Soon after the incident, people had voiced their theories, in plain sight of him, as though he were not only mute but also deaf. *No, you unholy fools!* he had screamed inside his head: no, I did not sacrifice it to propitiate a goddess; no, it was not to avert a *terrible portent*; no, I have taken no *vow of silence* nor have I attained *peace and enlightenment*, and most vehemently no, it was not *I* who cut it.

Accursed birth: how he envied the ability to write, how he regretted being illiterate. No better anymore than a servant, his functions these days alternated between keeping the Raja's grand-daughters entertained and keeping intruders at bay whilst the Raja visited his daughter-in-law's apartments. It was in these dual functions that he was occupied this afternoon on the terrace.

Securing a blindfold on the Tongueless One (as the Oracle was known these days) the Second Princess spun him thrice on his feet, let go of him and, stepping back, cried: 'Try catch us, old man!'

Arms outstretched and fingers curled claw-like, he took a faltering step. As the game progressed, the girls' whispers and giggles led him ever closer to the steps to a lower terrace.

He stumbled and fell. Peeling off the blindfold, he squinted up at the two figures against the white sky.

'Get up,' said the Second Princess.

'*Ngnu gnugn*,' he mouthed, struggling to his feet, '*Gngumga nga!*'

'No, you may not,' the Second Princess commanded. 'Come act as my steed.'

The one time he had resisted, early in their acquaintance, the wicked child had taken a stick at him. He went down on all fours, cursing her and her ilk under his breath; she clambered onto his back and smote his head with the palm of her hand. The rough paving skinned his knees. After four circuits of the terrace, she permitted him a rest. Her sister and she were considering what game to play next when their brother's milk mother appeared at a parapet.

The woman's child had become colicky that morning; she had left her in the care of another servant. Summoning the

Tongueless One with a clap of her hands, she spoke slowly and distinctly as though he were impaired of hearing: 'Pray-keep-an-eye-on-their-brother-while-I-go-downstairs-I-shall-be-back-in-no-time.'

'Wait for us!' called the Second Princess, dragging her sister by the hand. 'We too wish to see your dying baby!'

With that, the children raced up to the woman's side and the three figures disappeared down a stairwell. In the sudden lull, the Tongueless One was struck by an idea so outrageous it took his breath away. Snatching his shawl from where he had thrown it, he flew across the terrace to the nursery.

Decades of hard living had kept the Oracle light on his feet. Gathering the sleeping baby from his crib, he bundled him under the shawl and exited the nursery. No one—not even the sentries basking at the gates—saw him leave the palace and vanish down the hard-shadowed lanes of the citadel.

～

The milk mother returned with the princesses. One look at the empty crib, the woman's blood ran cold to her heels.

Already, the Second Princess had commandeered her sister to look under the other furniture for their sibling. With the girls thus occupied, the milk mother took to the stairs once again. There was no time to reconsider the course she must take. No one would believe her protestations of innocence; it was better this way, and, truth be told, she was tired of her existence. Collecting her whimpering infant from the minder, she ran through the kitchens and past the servants' quarters and latrines, praying no one would question her haste.

An overgrown garden in a rear courtyard.

The small mouth of a deep well was covered with some planks. The woman pushed them aside with her free hand—they clattered to the flagstones like thunderclaps—and climbed onto the crumbled masonry lip. Smothering her fevered daughter to her breasts and raising her eyes to the sky, she stepped off the edge. The well had long since run dry so there was no splash.

19

DONDRA

IN THE PORT OF DONDRA OF THE SIMHALA COUNTRY THE shipmaster sent his deputy and a dozen crewmen to seek audience of the king for His Eminence with a tribute of nine bolts of silk. Awaiting their return His Eminence and I partook of the sights on land. Setting foot on the pier it seemed as if it were upon water that I was walking and my gait was cause for much mirth in His Eminence. Only look at yourself I said to him for he too was struck by the same faltered step from our having only trod the decks these past five weeks at sea. Upon finding our land feet we proceeded to inspect the varied merchandise which are no different from our own country except that the natives here are forever smiling as if they have no worldly cares. Then we made a pleasing hour of a garden nearby. The greenery there was most luxuriant and in the vines and trees were birds of colours so brilliant that they appeared as if wrought of gold and gems. His Eminence has taken to conversing with me on sundry subjects of interest. There grows in Simhala he said a certain bodhi sprung from a branch from its sacred mother tree under which the Ninth Incarnation gained wisdom in our own country and that branch was brought here many years ago by a Kalinga prince and princess. Also a tooth of the Ninth Incarnation was brought by that same princess hidden in her hair and the tooth like the bodhi is a most sacred object to the natives of this country. Perchance we may behold this tooth and the bodhi I said. You should be so blessed His Eminence replied for only the holiest of holy may do so and who are you but a minder of bovines.

～

A party of women has put itself at our service on board our ship and His Eminence is much taken by the garlands of flowers and coral beads they have placed about our necks. The flowers are white and fragrant and gold-throated and the women wear these also behind their ears which are long of lobes from the weight of their gold rings. Here are fruit of many types of which some are tasteless and fish and rice and sweetmeats made of coconut flesh. There is also a wine of rice which causes much drowsiness. His Eminence wagered we will not be granted audience today for it is well past afternoon and has repaired to his chamber to sleep asking not to be waked. I write this having partaken of a generous feast while we await word from the palace.

∽

It is true what the shipmaster said. Everything is different in the western sea. It is three days since Dondra and I shall describe here the circumstances of our exit. The deputy shipmaster and crewmen returned aboard and said there would be no audience with the king for he was bereaved and it would be eleven days before the obsequies were complete. It is a lie pronounced His Eminence. How can you say so I asked of him. Because he replied the excuse of bereavement is an old ploy to keep at bay such visitors as one did not wish to receive and that they did it all the time in Parijatapuri. But there is no certainty that this king is lying I said to which he replied I had a long way to go before I understood the ways of the worldly and note how our tribute of silks has been accepted by this purportedly bereaved king and how the women plying us with food and wine seem unlike the citizenry of a kingdom bereaved. Why must one as worldly as you find imperfection in everything I posed of His Eminence. At my harmless utterance he narrowed his eyes and said just you wait and see what perfection awaits one who regards everything as it appears and perfect including your Sovereign who is anything but perfect but has perfected the art of making fools of all who love and trust him. I was taken aback and said in some haste Your Eminence pray speak not thus of my Sovereign for he has done you no harm except to rescue you from your own trap and

it is from his kindness that I am fulfilling my desire to see the
world which is a very big place. At this His Eminence shouted
how dare you speak of traps and matters of which you know
nothing. I was privy to the true circumstances of His Eminence
making this journey I replied so it would be prudent for him
and me to forget this imperfect moment and look only towards
making the remainder of our voyage in peace. Let us see for
how long said His Eminence. It must be painful I said to see
only the dark side of life and suffer this way. An unwise thing
for he turned upon me fiercely saying this is who I am do not
try to change me. I believed he would cease his complaint but
he went on to say just you wait it is you who are fated to suffer
most gravely from the hand of your perfect Sovereign and then
we shall see if your thoughts will remain on the dark side or the
light. His words left me of a sudden afraid but I kept my peace
and parted his company. He and I did not speak full two days and
only yesterday he ended his silence and bade me play upon my
pipe. I obliged for it is as you well know not in my nature to be
silent and brooding. Later he threw an arm about my shoulder
and remarked on the fine wind and the blue of the sea and
conversed as before in all friendliness about his life in Kataka
and Parijatapuri and his various exploits on the battlefield. But
I am chary for the friendliness he displays is not very deep and
nor can it be for he is overtly fond of only himself. I shall remove
these notings when the time is right but for the present leave
them be for it is easy to forget all that has transpired and from
forgetting I may give offence again. The blue of this Sea of Hind
I will say is bluer than the sea on the eastern side.

20

CADAMBAGIRI

GIVING THE REFERENCE A CURSORY READING, THE WOMAN TOOK it away with her for an eternity. When she returned, it was to show the Scrivener into a gloomy high-ceilinged hallway and, without a word, vanishing again.

A number of benches were pushed up against the walls. A huddled figure was seated under a window at the far end. Gathering his shawl about him, the Scrivener walked over and sat on an adjacent bench. His presence went unacknowledged: the young man, in a shapeless blue sheepskin, was engrossed in braiding a stockwhip. The cold grey morning dribbling in over his head lent a disconcerting underwater quality to the light.

'You, too, must be waiting for audience of Her Majesty?' ventured the Scrivener at length. He may as well have been talking to himself. Perhaps the fellow is deaf. Or fearful of yang-type men. Or perhaps the concentration required of the braiding of whips brooks no idle chat.

The braider checked the tension of the lash and adjusted the grip. His nails, the Scrivener noticed, were bitten to the quick. 'For use on man or beast?' he attempted afresh. His overture was again met with silence. Oh to divest those unlovely hands of the thing and test it across the rear…and then we'll see who'll ignore me.

The youth looked up. Still seated and gazing straight ahead, he unleashed the whip with a flick of a wrist. The lash sang through the air and flicked the floor with a crack a forearm away from the Scrivener's feet. Lashing the floor one more time, he rose stiffly and walked out of the hallway, the whip trailing behind him like a tail.

The Scrivener exhaled a long whistled breath. He felt strangely disoriented—as if he had fallen into someone else's dream. You're losing your hold on reality, he chided himself. Count backwards to a hundred slowly and if no one's come for you by then, you'll up and leave and never look back.

He was well into another hundred when the woman who had received him appeared at the doorway. 'Why, you are still here,' she said blandly. 'That is all for today. Come back in the morning.'

'To what end?' he called back, rising, 'Another wasted day?'

Her eyebrows rose in mock surprise. 'Consider yourself fortunate. It wasn't only your reference for we see many such, some more weighty. You must have said something to impress.'

'Who—?' he began, and then shook his head. It was just as well that he had jabbered no more than he had. 'Thank you, my lady. I am grateful…and shall remain so eternally.'

'Oh, don't count on it being permanent,' the woman answered. 'She might just as readily change her mind. Farewell.' She started to move away but stopped. 'No… Follow me, you had better see where you will be quartered, save me that added chore in the morning. Have you much by way of belongings?'

'Only the essentials of my calling,' he said, hurrying after her, 'and my fine mind and wit.'

'You will need all of it,' she replied drily, 'so guard them well.'

～

Salutation friend | A character of mixed extraction has presented himself with a reference which bears your seal | Said reference claims its bearer has served as scrivener to both yourself and your father the late Sovereign for full twelve years with diligence but for one fault of judgement | In test of his claims we hereby dictate this correspondence to his hand and to materials which he avers to have himself dispatched to us nine months previously at your behest | Only upon your response shall we deem it fit to depute the subject of this test to our service…

21

KATAKA

'How dare he!' Narasimha shouted, flinging the letter to the table and himself into a chair.

It was just him and the Secretary in the Morning Office. Justice manifests in mysterious ways, the Secretary said to himself, taking in the old familiar hand. Cunning half-breed, as usual placing yourself in a position of advantage over me. He crossed his arms over his chest.

'Have you nothing to say?' Narasimha snapped.

'What *is* to be said? The reference could in no way be faulted. I predicted we would hear of its destiny someday, although, admittedly, not so speedily. He is resourceful—always was, always will be—but we knew that already.' This is what comes, he did not add, of being forward-minded when timely measures would have sufficed; countless princes of your acquaintance don't think twice before divesting errant servants of tools *and* digits. As you must be different, so suffer the consequences.

'What are you thinking?'

'There is little to be gained from furnishing a reply.'

'No, that's an option not available to me. Think again.'

'You could deny all knowledge and thereby show yourself up to be—forgive me—dishonest. However, this being a personal, not state affair, it is not in my place to advise.'

He glowered at him. 'My mind is already made. The reply must come from your hand. The irony of it will not be lost on *him*. Begin.'

The Secretary studied his hand.

'Would you like me to divest you of it?'

The Secretary reached for stationery.

'Good man,' said Narasimha, and: 'Salutation friend... Him of whom you speak was indeed in my employ and the reason for his ceasing to serve me is indeed borne out in the reference which bears my seal. I wish him good fortune in your employ.' He rose and began pacing.

This is to compound a grave mistake, thought the Secretary, appending the signature seal. 'If we may turn to other matters of the day,' he said, 'your presence is required in Chandrabhaga for the heads of the greenstone deities. They seek word of when you may arrive.'

'Ah, progress, then. Ask them to expect us next week, anything to be away from…all of *this*. I am restless.' He cracked his knuckles. 'What news meantime of our seafaring friends?'

'No word since the last pigeon.' Those hapless cows. Not a day went by without him bemoaning their fate. 'They ought by now to have commenced the open crossing.'

TO LACADWIPA

OF THE MANY TYPES AND SIZES OF BOATS THAT APPROACH
our palace to conduct their trade in coconut and molasses and
messes of spiced fish and rice there is a type of boat which is
evenly flat and covered with roof from fore to aft and moves
with great swiftness to be the first by our side and these call
to my mind cockroaches clustering to some fallen viand. The
appearance of these is cause for much joy midst the crewmen
for the crafts contain not edible feasts but women. Because no
woman is permitted aboard our palace the boats may only draw
close and when these are suitably positioned the shipmaster
assembles his crewmen and draws numbers from a bucket and
these men descend by ladders to the women. The ladders are
drawn up until a sign is given for the men to climb back. Thus
our crewmen return in good spirit to their posts and duties.

∼

A matter pertaining to the shipmaster. We came upon some
islands like grains of rice floating upon this blue emptiness.
Growing on them are trees of lac and thus the name Lacadwipa
of the islands. Dropping anchor the shipmaster and his servant
made by oar boat for the longest island. In their absence the
lookout dwarf who had descended from his nest revealed to His
Eminence and me that upon that island was buried the father
of the shipmaster who was likewise a shipmaster like his father
before him and it is the practice of the son to pay tribute at the
grave of the father and upon his own death whether on land or
at sea his body must be buried beside his father and not given
to the waves. The lookout dwarf added not without spite that
the one-eyed tyrant should be fortunate for so much as a scrap
of sailcloth for his wrapping when the time came for it.

CADAMBAGIRI

THE ARCHIVES WERE NOT IN ACTUAL FACT GUARDED BY SNAKES, yet it had suited the old caretakers to perpetuate the myth. The women were unlettered, in any case, and wouldn't know a treaty from a charter if either had leapt up and bit them in the neck. The Muniments Room had, as a result, accumulated eight years' worth of dust and cobwebs. The Scrivener chanced upon it in the course of exploring the bleak north wing of the palace, and only because he had had nothing more pressing to keep him occupied that day.

From a quick assessment of the room's contents, he surmised that the staggered bundles and tumbled stacks had been dumped there and forgotten following the Great Fire of 1237: everything he touched breathed up a whiff of burnt wood and incense. He might have meddled some more, but the dust tickled his nose and he sneezed; an agitation of smoke-grey flew up through the gloom and out of a broken skylight under the ceiling. What better guardian of the written word, the Scrivener exulted: where owls reside, there can be no snakes. That evening, he sought, and was granted, permission of the Sovereign to further investigate his find.

In a fortnight of salvaging, sorting, deciphering and arranging, the closest the Scrivener came to a snake was a length of shed skin and some yellowed eggshells. How adroitly a myth can be spun to feed laziness, how little it takes to sustain a myth. And then, as abruptly as its transformation had begun, the room was rid of its dismal aspect. The shelves lining the walls were sprinkled with neem powder against weevils, the documents shelved by subject and date, the floor polished, the air fumigated and a circular table in the centre repaired and graced with a branched lamp stand. It was months since the Scrivener had dipped reed to ink. He wrote quickly:

My dearest boy. I am uncertain as yet of how I must reach this to your hands but a way will doubtless show itself in good time. As your eyes take in these feeble words I pray you will find it in your heart to forgive me for not alerting you more fully of the life that awaited you upon the close of your voyage. Only imagine how it seared me each time you spoke of returning and what torments I have suffered since that last sweet evening before you were permanently taken from my sight. I pray that your journey thus far has been blessed with fair weather and is free of cares the better to arm you for your altered circumstances. Upon your landing conduct yourself with decorum and politeness always and perform every task you are set by your new master with cheer and grace. The Sultan Splendid it is said is a good and just man and I have little doubt that you will be well kept. May you soon forget your former life and find joy in your new surroundings as indeed I have these past weeks. You were right in doubting me that evening for I too have embarked on a new life in the palace of Cadambagiri where I serve as scrivener to the Sovereign lady. My work here is no different to that which I rendered to your cousin by marriage although my new employer is harder to please. In her service are a number of women and only a few men. Here I have no students to tutor in grammar or penmanship. Each evening I make a leisured visit of the palace menagerie where the strangest residents are two aves which are tall as elephants and fearsome of presence. It would be remiss of me to not mention that Pol has died of old age. Perhaps I shall keep a small monkey on a gold chain after the model of our Minister Lady of the Treasury. I will write to you everyday until such time that a suitable courier presents himself. In this way you will know that you are in my heart daily. If the stars are kind you and I may one day speak again…

∾

But what of Treasury—he who had purchased his freedom from Narasimha's ship?

No sooner had his feet touched Vedapuri, Treasury had fallen into step with a caravan of merchandise fresh off a Samudera ship. The convoy, consisting of carriages as well as palankeens, was on a cross-country march to Bharukachchha in the northwest. Presenting himself as an out-of-luck Cadambagirian merchant who had lost his companions and possessions at sea, Treasury had secured not only the trust of the Muslim masters of the caravan—aside from the rags on his back, he carried neither weapon nor ornament—but also some stitched robes and the comforts of a commodious two-in-hand near the head of the convoy.

The carriage already contained two fleshy merchants who may have been twins: so great was their camaraderie that the duo sat with shoulders pressed and arms linked, had the same measured diction and wore identical square beards beneath their shaven upper lips. Leaner and meaner from his misadventures but not a bit out of spirit, Treasury had quickly ingratiated himself with the affable pair and clung to their company as if they were long-lost comrades.

The caravan guard, he had noted from the outset, was almost a small army, bristling with long spears and scimitars, more closely around the middle section which comprised the palankeens. On his inquiring after the merchandise they contained, the twins had laughed as one man and, altogether ignoring Treasury's line of enquiry, plied him with tart wedges of citron—of which they enjoyed a near-constant supply—before launching into a fresh cycle of rhyming couplets—of which they possessed an endless supply. Knowing better than to persist, Treasury had dropped the subject. The journey thereafter was a most illuminating one, for his own peregrinations until now had been shorn of all comforts and niceties.

The caravan might have easily covered more than its daily quota of twenty-two miles, but for its frequent stops for prayers and meals. How extraordinary, thought Treasury, that they make much ado about something as mundane as a night's rest: from the selection of campsites for elevation and scenery to the unloading of tents and private latrines; the cushions and carpets and mattreses and quilts to furnish the tents; the spittoons, lanterns, fly whisks and peacock-feather fans; the sealed jars of fresh water and the flagons of cool wine; the platters of dry fruit and nuts and sugar-candies… It was also in this company that Treasury acquired a taste for wild game (peacock and blackbuck, especially) prepared over live coals and smoked with dry herbs and ghee. There were quail eggs boiled in their shells and then peeled and dressed with salt and spices. There was a type of pickled black grape with a seed like stone (on which Treasury almost broke a tooth the first time he bit in), and a bread so sheer that one could behold a buttery January full moon through it. While they feasted, the merchants' servants played finger-drums and doleful stringed instruments; and after they had eaten, other servants rinsed and dried and perfumed their masters' hands. So much for Treasury's inclusion in their habits. Only when the convoy broke journey to unroll their prayer mats, he removed himself to a polite distance on the pretext of communing with his own heavens. It was during one such interlude that the contents of the palankeens revealed themselves.

They had stopped at midday by a pond outside a village. As was their wont, a clutch of peasants had gathered to stare at the travellers in inscrutable silence. Of a sudden the shutters of all twenty palankeens, grouped in the shade of a spreading tamar-e-hind, had flown open like beetle-wings to spill their cargo of small pale women—identical of build and slant-eyes and red mouth slits—all of whom began to heave and vomit. At this grotesque display, the gawping villagers had fled screaming, '*Devils! Devils!* Hide our children and babies!' Soon, the women were done regurgitating and climbed back into their palankeens, leaving a sickly sweet breath of rotten onions to the air. That night, emboldened by drink, Treasury implored his companions to let him lie with the palankeen women.

'You horny cur!' cried one of the twin merchants, pinning Treasury down in a playful neck lock for the other to tickle him in the ribs. 'Do you take them for common harlots to make with one as shrivelled and unwashed as yourself?'

'They must be,' Treasury replied, giggling and wriggling to free himself. 'Why, there are eighty of them…four to a palankeen. I wager your friends and you have your way with them while I sleep; all I ask for is but one pair for a night, a *single* night. I have forgotten what it is!'

'You speak as any infidel pye. For one thing, they are not *women* but catamites of the highest pedigree. For another, they are all virgin and must remain so until we have delivered them. So hold your prick and speak no more of this unless you wish your neck to be slit.'

'But where are you delivering them?' Treasury persisted, chafing his neck.

'To Bharukachchha, where else. They'll be out of our hands and board a dhow for the Yemen, they are bound for the harem of a particular Sultan of Araby.'

'Might it not have been more prudent to convey them by ship?' said Treasury, something of an expert on the subject from his eventful month at sea. 'Surely their beauty and worth will be much diminished from jiggering and vomiting their way across Hind?'

'Well said. But the last time the goods voyaged from Samudera to the Yemen, its ill-fated vessel was blown off course in the Sea of Hind and fell prey to some pirates of Aphrike and that was the last anyone heard of them. Hence our caravan this time, and then upon safe waters, always in sight of land.'

'But what if we are waylaid by brigands? The forests are filled with all manner of wild beasts and pestilence.'

'Brigands?' the pair chuckled. 'And *forests*? Mind well, this is only the first of such deliveries; we'll soon be more common a sight than crows in the sky.'

'How so?'

'You will see by and by.' They smiled their twin smiles. 'Cadambagiri, did you not say? We pay no toll there, for our Governor, may God keep him well, and the Sovereign there, may God keep her well, have a treaty. You must know that, being as you are of that country.'

'I certainly do,' Treasury replied. 'A treaty sealed with priceless aves.'

'Possibly so. The next time we pass through, we will be sure to seek out *your* hospitality. Now go to sleep.'

A few days later, Treasury sensed the nearness of Cadambagiri in the air even before spying one of the watchtowers in the thorn fence marking the boundaries. The sight gave him scant joy. His mood sank more fully when the blue-grey hump of the palace-hill hove on the horizon like a fallen elephant. Parting his company on the toll-free highway, the twins each gifted Treasury a keepsake: a small damascened knife with a curved iron blade, and a lifelike phallus carved of hippopotamus ivory. 'For your wife to employ before you go away next time,' they chortled, slapping each other and miming lewdly, '…and then she'll have use for the toy as well.'

Directly upon arriving at the citadel, Treasury made for the brothel his comrades and he had patronized that night, months ago, prior to their flight to Parijatapuri. He had come full circle: the same harlot, the same creaking bed, the same rancid smell of hair-oil mingled with stale lust and sweat. Later, in the public house next door, he was rewarded with news of his family—and news also of one of his former colleagues.

～

Granted clemency and released from confinement, the former Minister of Defence had mended his ways so completely as to set himself up as a holy man. His hermitage nestled in an acacia grove not far from the citadel. It was there that Treasury found him—shrunken of frame and painful to behold in an acacia-thorn cape which lent him a disturbingly hystricine air. The ill-lit hovel smelt overpoweringly of wet sheep. In attendance on the holy man were his children and wife—spared of thorn cloaks, yet all three of them wearing expressions of pious content.

Defence seemed pleased to see his long-lost colleague. 'Come, brother,' he rasped, 'only last night, you appeared in my dream. Verily it is god's grace that you stand before me in the flesh.'

'Enough,' said Treasury brusquely. 'As you know, I cannot present myself at the palace. Is it true what I have heard that my wife and children are slaves of that witch?'

'Not slaves, nay. After you and our comrades went into exile, all your womenfolk and children, my own included, entered the services of our Sovereign, for what choice had they in their destitute state? So, not slaves, no…and don't call her a witch. They serve the good lady in all correctness in the same positions that we ourselves held until…until *you* led us astray. There is also a man of mixed blood in her employ. She has him at all times by her side, and who knows where else.'

'But you have your family,' said Treasury lamely.

'Only because I begged them come take care for me. Word reached me that the four of you had fled to Parijatapuri whilst I languished in the company of porcupines. Ah, those dank dismal months…' He paused, adjusting the neckline of his thorn cape. 'So yes…Parijatapuri. A name I had sworn never to take—may my accursed tongue turn to ash—for was it not *she* who plunged us to our lamentable plight? But leave that be. The past is history. Are the others with you or do you grace my humble abode singly?'

'Singly,' Treasury said, still smarting at the unfair reference to him. Where had he led anyone *astray*? 'The others send you their respects,' he added. 'Our lives too have altered since we quit her service. I have come only to reclaim my family. But you say there is a man there…?'

'Yes, there is. So bide here the night, tell me all that has transpired since last we met, for my only visitors are women with cruel husbands. Who would have thought there are so many in the citadel!' His eyes twinkled in the foetid half-light. 'To each of my devotees, I present a thorn from this cape to place inside her tormentors' footwear or bed, so that it's not only their conscience that is pricked. It is only fair, do you not think, that the voiceless be avenged?'

'I am relieved to see you haven't lost your wit,' said Treasury. 'Let us converse at length the next time I visit. I must take your leave. Stay well, my friend.'

Outside the hut, Defence's children were force-feeding a white lamb some sharp green grass blades. Their mother was nowhere to be seen. On an impulse, Treasury took a step back inside.

'I have something for you before I leave,' he said, reaching inside the folds of his borrowed garments. Presently, he emerged, smiling, and stood watching the children and their lamb. 'Come see this, little ones,' he called softly.

In the acacias, the sparrows and babblers continued to chatter and chip.

24

CHANDRABHAGA

The Chief Architect had brought his son with him: a slip of a boy, waist-high to the man. 'Forgive us this intrusion, Majesty,' he said, nudging the child forward gently, 'but he will neither eat nor sleep until he has spoken with your noble self.'

Without greeting or artifice, 'Have you a son?' asked the child in a self-possessed way. The father gasped; the Master Draughtsman almost choked on the betel nut he was chewing.

'No, I do not,' Narasimha replied, briefly laying his right hand on the child's head.

'Why not?'

He laughed. 'It's a question I have often asked myself.'

'It is good to have a son. As I assist my father in building the Sun God's chariot, so yours can assist in ruling our land.'

'Has he been groomed to speak thus?' Narasimha asked, glancing up with a smile.

'Pardon his tongue, Majesty. We know not whence such ideas spring to his head. In the matter of building, however, he possesses a grasp of the science well ahead of his age; he must have been my father in the previous life. His greatest fancy of late is to install the gold lotus finial to the sanctuary tower when the time comes for it.'

'How old are you?' asked Narasimha.

'Six summers of age. I was birthed the day you broke ground for the chariot. Seeing how much remains to be finished, I may well be twelve by the time it is ready for the crowning ornament. Pray say I may affix it.'

Six years. His smile tightened. 'You have my word for it; I shall seek you out wherever you may be for that undertaking.'

'Where else will I be but by my father's side?' said the boy.

Then there was the matter of the floating image.

❧

After months of experiment, this was the best they had come up with: a scaled-down simulacrum of the sanctum and a handspan-high approximation of the iron icon of worship.

The eight-sided chamber was built of garnetstone and iron bricks. Where one might anticipate windows were seven blind-niches of lodestone instead. In the middle stood a lodestone plinth and directly above it, a ceiling-medallion of the same element. A length of silk was draped over the plinth. At a sign from the Master Forger, a servant lowered the iron mock-image to it.

A moment passed, in which nothing happened. The Master Forger stepped up and, without touching the mock-image, drew the silk away from under it. At the Sovereign's silence, he once again passed the silk through the hair's breadth of space between the plinth and the image.

'And the object of this trick,' Narasimha said, barely disguising the sneer in his voice, 'would be what, precisely?'

'To illustrate that the iron image can be induced to defy its weight, Majesty,' said the Master Forger. 'From the artful arrangement of lodestone and iron beams in the tower, and lodestone also for the crowning stone and platform—'

'At this scale, perhaps,' said Narasimha, ducking backwards out of the door of the confined space, 'but on the scale of the works under way? For years of libations and adornment? Decades into centuries? Posterity? Do you aver it will not settle to the base as a pebble thrown to the sea?'

The company waiting outside the mock-sanctum was silent. 'No,' Narasimha continued. 'Such effects lose their novelty in a matter of days. By all means continue your experiments, but only in so far as they advance our science. Side by side, it would be prudent to consider an alternative.' He turned to the Chief Architect. 'If you will permit it, I wish to converse again with your child.'

∼

Three portrait heads, sculpted of blackened and hardened beeswax: Dawn; Noontime; Eventide. They must, in due course, be copied to the corresponding greenstone figures for the terrace-shrines. The first wears a diadem and a hint of a smile. Noontime, frowning, and Eventide, drowsy, sport identical crowns enriched with ornament. All three heads are embellished on the sides with lotus medallions and swirled pennants.

Narasimha stood before each likeness, mirroring their expressions unconsciously. How terrifying to be gazing upon these waxen triplets of myself. How terrifying that wax, like flesh, will one day lose form and cease to exist. How reassuring that the stone versions of this set will remain unchanging… His reverie was interrupted by approaching feet. He turned with a sigh from Eventide.

The Secretary ushered in the Chief Architect's boy. The father hadn't accompanied them.

The self-possessed child was the first to speak. 'There is a story,' he began, 'of Sambha the son of Krishna, cursed by his father with leprosy. Sambha stood twelve years in the Chandrabhaga and prayed to the Sun God for release from his plight. After he was mended, he built a temple for lepers to worship the god in. It is that whitestone image that you may consecrate afresh in the chariot.'

'I too was told the story when I was your age,' Narasimha said, 'and the reason my mother chose this place for the chariot. But it's only a fiction. There was no temple, there is no image—'

'A hundred paces southwest of the plinth.'

'Do not interrupt me—' He stopped, pressing a hand to his forehead. 'Forgive me. Pray proceed.'

'There, under the mound, lies the old temple in pieces. The god on his lotus throne is undamaged. Anything else for the sanctum of the chariot would be a conceit.'

'Who *are* you?'

'I am Dharmapada,' said the artless child, 'the son of Sadashiva Samantaraya, your Master Architect.'

Presently, a fallen temple was excavated. The limestone image, buried in the sand, was undamaged.

∾

One of the guilds of draughtsmen was busy with a series of scenes of courtly life. The preparatory drawings, large rectangles of stiffened muslin, were pegged to the walls at eye level. They showed the Sovereign at prayer inside the Great Temple of Charitrapura. The Sovereign being weighed against gold in a ceremonial balance. The Sovereign dedicating a grant (held up by the Secretary). The Sovereign accepting a garland from a priest. The Sovereign on horseback. The Sovereign in a palankeen…

He stopped before one of the drawings.

Half-life-size, a man and woman stand at ease on either side of a flowering banana tree, itself framed by a trefoil archway. A breezy day. The woman's veil billows about her head. The man has, only moments ago, thrown a shawl across his chest. From their expressions, the pair have mastered every secret of marital bliss.

'And who might these happy fools be?' Narasimha said.

'Yourself, Majesty,' replied the Master Draughtsman with a nervous smile, 'and Her Majesty.'

'The scene is incomplete.'

'How so, Majesty?'

Divesting a draughtsman of his charcoal stick, Narasimha worked in the outlines of a child between the woman and the man. 'What would we do without sons to carry forth our names?' he said, tossing the stub aside and turning to the Chief Architect. 'In fact, I deem this instead to be turned a portrait of yourself and your kin.'

The Master Draughtsman and the Secretary exchanged a look of bewilderment. The Chief Architect bowed and bobbed his head in delight. A stickler for detail. 'May I point out, Majesty, that I sport no moustache.'

'A simple matter of erasing it,' Narasimha said, moving on:

'And what mischief is *this*? No, let me hazard a guess…? The court buffoon? Or more likely my Right Hand?'

Through it all, the Secretary stood lost in thought before the charcoal family. So—he said to himself—the unimaginable has at long last happened. Or had it? Either way, some discreet inquiries were in order the moment they returned to the palace. Retrieving the stub from where the Sovereign had tossed it, he added a nose, eyes and mouth to the charcoal child.

~

'I have been thinking,' Narasimha said. Always a bad sign, it was best to remain silent. They were taking in the evening breeze on the beach, close along the surf so they left no footprints. 'It will be a year since Katasimha. Lakhnore is safe in our hands. The time has come to push ahead. Lakshmanauti next, permanently unsettle the Turk from his seat.'

The Secretary's frown deepened. Another unprovoked attack. It did not bode well to keep tempting fate, not when you have no heir as yet; the contented family under their banana tree was only a sketch. Did the Sovereign secretly desire a hero's death?

'Aside from consolidating our gains,' Narasimha was saying, marching ahead, 'a fresh assault will hasten the completion of *this*.' They were passing the temple site. 'If it must take another six years…it isn't as if my coffers replenish unaided.'

'When do you wish to embark on this…*replenishment*?'

'The first day of the new year would be appropriate. What have we today?'

'The fourteenth of February.'

'In six weeks, then. Let us return to the capital and prepare.'

'The capital?'

He threw him a look over his shoulder. 'Yes.'

'Might it not be expedient to proceed to Lakhnore and to there await—'

'Since when,' Narasimha snarled, spinning around, 'have I set out to battle without the Consort's blessings?'

'Forgive me,' said the Secretary. 'I spoke without thinking.'

'And making a habit of it. We leave at daybreak.'

'The Aphrikes too?' he asked, hurrying after him. 'And the masons and forgers?' Each time they launched a campaign, the labour gangs suffered the worst casualties. It was hard these days to distinguish between the lepers and the battle wounded.

'No, leave them be. A novelty repeated becomes a contrivance. And no labour gangs this time.' He gestured towards the temple site. 'Enough! I want this finished without further delay.'

25

KATAKA

A KALACHURI, NOT GANGA BY BIRTH, AND SOLDIER FIRST AND
then brother-by-marriage, the man pacing the War Office was
possessed of looks and bearing which had women of all ages
(and not a few men) mentally engaging with him in all manner
of submissive acts. They took his name under their breath as a
charm against the evil eye. When they stood aside for him to
pass, they inhaled deep to memorize his scent. Horse-sweat.
Saddle wax. Burnt iron. Stone-oil. It was him—*Paramardideva
… oh lord Paramardideva!* that they invoked in their heads as
they lay under their pig husbands, inwardly cursing fathers and
fate for marrying them to the wrong man.

The General for his part was blind to his effect. When he
wasn't leading Kalinga to victories, he kept to Ekamra and
his extensive landholdings—tilling his fields, rearing Persians
to stud and dogs for the chase, and drilling the city's young
bucks in mace and hand-to-hand combat. There was talk of
irregularities—taxes, favouritism—but it was all overlooked.
He kept his wife the princess Chandrikadevi like a goddess and
permanently gravid.

Arriving a day in advance of Narasimha's return from
Chandrabhaga, the General had quickly acquainted himself
with local happenings. Some of the news amused him. Presently,
the door of the War Office swung open and the Sovereign was
announced in.

The General stopped pacing and strode up to Narasimha. 'At
long last,' he said, clasping him briefly by the upper arms and
then slapping his shoulders heartily. 'And what's this I hear about
your puppy Parijatapuri sailing to Kilwa on our ship?'

'I sent him,' Narasimha said, taking a step back. A decade
older, the General had a way of making him feel less than

adequate…as though he were being constantly assessed for his suitability as Sovereign. He tended, not unconsciously, to roughen his timbre and lower his pitch: 'He was beset by certain worries. He was only too happy for respite from them. I sent him as my envoy.' He paused, and then added, 'He went willingly.'

'If you say so.' The General grinned, presenting yellow ranks of teeth. 'I keep telling you always, never explain or justify an act. Nonetheless, had you asked me, I'd have offered a more suitable envoy in one of my boys. I hear you've dismissed the half-breed?'

'One takes what action one must at one's own counsel. And peril.'

'Well said.' He smiled. 'You summoned me. I trust it is not to retire your general next. Incidentally, I have brought you another spirited young thing… A bay, sixteen months of age.'

'My thanks.' Narasimha sat, indicating a chair. 'I shall come to the matter directly. The time has come to take Lakshmanauti.' His hands closed around the lions-head terminals of the armrests. 'Is it true the name has been changed? What sort of name is *Lakhnauti*?'

'One easier on the tongues of Turks. When do you wish to take it?'

'The first anniversary of Lakhnore. The Privy Council and Defence will have a thousand reasons to object. It is your job to convince them.'

'Convince me.'

'Oh? I can hardly be faulted—' He studied his hands. 'There is the temple to finish. Since Lakhnore, the privy purse is all but empty…but don't let the word get about, no one respects an indigent king. So this is what I've been reduced to, a bounty collector. Therefore Lakshmanauti.'

'I am not convinced.'

'With the Turk's capital in our hands, the thrust eastwards will be eased. I hear the floodplains there have been turned to fields of rice; it is five years since they've suffered famine. Whereas Kalinga…' He spread his hands.

The General gave him a long appraising look. A peculiar creature, this brother-by-marriage. How much longer before his spell of fortune ran dry? 'It is my beholden duty to advice caution,' he said at length. 'It has come to our ears that your friend Tughan Khan has been cultivating his overlord in Dilli. An unprovoked assault would be intemperate.'

'Caution? Intemperate? *Unprovoked*? You, of all men, speaking the gilded language of my priests? Don't tell me you are…scared?'

'As sultans go, Ala ud-din Masud is the most ineffectual that Dilli has had to date, a slave to fine wines and sweetmeats. It suits your friend to be his principal procurer of dates, grapes, pomegranates—'

'I am not interested in his dietary habits.'

'Please.' He held up a hand. 'Only last month, three hundred sealed flasks of wine from Sicily, so sweet and warm you could taste the sun in it, travelled from Lakshmanauti to Dilli for the coming of age festivities of a favourite concubine. Your friend the Turk personally accompanied the gift. He has made himself indispensible to the sultan and in return enjoys his personal protection and ear and much else beside, if only to ensure a steady supply—'

'Cut off the supply. And quit calling him my friend. A sovereign has no friends.'

'Except the one.'

Narasimha laughed. 'If that is a reference to yourself, it was you alone whom my father trusted and it is you alone I must trust in matters as these. That does not make you my *friend*.'

For a fleeting moment the General's face seemed to crumple into itself. 'Of course.' He brushed a knuckle to his nose and nudged the points of his moustache. 'But back to the matter at hand. The fortifications in Lakshmanauti are of a new order and scale…unlike Lakhnore, unlike anything you have seen. The citadel rises on the east bank of the Bhagirathi; the palace inside is defended by two concentric walls, each forty cubits high and with a ditch between…a hundred cubits wide, filled with crocodiles. There are four drowning pools and two whipping yards. There is talk of a tunnel all the way to Dilli, although I have no way of confirming it as yet. The assault must rely on stealth, not shock and surprise. To that end,' he spread open his hands, 'we must sweep sideways and northwards, one district after the other. Surround. Secure. Proceed. Repeat. Not a single frog must slip through to croak the alarm ahead. Twenty-five thousand foot soldiers, three hundred elephants, a hundred chariots in the advance ranks, none of your stonemasons and slaves. There is also a fire device I wish to put to the test.'

'You worked all this out in a moment?'

'I've been anticipating it for some time.'

Narasimha straightened his back, ran his hands through his hair. 'Where would you like me? Horse or chariot?'

'I was coming to it. There is the river to ford. The approach is open country not forest; we will be sighted for miles. The crossing must be made at night, a bend in the Bhagirathi, half a mile upstream; foot soldiers and elephants only. On the matter of your position, upon taking the last but one village southwest of the river, you will remain there with a deployment, secure the hostages and bounty, hold court, whatever else to establish your presence.' He paused, gauging the effect. 'Look, I know… But your old friend will not be as amenable as the last time. Anything can happen.'

'Yes. I wouldn't want my army rendered headless.'

'That will *never* happen.'

'Nor must we render my *empire* headless.'

Again that slight smudging of features. 'Bear with this deviation for a moment.' He leant forward. The chair creaked. 'Your sister and I have been meaning for some time to broach the subject. Knowing your situation, it would be an honour to offer you one of our own set. The second born especially has all the makings of…is worthy of carrying forth his Ganga lineage. We only ask you to enact the instrument of adoption at the earliest.' There. He had said it at last. He slumped back, passed a hand over his brow which was beaded over in sweat.

A sovereign may not exhibit rage. A sovereign may not speak harshly. Whatever the provocation, it ill behoves a sovereign to strike a subordinate.

Narasimha stood. It signalled the end of this part of the meeting. Presently, the doors of the War Office opened to admit the Privy Council and the Ministry of Defence.

26

PARIJATAPURI

FOR THE MURDER OR ATTEMPTED MURDER OF A KING, THE penalty is death. The last public execution was conducted in 1223: a priest, for the murder, by quicksilver poisoning, of the Raja's grandsire. For most of the present generation, the imminent execution was a novelty.

The wrestling arena, appropriated for the event, was packed. Rumour was rife. The accused was an illicit lover of the Crown Princess. No, an estranged half-sibling. No, the kidnapper *and* murderer of the Heir Apparent. No, a lust-madded hermaphrodite who had snuck into the palace: what better explanation for that mock-phallus and gelding-knife...

A single drumbeat, followed by a bleat from a trumpet.

Jostling for space, the spectators craned their necks. Look! the very personification of evil! Look away quick! Don't let him look you in the eye... Die! Die!

His hands bound behind him, Treasury was led to the block by two sentries. Until this morning, he had expected a reprieve, some change of heart in the good lady. Instead, this. He held his head high, a smirk on his face. His eyes blazed: so many people, just to see him! 'Victory!' he yelled.

'Hush your cunt mouth,' growled the sentry on his right.

'You'll be squealing a different tune in a moment,' supplied the other, adding a vicious jab in the ribs.

Treasury recovered his breath and found his voice again: 'Freedom! *Justice!*'

The crowds went mad. Treasury grinned. A shame he couldn't wave up to the tiered ranks. Men, women, girls, boys, wizened crones, even babies at breasts. The block was several paces away. It seemed such a waste of his illustrious life. Shaking his head, he cast his mind back, for the hundredth time, to the events which had led up to this.

After murdering Defence and his family, Treasury had made short work of the road to Parijatapuri. Despite his wasted state, the guardsmen at the palace remembered him as a kinsman of the Crown Princess. 'I bring word of your Crown Prince,' he said to them. 'I beg you present me directly before Her Radiance.'

She was alone in her chamber. 'You?' she said, frowning. 'You look a sight. Is the deed done?'

'Where do I begin, my lady,' Treasury replied, playing for time. 'On my way here, I was set upon by bandits who robbed me of everything and left me for dead. It is only from your grace that I am alive. I owe you my undying allegiance—' But she'd stopped listening to him. 'Quick,' she said, pointing with a forefinger, 'Hide!'

The beaded curtain fronted a privy latrine. Treasury almost stepped into the hole in the floor; steadying himself, he reached into his pockets. He scarcely dared to breathe, catching the short sharp exchange between Her Radiance and the newcomer. 'He is there,' Treasury heard her say to the Raja of Parijatapuri, and, 'Protect me!'

The moment the Raja whisked the curtain aside, a blunt blow to his forehead knocked him out cold in an instant. Her Radiance began to scream and scream; jumping out over the prone Raja, Treasury pointed the damascened knife to her breast. She promptly winded him with a kick to the groin. As he crumpled to the floor, she ran from from the chamber, screaming her head off like a woman of the streets. Before he knew it, Treasury was overpowered by a thuggery of servants.

When they served him his sentence, he had begged audience with their mistress: everything could be explained, it was all a misunderstanding, he was a trusted ally. But they laughed and said Her Radiance neither knew him nor deigned to make his acquaintance.

He blinked and faltered. By a cruel concision of time and space, the block had reached his feet. His captors pushed him to his knees, pressed his head to the cold granite and held it there. No call to be so rough, he wanted to say, he was a man of refinement, but his tongue was dry.

Under his right cheek, the stone was slightly concaved to accommodate a head. It smelt, inexplicably, of watermelon and tender coconut. He squinted. Was that a melon seed stuck to the granite? He wished he hadn't seen it; it infuriated his sense of neatness. As if to mock him, a great cheer filled the air. A shadow fell over him. He felt his bladder empty itself.

The regular execution elephant had died some years back. For the past two days, they had primed the replacement on melons and coconuts. But this was different. Something inside the novice's head told her to resist: her upraised foot touched and then hovered a breath away from the tonsured human head.

Who would have imagined the crazed sole of an elephant could be so smooth and yielding. Treasury squeezed shut his eyes, at once recalling the sight, long ago, somewhere, of a trail of elephant footprints like great silver coins cast to the dust one cold gold morning. His eyes welled at the memory. The executioner's foot settled lightly again. It felt oddly comforting and smelt of freshly cut hay. He would have liked it to remain there but a shaft of light blazed through his eyelids. Something wasn't going to plan. He wanted more than anything else to pull that grey mass of hard-bristled skin and chipped toenails to his hot face and hold it there for dear life but his hands were tied. The voices above him turned sharp and urgent. A secret tongue, of men and elephants.

They finally saw where the problem lay: the elephant was reluctant to bear down upon the face with its protrusions of nose and lips, eyelids, eyelashes. They turned the prisoner's head so that his other cheek was pressed to the block of granite.

No melon seed; instead, directly ahead in the galleries, a big-eyed child staring straight at him. He felt strangely vindicated: he would visit her nightmares for the rest of her life.

The foot returned. His scalp tingled. And then this unimaginable weight. Something gave. His eyes bulged before sliding out of their sockets like grapes from their skins.

~

The poor Raja. The clout he had taken from the ivory phallus had been compounded by his fall backwards to the floor. No one knew how long he had lain unconscious before he was revived.

Not soon enough, it would seem. It had resulted in the dreaded living-death, robbing the Raja of all sensation and movement. The left side of his face had fallen askew and refused to realign itself. To keep his mouth from hanging open like a common idiot's, the Crown Princess devised a bandage—under his jaw and behind his ears and fastened in a bow on top of his head. The Second Princesses embellished it with a jewelled butterfly-clasp. As for the girls' baby half-sibling, meantime, there was still neither sight nor sound or, for that matter, of the Tongueless One who had spirited him away.

Whereas the strain of *not knowing* would have driven any mother out of her mind, the Crown Princess calmly took it upon herself to remain at all times by her father-in-law's side as his guardian and attendant. With the novelty of the execution behind them, the good people of Parijatapuri clamoured for audience at the palace gate, in order to confirm with their own eyes that their Raja had survived the attempt on his life.

The Crown Princess graciously obliged. In the days and weeks to follow, the citizenry and visitors alike filed reverentially past the motionless figure who might well be dead, but for the eyes which wetly, cannily, took in every gawp and prostration and offering of flowers, coin and cowries. No one asked why the Raja was sat in a wooden crib even though his gem-crusted gold throne stood a few paces behind. No one questioned the indignity of the bandage with its jewelled butterfly. Through it all—day after day, dawn to dusk, with intermissions only for feeding and cleaning—the Crown Princess sat by her father-in-law's side, wearing a smile of infinite patience.

The mask cracked when the Raja soiled himself before his chamber pot could be replaced under the crib. First, she consigned him to an outhouse in a rear garden of the palace. Next, she sat in the royal throne and proclaimed herself Princess Regent. Keeping it warm, she explained, for her consort the rightful heir. Then she penned a letter to the Crown Prince, entreating his return from Kataka in haste. It went unanswered, even after a fortnight. She penned another, this one to Narasimha, asking him to return her husband. When it too went unanswered, she concluded her mercenaries had accomplished their errand.

One hot March afternoon, a courier pigeon arrived. The message, ragged in transit, made no sense: *Upon ship with quarry in*—They brought it, together with the messenger, to her notice.

The bird struggled in her grasp. 'You worthless thing flying into the wrong hands,' she muttered, kissing its beak before twisting its neck.

27

TO THE NAMELESS ISLANDS

AFTER FULL TWENTY DAYS IN THE SEA OF HIND WE MADE landfall on one of the Cowrie Islands in time to replenish our water bins. The natives of this island are comely and greeted our shipmaster and crewmen with much familiarity. At the behest of their headman our cattle were brought ashore so that they may feast of fresh grass of which they have been thus far bereft. To see them run and skip as lambs not bovines was a gladdening sight and even His Eminence who remains stiff and distant cracked a smile. Perhaps the firm ground has lightened his mind for come dusk he bids me play my pipe for the headman whose women attend upon His Eminence and myself and ply us with meats and fish for these few days of respite from our ship. For this kindness and in recompense for sweet water from a stream His Eminence vouchsafed one of our six stud bulls to the headman. It is with heavy heart but silent tongue that I stood witness to the exchange.

∾

There is a type of coconut native of the Cowrie Islands which is deemed precious for its immodest size and shape. One such coconut was given by the headman as tribute to His Eminence who upon repairing to our ship declared the thing was of little use to him and gave it to the shipmaster who fell upon it gladly. This coconut is called a sea coconut and bears a likeness to the parts of women. Tomorrow we must weigh anchors again.

∾

The weather has turned against us most cruelly. Not even during the hottest months in Kataka is the air so dry. It brushes the skin as if it were a flaming torch and to step outside is to become shrivelled like a grape. The act of crossing the deck to the privies is an effort as are the functions of eating and sleeping and speaking. The heat is most fierce come noontide and remains so until twilight. It is only at night that the wind cools and our sails fill and then we make haste in darkness. Having come this far I cannot cease to write for I write for you who taught me to write so that you may see through my eyes all that I have done and seen. The heat today is at its fiercest and the reed keeps slipping from my hand.

∼

Upon emerging from my chamber yesterday I beheld in the as-yet cool morning light a most frightening sight for assembled upon the deck was an army of black aves with red bills and red sacks upon their breasts the likes of which I have never seen. Nor has His Eminence who made bold to approach the set which set up a fearsome flapping of wings and snapping of bills yet made no move to take flight for they seemed fearless. The crewmen were chary and went about their business neither singing nor arguing as is their habit. It was only when dusk fell that the birds climbed onto the side and threw themselves to the backward wind. After the last had quit our sight the lookout dwarf climbed down from on high and the shipmaster and he spoke in low voices. My curiosity was great and upon enquiry I learnt from the deputy that the black aves portend ill to any vessel upon which they alight for they are the spirits of women who had died at sea. Thus the unease of the crewmen. Seeing as this is the maiden voyage of our ship he said the lookout dwarf has called for a blood sacrifice to counter the ill-effects of the aves. Upon hearing this my own blood turned as water for I knew in my stomach that the victim of sacrifice would be one or other of the crewmen whose number would be drawn from a bucket. But I was wrong and a more cruel tragedy awaited for the shipmaster approached His Eminence and sought leave to sacrifice one of my damsels. For my part I wept and protested so His Eminence stood up to the shipmaster and reasoned that no bovine be sacrificed for so foolish a belief and that the birds had only sought refuge upon our deck and caused no harm to any life or limb. But the shipmaster was adamant and to prevent an uprising His Eminence conceded and despite my entreaties and tears and pleas one of the five remaining stud bulls was picked and with the lookout dwarf conducting the ceremony its blood was spilled and the carcase quartered and thrown over the side with the dwarf all the while loudly chanting. Forthwith there appeared a sea monster with gaping mouth and cruel teeth which threw itself upon the parts and entrails as a wild dog might upon a hare so that the water churned red and the air filled with the cries of seabirds and of the dwarf and the crewmen. For a time afterwards the monster remained in sight under the red water making circles of our ship as if its blood lust was not yet fully sated. Only after it had departed did the dwarf give word that the ceremony was concluded and anchors were drawn and the sails lifted so that we could at long last proceed. These sights shall remain with me for as long as I breathe.

His Eminence has taken to his bed as of yesterday. His stool is bloody. I hear him cry as he is helped by his servants to the privies and back and so a bucket and water are brought to him instead. He is biddable and makes no protest when I administer the medicaments to ease his pains.

At noon His Eminence bade me fetch from his clothes chest a silver scroll case and to unseal it for him. From it he removed a missive all very beautifully writ in red. Because the writing is Persian I could not assist in the reading and made to summon the shipmaster or his deputy. That will not be necessary His Eminence said and bidding me to hold the lantern close began to read softly the while following the writing with his forefinger from right to left. His diction I shall vouch seemed fluent. Next he asked for crimson ink and reed and sealing wax all of which items I duly furnished. His Eminence scored some words of what was writ and wordless returned the missive to the scroll case. Then he bade me to seal it again and with trembling hand pressed his thumb ring to the wax the while saying I must hand this to the Sultan Soleiman of Kilwa and to none other than that personage and to return forthwith to Kataka with the gift of a particular camel from the Sultan to our Sovereign. Why are you telling me this I said but he did not reply and thus I knew the answer for myself. He who has forsaken the will to live is already dead. I felt a great sadness for His Eminence is a good man despite his timidity of heart and mind.

∼

It will be three weeks before we sight land. Today a rain has begun with great force and one heifer has died and the numbers of the gift is fallen to forty-three. The crewmen I feared would eat the carcase for they are possessed of neither caste nor creed but they threw it over the side to the sea. I did not care to see whether it sank or floated or was taken by some monster fish. I fear I cannot write for some days.

∼

His Eminence summoned the shipmaster and deputy and me to his chamber and with our servants bearing witness bade me wear his ceremonial necklace and thumb ring and also a different finger ring. In this manner the weight of conducting the embassy of our Sovereign has fallen upon me and I have given His Eminence my word to carry out these matters with due care. Thus assured His Eminence sought my forgiveness for any unkindness and pain he may have visited upon me and before I could utter some words of courage he quietly departed this life. It fell upon me to cleanse and dress his body. Because we are still some days away from the Nameless Islands the funeral was conducted at sea itself. First we wrapped the body in a square of sailcloth and tied a stone anchor to the feet. Then some prayers were uttered by the deputy and one of the shore-sighting crows was brought from its basket. It cawed six times and flew to the clouds whereupon the shipmaster gave the word for His Eminence the Crown Prince of Parijatapuri to be given to the Sea of Hind.

Part Four

28

KILWA

TODAY THE FIRST DAY OF APRIL AND FULL ONE HUNDRED AND thirty-seven days of our embarkation from Khalakatapatna the island of Kilwa appeared on the horizon as a long black shape which I took at first sight for a ship-eater fish dead on its back. At our approach the lesser shapes gathered about it grew as vessels of every type and size and these were more numerous than I had seen at our many ports of call between Khalakatapatna and the Nameless Islands. Our progress between the vessels occupied all of the morning and it was well-nigh afternoon when we paid our custom and were admitted to a dockyard and thence to this jetty where our ship must be tethered for the length of our embassy. The shipmaster stilled my eagerness to step on to land and dispatched his deputy to the palace of the Sultan bearing word that a ship of Kalinga bearing an emissary is arrived with a gift of bovines from our Sovereign. But the emissary is dead I countered whereupon he reminded me of my embassy by proxy. There is no escape from whatsoever trials await me and come dawn I must wear the necklace and rings and submit myself before this Sultan Splendid. The thought is not pleasing for I know not a word of greeting or jest in the languages of this place. I have no desire for food or drink. Now I must sleep the better to ready myself for what tomorrow must bring.

～

The second stowaway who served as foot servant to His Eminence interrupted my rest and bade me hurry with him to the side of the deck to behold a sight. There passed below us on the jetty a line of slaves in chains each bearing upon his shoulders paired ivories of great length and in thickness as much as my waist as if those were plucked of some monster elephants. The elephants of Aphrike the servant said are unlike our elephants and this difference is marked in their ears which are the shape of Aphrike. How do you know this I asked of him to which he replied never you mind. In all we counted a hundred paired ivories and as many men making into a neighbour ship which the servant said was bound for Araby. How do you know this I asked of him again to which he replied I have conversed with the merchants on the jetty while seeing to the bovines which were removed to the palace whilst you slept. On hearing this I was saddened to have not bid my wards farewell before they were taken from me or had a word of pleasantry with their physician and servants. Here I close this account of our first day during which I have as yet not stepped upon land.

～

My fears of yesterday have eased from the events of today which I must recount with care in the way they happened for my mind is a monkey and cannot be trusted to remember everything. First at daybreak I was roused from sleep by my servants who informed me that a guard had arrived to convey me to the palace and I must ready myself in haste. On my way to the privies I spied this so-called guard waiting on the jetty and found it to be not one guardsman but twenty giants disposed about a golden chair on wheels. Upon readying myself I forgot in my anxiety to wear the necklace and rings but the stowaway servant was at once on hand to assist with these and to hand me also the scroll case for the Sultan Splendid. I bade the fellow tidy himself and join my toothsome chaperone and four servants already by my side and so he did at once leading the way down the bridge so that I may not trip. I was glad to once again feel the ground neath my feet but only for a moment for the waiting guard bade me climb into the chair on wheels and in it conveyed me into the lanes of the citadel with one man drawing and four others holding aloft a scarlet cloth between four long golden sticks to keep the sun off my head and the rest of their party disposed fore and aft. At our progress the people there pressed themselves to the

walls on the sides and these were of all types and very pleasing
in cloths of blue and white and some painted blue of face and
all wearing much gold and ivory and jewel beads. Then we came
to a flight of steps and I was asked to sit in a palankeen waiting
there and in this was borne up by a different guard directly into
the palace. Now this palace is a city in a city and we entered it
through a great doorway and thence through more doorways
within doorways each of decreasing size but increasing ornament
and leading into courtyards of greater size and everywhere
were men coming and going and selling stuffs of all types and
there was a lion chained to a wall but it was asleep. We came to
stop in a garden of pomegranate trees and some fruiting vines.
Climbing out of my palankeen I looked around for some sign
of what I must do next when the stowaway servant made a sign
with his eyes for me to look up to my right. There from a balcony
some women were looking down and smiling and waving and
I waved back at them and this caused them to laugh gaily. Now
there appeared among them a personage I guessed at first sight
and correctly was our Sultan Splendid. And a very splendid
man is he of middling height and age and slender of build and
shining lightness of skin and shaven of head and nose like beak
and sad eyes and a beard of some length and in a robe of white
and in his right hand he bore a stick like the dry tail of some
beast with which he flicked the air in a most elegant way and I
knew at once to bow low in the manner of visitors before our
own Sovereign. I was unsure of what to do next or say but the
stowaway servant divested me of the scroll case and unsealing
it proceeded to loudly read the missive therein. I knew full well
that this was not the way but stood in mute surprise for who
would have known the fellow was lettered and that too in the
Persian script. As I looked from him to the balcony it was not
clear what the Sultan was thinking but upon the conclusion of
the reading he gestured with his stick for us to be brought up to
him. Only then and pressing close by my side did the stowaway

reveal that he had formerly served as a minister in a country in Hind until certain events had reduced him to a loader of hay adding that it would hold me in good stead to keep him near at all times for he was well versed in the ways of kings and had already proven his claim by giving voice to the missive. Albeit without my leave I replied but be that as it may I shall have you as my language bridge and for this office the fellow was most glad and asked how I would recompense him. Justly I replied. And just as well for forthwith upon our entering a hall of audience the difficulty of my embassy became evident to me. The Sultan Splendid was seated at the far end in a chair with his feet upon a lion skin and in his company were over a hundred elders looking upon me with hard black eyes. Behind his chair stood two giants bearing swords and I took them to be of black wood and paints and gilt until one of them blinked and these giants were the personal guard of His Splendid. Also present right and left of his chair were two old men but no higher than my waist and attired like the giants in coloured cloths and jewels but unlike the giants these were without swords and restless. I bowed again before the Sultan and my thoughts went for a moment to how His Eminence might have conducted himself in this presence had he not departed his life. The thought brought a smile to my lips and this pleasing expression I kept in place for the length of our audience for it was not required of me to say a thing but only to nod and bow each time my new-found assistant conveyed to me that which was said by the Sultan in his deep slow voice firstly to express his joy in the bovines and then to enquire after my health and lastly to welcome me into his palace to rest and strengthen myself for the return voyage. One of the little men then stepped up to take from my assistant the scroll case and handed it to his pair who in his turn removed the missive and held it up for the Sultan to read of himself. As he did so the Sultan smiled and nodded and frowned once and then smiled again and nodded. Then the missive was returned to the case and remained with the second little man. Next the Sultan commenced what was from its tone and rhyme to be a very long poem. For all their sweetness the words lay beyond the reach of my language bridge but suffice to say it greatly charmed the elders in their chairs for upon its conclusion they gave praise as one with their hands held high and nodding their heads. His Splendid I have since learnt is given to composing such poems whenever the mood and occasion presents itself and the arrival of the cattle is said to be one such time. Our audience thus concluded we were shown downstairs and directly towards these apartments in a garden courtyard and here we may rest for some weeks. From five months at sea I am only grateful for the fresh not salt air about my face and shade and cool water always to hand. There is a common privy in the corner and also a bathhouse beside and chambers separate for my chaperone and four servants. My interpreter has chosen without my leave to share my chamber but not bed with me. We are not wholly alone in this yard for there are present in their own apartments some other embassies from the western countries of Hind and these have their own servants. Everywhere are cats the colour of ash but these are unfriendly. There are no more women to be seen. Here I conclude my first day as Emissary by Proxy.

∼

We have bided here four days. For there is naught to occupy me after our daily audience is complete I have taken to making a visit everyday of a different side of the palace which I have already noted is a city. Now this palace is built of a stone which they say is made by sea insects and the walls and ceilings are evenly covered in white lime of seashell. Everywhere are pillars and arches and steps and the ceilings are made very fine like the inside of seashells and in the chambers are small windows at different heights. The air is cool and always sweet from some oils burning. In the shadows at any time of day are many pleasing young men like myself sitting and silently staring or with eyes closed telling their beads or speaking softly each to each or writing and these I have learnt are officers of the palace. Between the arches are small yards with fountains playing and pigeons grumbling and here gather older ministers in quiet serious talk the while sipping a black liquid from small goblets. There is a courtyard more squared than the rest where all these men gather to pray thrice a day but the temple of the Sultan and his family is said to be private. Our repasts are prepared and served by our servants with our rations from our ship and also fresh figs and melons with comb honey and breads and wine the last of which is very sweet.

～

One week has passed and I am well revived from food and sleep. After the first morning I have not once again seen the women of the balcony who must be the wife and daughters of His Splendid. Upon my mentioning this my language bridge laughed and said any women I had seen must have been visions in dreams. But you showed them to me I said to which he replied it was a trick of my eyes and there are only men and boys in this palace. This is not true for I have heard the voices of women singing at night above these apartments and when I stepped outside in the darkness last night and soft played upon my pipe the same melody a square of red silk made as a ball was thrown from the darkness and when I picked it its scent was a womanly scent. This silk I have kept to myself lest my interpreter who is given to speaking too much even in sleep makes some mischief. Word is come that our shipmaster has taken our ship to the southern side of the citadel to ready it for our return journey and the day for our embarkation is set for first day of May.

～

Today I was possessed of a desire to see the sea. Because these apartments all look into courtyards and passageways it was some time before I chanced upon some steps to the roof and thence by way of bridges from one terrace to the next I made my way towards the west of the palace at all times noting the men going about their duties below the bridges and praying I would not miss my step and fall to their midst. When at last I stopped it was upon a broad terrace and there is a water tank of eight sides with steps leading into it and surrounded by pillars and arches but open to the sky and open also in its northern prospect towards the sea. Seated upon the steps inside the tank and some of them swimming were some elders and these men looked up at me and from their signs and laughter I could tell they were asking me in to join in their bath but because I was unsure of the depth and also timid before so many of the yang type I bowed and stepped back and away. The sea from this place was of a colour more brilliant than the sky and the sailcloths of boats upon it were like silver fish.

29

KATAKA

THE SECRETARY'S LETTER WAS DATED THE FIRST OF APRIL; today was the tenth. The Consort read quickly:

Your Excellence | Since my last dispatch there is improvement in the mind and heart of he who protects | At all times by his side is his brother by marriage | Together they have been out on the hunt every day and from the baying of the dogs and the blood smears on their faces it is from a fine hunt they gallop to the fort | For I am loath of the sport and averse to the sight of butchery there is naught I can relay on the nature of the bag | Suffice to say there is much feasting and smoke leaf | Thereafter the two repair to a balcony to roll the dice the while laughing and joking like youths for these are their sole diversions before the greater hunt ahead | Each night thus far the lion has lain restful under the stars for he has chosen to bed on an open terrace | The brother by marriage has his own quarters with his deputy and closest men at hand for he constantly fears death by treachery | From where I am quartered a window permits me a view of our massed army at rest for the night with the horses and elephants formed as a bank behind their encampments | Further beyond lies the blackness which is our infamous bamboo forest | As in the past I must remain in Katasimha and attend to messages until the lion returns in victory | The march northwards is due on the full moon | I close this seeking your prayers for the lion and his company |

30

KILWA

TODAY I WAS SUMMONED TO PRIVATE AUDIENCE WITH THE Sultan Splendid but only so private as his guards and little men and my language bridge permit. After I had made my salutations His Splendid enquired if I wanted for anything by way of comforts to better my stay while our vessel is readied for the return to Hind. Then he bade me describe to him our Sovereign and this I did in my best words and omitting the matter of bent legs and also such matters which show our Sovereign in a human light. My speech pleased the Sultan who had imagined his compeer to be all that I had described of his bravery and wit and horsemanship. Then the Sultan enquired after the wives and children of our Sovereign and to this I replied that he has just the one consort who is also my cousin and they have as yet no child. Next the Sultan enquired after my own wives and family. I have neither I said. Be that as it may a winsome young prince as yourself is a most fitting emissary of my compeer Narseen said the Sultan taking the name of our Sovereign in that way. I began to reply that I had but turned emissary by proxy when my language bridge quietly said to me that there was no call to confuse the Sultan with that affair. I heeded his counsel and gave thanks to the Sultan for his kindness and declared that it was I who is more fortunate to discharge the present embassy. At this the Sultan replied that I have fared well and it remained for me to ferry back a beast for which my Sovereign had expressed a desire in his missive and on the subject of this missive perchance I had fair idea of what had been covered over in ink. The interpreter who knew naught of that matter looked to me for a reply so I replied in all honesty that I was ignorant of the contents of the missive save that it was from my Sovereign. My response seemed to not to satisfy the Sultan who looked from my interpreter to me and then held the missive up to the light for some moments before letting the matter rest. Then the Sultan conversed directly with my man in their common tongue and the latter I could see was turning most unctuous with each passing utterance. My sense of their exchange was not far from correct for no sooner had our audience concluded and we were shown outside the interpreter declared that he would soon quit being my assistant for he had submitted his talent most humbly to the Sultan and it had been accepted. For how long I asked him. For the rest of his life he replied and added that he would not be going back to our ship. So be it I replied and I wish you well. I seek neither approbation nor blessing from you he said of a sudden ungracious and that he was not a Kalinga subject and therefore free to do as he pleased. Even if it were upon a Kalingan ship that he travelled to this palace I said whereupon he fiercely bade me hold my tongue or else. Or else what I asked him. Beware he said and that he had saved me from declaring my true office as glorified servant and it would be prudent of me to address him with respect or else. So be it I said and let it rest for this entity is possessed of a most unpredictable temperament. Our shipmaster will be pleased to learn he has one man less to ferry back to Hind.

～

I was readying myself this morning when my wily chamber-mate appeared at the doorway. I shall remain your interpreter he said for without my skill oh such troubles you shall call upon yourself. So be it then I replied at which he laughed for that has become my stock response to him. But hurry now he said and come with me. To where I asked noting the guard of men behind him. On the instructions of my new master the Sultan he replied I am to take you to the animal market. Why so I posed of him. For one so pretty you are also stupid he said and only so that Your Eminence may personally select a zarafa to take back to your great Sovereign. A zarafa I repeated. Yes a zarafa he mimicked and I have not all day to waste for I am an important man. And so it was that I set eyes for the first time upon a beast which is neither horse nor camel nor wolf nor cat but methinks you know this already and as you will see for yourself when I bring her back I shall proceed to the event. I was borne out of the palace in the chair on wheels with the language bridge following behind. The market is in the west of the citadel and is a most clamorous place where blood and excrement make a mud-coloured stench through which we progressed the while pressing a cloth of pomade to my nose to keep from vomiting and waving a feather fan about my face to keep the flies away. Directly upon entering the market my eyes and ears filled with the colours and cries of aves for here were cages upon cages and pens beside pens of saffron and green aves less than my little finger in length and parrots and spotted hens and ducks and geese and past a yard of aves of the same feathers as my fan and long and bald of neck but small of head yet manlike of legs and taller than a man. Indeed upon some of these some men were riding clutching the necks of their mounts which are like snakes. See those tall hens I called over my shoulder to my language bridge and he replied oh these are nothing for he had seen birds far greater in size which kill and devour the flesh of men and had even killed and feasted upon a friend of his. When I turned about to see if he had spoken in jest he laughed like a mad man and declared how grateful he was to never again set eyes upon the shores of Hind. Thence we progressed into the animal market. Here were tethered some black horses painted with white lines and cages of forest men and women and even their infants covered only in black hairs and some pigs with tusks like those of elephants and a water horse in a type of well and most plentiful of all were lions in cages and also leopards on chains but naught one tiger or elephant. Imagine for yourself the noise and smells of this place. From there we arrived upon a jetty and here were more cages covered with sacking. The jetty was crowded with boats and into these were being loaded those cages as also some white camels and donkeys and in the water I espied a dead dog or maybe a pig swollen with flies. Through the crowd of rude men of different types we came upon a place with high walls and high wooden gates with a small door inset. Here we were met by an Arab of some rank and means from his manner of speech and gold-tipped ivory cane and he seemed informed of the purpose of our visit and after I had climbed from my chair he bade us enter through the door in the gates. Inside I beheld a sight like magic and I must have shouted in my surprise. For there appeared before my eyes these animals of great height with long legs and sloped backs and necks like trees. These were the zarafa and each was possessed of like beauty of eyes and a pattern of pelt like groundnut shells and each wore a collar of red leather with a silver amulet. Some were drinking from a trough not unlike that of my damsels under the neem but here there was no tree for shade and the zarafa drank with forelegs outspread and necks bent so as to reach the water with their horse lips. To one side were more zarafa feeding on bunches of babbula leaves tied from wooden stakes. Their tongues are blue and like snakes curled to partake of the leaves. Whilst I watched the animals in wonderment the Arab spoke to my interpreter who bade me to hurry and make my choice of one zarafa to take to our Sovereign. This was a difficult choice for all were of equal grace and height and it was all I could do but gaze and gaze so the Arab made a selection of one and it was led forth by his servants. This particular is a cow three years of age and eleven forearms of height and in colouring lighter than the rest of her type and Fathema by name. The choice thus made we repaired back to the palace but without the zarafa who they say will be led to our ship when that is readied.

~

The deputy shipmaster paid me a visit today for word had reached our shipmaster that I had been to the animal market.

We had no orders to take aboard a zarafa to Hind he said. You have now I replied. And how will you keep it alive for the four months at sea he said. I have no experience in the husbandry of zarafas I replied but what had served my cattle well should serve one zarafa equally and if its fodder is tied on high as I had seen in the market. And what if its neck gets tangled in the riggings said the deputy or if it breaks its legs or falls in a wind and cannot be uprighted and what if and what if and what if a hundred things that may not happen. To all this I replied it is the order of the Sultan to reach the animal to my Sovereign in safety and it fell to the deputy and the shipmaster to fulfil the brief. The brief indeed he replied adding that he would bear no penalty if the zarafa came to grief. And mind you well I replied for I shall brook no talk of blood sacrifices whatever woe or care befell upon the return journey. I was wise not to be returning to your ship put in the interpreter in his unkind way. Leave me alone I said to him. After you do one thing for me he said. What thing I asked at once vexed for the wretch takes every chance to taunt my embassy by proxy. He pointing a finger to my toothsome chaperone who was standing by. What of him I asked. You have no need for him anymore than he has for you he replied for you have four servants to tend to your every whim whereas I have none and fancy this fellow for myself. So be it I said for I could see the giant is happy these days midst his kind but this I did not voice lest the wretch sought some other ransom of me. So be it he replied mockingly and clicking his fingers bade the chaperone to his side and this the latter obliged without so much as my leave. Having witnessed this petty exchange the deputy shipmaster left our company grumbling into his beard about making measures afresh for stabling the zarafa upon our ship.

∽

I have not written a week for there was naught to write. Word is come today that our vessel is readied with caulk and new sailcloths and rigging and also to hold the zarafa and I must prepare for our embarkation in five days. I am happy but also sad for I have seen little beyond this palace and the animal market. When this regret I expressed to the Sultan Splendid at common audience today he replied you will doubtless have only good words to carry to my compeer Narseen and return again as his emissary. I have one question for Your Majesty I said. How be it that you rule an empire and yet do not ride out to battle as does my Sovereign. The Sultan replied that he had governors to fight his battles and he was no fool to risk his life in common skirmish as does my Sovereign. These words of the interpreter caused me to doubt if the Sultan had indeed said this. Upon my return it is my wish that you tutor me in Persian script and speech so that I may conduct these embassies without assistance. Also in Chin for I should like to read Wangyanli. I had other questions of the Sultan but these I did not voice for my words may be altered from crossing the language bridge.

∽

An incident last night has me troubled of mind. Have you ever killed a man asked the language bridge as we partook of our evening meal. I have not I replied. I have he said holding up two fingers and claiming one man in Khalakatapatna and more latterly His Eminence the Crown Prince on board our ship. I stared at him and he gave a jackal laugh causing my marrow to turn cold with fright. There is naught you can do with this knowledge he said laughing in his mad way and no one will believe you if you tell on me and nor do you have the language to betray my confidence so keep it secret or else. Or else what I asked quietly. Or else I will cut your ears from your head while you sleep he screamed pushing his face to mine so that I had his spittle on my face and the smell of hate in his breath. I moved back but he pulling my head forward with a hand behind my neck and still screaming said I give you leave to tell your great Sovereign that it was I who killed his bosom friend and my reward for the deed is freedom from Hind. Hearing his voice his newfound servant and my own rushed in and he shouted that he was narrating a story and thrust me aside laughing loudly to drink directly of the jar of wine.

∾

Today I was asked to inspect tribute from the Sultan to our Sovereign. Of these items are forty-six gold bricks in a blackwood chest with gold lock and key. One lion pelt with face and tail for the throne of our Sovereign. Two redwood chairs with shell and blackwood flowers inset. Two leopard skins one male one female both edged in gold bead. Eighteen paired ivories. One stoneglass goblet which is said to turn black if any poison be poured in it. A silver hand-mirror and ivory box of perfume phials. A silver box of grey amber of whale. Three Arab syces to attend upon the zarafa. Lastly a missive for our Sovereign in a sealed scroll case.

∾

I was readying my things when the language bridge entered looking much subdued of spirit. Tomorrow I shall be rid of your presence he said but I shall be sad for whom shall I tease and trouble after you have set sail. You can sail back with us to Hind I said to which he countered I have given my word of honour to the Sultan but hurry now and give me a token of our friendship for I have not all afternoon to waste in your company. What would you wish I asked. That which you bed with nightly he said with a cunning look and without my leave removed the square of red silk from where I had kept it in my clothes chest. Then breathing of it deeply he drew it over his head as to wholly cover his face and left the chamber at a dancing step the while laughing as one possessed of madness. If he truly caused the demise of His Eminence as he claimed I pray the guilt of it drives him fully out of his mind.

∾

Today I conclude my embassy at the palace of the most gracious and splendid Sultan of Kilwa of whose goodness I have partaken these past four weeks. Thus fully refreshed I am eager for all that the seas hold in events and sights and I pray for fair wind and kind waters and the safety of the zarafa Fathema upon our journey to Hind.

31

LAKHNORE

THE GENERAL WROTE HOME TO HIS PRINCESS:

My Moonshine | The news is not heartening | We have
returned to Lakhnore and will bide here awhile before the
march homewards | Your brother is in a black mood and
speaks only in expletives and for the rest either eats like an
elephant or sleeps like the dead | Although unharmed of body
he is wounded of pride | He refuses to travel in this dark frame
and has decreed I may not leave his side | His mood effects
mine and I desire more than anything to have you comfort
me with sweet words and embraces to balm my shame | No
shame can befall a man as your lord you may say for have I
not led Kalinga to victory without once failing your brother
and your father before him | Except this once for we have
received a slap in the face of our pride from Tughan Khan
himself | The Turk upon sign of our approach sought aid of
his master in Dilli to repel our advance on Lakshmanauti |
That assistance did speedily arrive by way of the governors
of Awadh and Manikpura each with his massed army of
infantry and carriage and horse and elephant | The sight in the
distance of their dust caused our men to tremble and shake
like reeds | Thus outclassed by three armies from three sides
we had no choice but to retreat south and cart what bounty
and hostage we had | Your brother was quick to accuse me
of cowardice and envy of his might and other manner of
deceits to all of which I willed myself to hold back my fists
| Any advancement I had achieved in the other matter is
thus retarded for although I remain by his side there is little
speech | To compound these setbacks my own temper is
further muddied by an utterance this evening of a fool temple
priest | Seeing his hand tremble as he held a bowl of nectar
with which to anoint my forehead I asked him to reveal the
cause of his fright | At this the wretch let fall the bowl and

wailing like a widow revealed that he had seen in the nectar a vision of my death | How so I demanded but all that issued was another cry before he fell to his knees and began to kiss my feet | I pulled him up by his topknot and commanded him to fully reveal his augury if he valued his life | Upon a battlefield in ten years to the day he said | Thus relieved that my end is neither imminent nor due in some ignoble way I laughed and released the wretch | My deputy and sentries were witness to the event and I roundly mocked these false beliefs | I know you are of like mind so pray that you may not become widowed before your time for I have as yet more battles to win and sons to beget | At a propitious time I will again broach the other matter with my royal kinsman | He speaks of breaking journey in Chandrabhaga to heal from his defeat | It would be wiser to repair to the capital I said but his mind is made and you know him when he turns adamant | I shall accompany him there and if he will permit it return to Ekamra thence | Await me with perfumed breast and clove-scented breath my love my life my dew-bathed moonshine | Your lord and master and most vigorous thunderbolt...

32

THE *ARKAJA*

In place of our former chambers and pavilion behind the figurehead now stands a stable for the zarafa with high roof and half gate. For her water and feed are two buckets from the cowshed tied to ladders on either side of the gate. The walls inside are faced with bales of hay and upon the floor is a bed of cut hay. The zarafa had been stabled thus three days in advance of our setting sail. One of her three syces tends to her water and feed. Another cleans out her dung and lays fresh hay. The third of whom she is fondest massages her legs and anyone else who attempts to touch her may receive a kick from her forefeet. My own quarters are nowadays below the deck with the archers and fire-throwers all of whom I have latterly learnt are not crewmen of the shipmaster as I was given to believe but guardsmen of our Kataka palace. These men may well have quartered in the cowshed but for seventy women of Aphrike housed there. Upon my inquiring after their presence the shipmaster replied that they are in lieu of the weight of the bovines and in the lowermost deck in lieu of fodder is an equal weight in sacks of sand. We drew anchors at midnight and by daybreak entered the open sea in the company of over four score vessels all sailing northwards and east and all our crewmen shouted greetings each to each for safe passage.

～

It is five days since I have set reed to paper for this broiling heat neither lifts nor for restful sleep makes and I have a head cramp which defies all my balms and medicaments and I have no appetite. Before the air over the deck was sweet with the scent of cattle and hay. Not so now for it is fouled by the smell of human excrement. I chanced to look today into the cowshed only to recoil from a most pitious sight. Upon my speaking of what I had seen the shipmaster with hard eye and voice forbade me to venture there again but to remain always with the zarafa or in my quarters below decks. I am not far wrong in finding his manner and speech much altered as though he were a stranger to me and save for his one eye I might believe it. I have since learnt from my servants that the women are as fodder for the shipmaster and his men and only the soldiers do not partake of that which nightly takes place. The women—said my servants— are daily given but a handful of rice each and one bucket of water between them and some days neither food nor water and because they are tied each to each they must sit in their ordure and when any of their numbers dies she will be thrown over the side and it is such women who return as black aves the likes of which foretold the demise of His Eminence. On hearing this I was seized by a great despondence and prayed that such a fate does not befall me. It will be four months before we make landfall in Khalakatapatna so I must stay fearless.

~

At sea a fortnight and there is as yet no sight of land. The glare from the water causes my eyes to weep and the application of antimony is of little aid. I believed we ought by now to have dropped anchors by the Nameless Islands and upon my voicing this thought to the deputy for I no longer speak with the shipmaster he replied that we were making across open sea north-eastward to Hind for the pace of our vessel had been altered from certain works upon our masts and sailcloths to benefit from a wind they call mawsim blowing upon us from the land of Aphrike. Only then did I see the four masts are shorn of some cubits and the sailcloths thereof also made different and indeed we appeared to be moving apace and I had failed to feel or see this until then. In thirteen days we shall make sight of Hind said the deputy and his words brought me some gladness.

~

I dreamt last night that my erstwhile wards were set afire in the eight-sided tank in the palace of the Sultan Splendid. Their cries were akin to the cries of the women in the cowshed which I have chanced to hear some nights. The kindling in the tank was not wood but these papers but their size was that of sailcloths and all that I had writ upon them in my neat hand was turning to ash. Performing the sacrifice—for a sacrifice it was—stood the deranged language bridge assisted by the lookout dwarf and also the Arab of the animal market. There was naught I could do to save my damsels or even my papers which flew to the sky as they burnt as black aves even as more papers were thrown to the flames and it was then that I awoke with a cry and covered in sweat. I was at once overcome by guilt for not once during my time in the palace did I visit or so much as ask after the cattle and their physician and servants. Sleep then was hard to reclaim so I climbed out to the deck and made into the stable of the zarafa and sat there in the company of her syces thus passing the remaining hours in quiet until daybreak. Methinks the dream is a portend and I must closely guard my effects.

∾

Full twenty-eight days since Kilwa six shore-sighting crows were brought out to the deck and freed of their cages. Circling twice and together cawing they made as a line towards the east. The crewmen who had gathered with eyes to the sky rejoiced in their mixed tongues and it was clear to me without asking that our destination was nigh. Around midday there appeared a line of gold where the sky touched the sea and all the sailcloths were lifted to hasten us to it and one by one the sacks of sand were brought upstairs and dropped into the sea. Meantime the night-soil servants led the women from the cowshed tied each to each and threw upon them buckets of salt water and when the women were done washing and dried themselves with scraps of sacking they were given a ration of coconut oil to rub into their hair and skins. Thus made fine they were bade to sit in a coil on the deck and so they sat neither speaking nor smiling but I could see they were glad for the sunlight. Some were about ten years of age and

some the same age as myself and the eldest among them has
silver in her hair and I counted in all fifty-seven women. Nearing
land I saw from the buildings all limewashed and low that it was
not to Khalakatapatna that we were bound and upon enquiring
of the deputy what place that might be learnt it was the seaport
of Bharukachchha of a western country and there we would drop
anchors for water and trade. What manner of trade I asked but
he moved away for some boats were making fast for our ship and
I learnt from my servants that they had come at a mirror signal
from on high. In these boats were men with square beards and
when they touched the sides our ladders were let down for them
to climb. These men and the shipmaster engaged in talk for some
time and then their commander walked between the women
and pressed the flesh of their limbs and looked at their teeth
the while frowning and shaking his head at the shipmaster who
walked behind as humble as a servant. The man then summoned
one of his own who carried a sack and from it drew out ropes
of coin and these were counted by the deputy with more talk
to follow and more coin being thrown upon the deck. Then the
women still tied together were let down the ladders and all this
I watched through the gaps in the stable gate where I had sat
myself with Fathema and her servants. Now their commander
walked towards the stable with the shipmaster and I could see
from his gestures that he wished to lay claim of the zarafa whose
neck and head were outside the half-gate and more than once I
heard the shipmaster take the name of our Sovereign. My inner
voice told me to step out and so I did taking the men by surprise
and more so when I ordered the visitor and his company to quit
my ship. He gave a laugh and asked in Sanskrit who be you
native monkey to which I responded no monkey but the true
master of this ship and may this be the last I see of his back.
We shall see about it said the man and speaking harshly to the
shipmaster climbed down from our ship followed by his men.
You have slighted an agent of the governor of Bharukachchha

the shipmaster shouted to me. They will lay siege of our vessel and take the zarafa as bounty. Over my ashes I said to myself and aloud ordered the shipmaster to turn our ship. I will not do it he said for we have already dropped anchors and must refill our water bins. But his voice betrayed some trickery so I bade our soldiers to keep him and his crewmen under point of their arrows for I was now master by proxy of the ship and it is my word and command they must heed in all matters hence and not of the one-eyed seller of women. I know not from whence I found the words but I became in that instant more of a man than I had these many months past and with the taste of courage still fresh on my tongue I once again commanded the shipmaster to have his men turn my ship if he valued the eye left in his head. He did as told without protest but looking over the side we saw the boat of the agent had gathered more of his ilk and all were making to assault my ship. But their attempt was short-lived for my archers and fire-throwers let rain upon them their talents and in this way we made quick from those odious waters and thence southwards for the port of Kulam with land always in sight to our left.

∼

We were but a day short of Saymur when a mast broke in half in a great wind and fell upon the cowshed making a hole the size of an elephant. The crewmen made to free the fallen half of its riggings which were pulling hard and causing the other three masts to sound as if they might break like twigs. The shipmaster and deputy were screaming to the crewmen to be quick at it when the second and tallest mast broke sideways and the lookout dwarf in his nest was thrown to the sea and not seen again. The deck by now was fallen about with men from the rocking but my fears were only for Fathema whom I could not see for the torn sailcloths beating in the wind. When at last I reached the stable I found the gate secure and the zarafa and her syces all atremble inside. I climbed over the gate and

in their company sat praying that we may not sink for I did not
wish to meet my death of drowning. It was a long time before
the wind eased and only then did some oar boats approach and
pull us for three days into the port of Gopakapatna of a southern
country. My fears had grown for Fathema these past days for
she took neither water nor feed and it was with much trouble
that we brought her by boat to land and thence to this grove of
coconut by the custom house where her tremors settled and she
regained her spirit from drinking of cow milk from the many
herders who throng this place. Having myself feasted on my
first wholesome meal in many weeks I fell into a deep slumber
in a common hall in the custom house and waking only when
a man came to say my shipmaster awaited. I stepped outside to
see our tributes from His Splendid thrown hither and thither
with my own cases and the shipmaster standing with his hands
on his waist. Have you my ship made seaworthy I asked to which
he replied your ship is worthy only as firewood hence. How
then must we to Khalakatapatna I said and he replied go seek
for yourself a fine palace instead seeing as you are possessed of
enough means to live as a proxy prince for the remainder of
your life but come hand me our dues now and I shall be away.
What dues I asked. For your safe passage he replied. You have
enriched yourself through the sale of women so quit my sight
forthwith I scolded. The pox be on upon you and may you lose
an eye for your pride he said and spitting upon the ground
ordered his crewmen to take of the paired ivories and any other
items they pleased. Now I gave a signal to my soldiers standing
by and thus was that wicked company removed from the place.
A crowd had gathered meantime to watch the rude display and
when they too had parted I sat of a sudden weary on the steps.
Presently a man in poor cloths of black came stood before me
with eyes closed and hands outstretched. I knew him on sight to
be a nasrani priest for His Eminence Parijatapuri and I had seen
his type in Dondra and around their neck these priests wear a

wooden cross which is a mark of their creed. I have no alms to give I said and this nasrani replied I come not seeking alms but to pray for your profit. I shall need more than prayers I said for I must to Khalakatapatna in haste but my ship which you see there is unfit to sail. I have learnt of your woes the nasrani said but the mawsim is due to bring rain any day and no vessel will put out to this sea a month at least. What must I do meantime I said. It is quicker to walk to Machalipatna and thence to Khalakatapatna he said. Is it far I said. Forty days hard east across the Dakkhin he replied and that he had occasioned to make the crossing twice. I have with me a most precious beast and she might perish of the walking I said. The nasrani laughed and said your zarafa will benefit from it for she is a creature of the sun and the plains so do not tarry but change some of your things for coin for there are tolls to pay along the way and nor will you be alone or want for food for the last caravans before the rains are as yet plying between this Port of Cowherds to the Port of Fish but hasten now and purchase a cart and oxen to carry your wares. Then he gave to me a cross of silver to place about the neck of the zarafa and for his counsel in my time of need I gave to him the silver box of grey amber of whale. This substance he said accepting it he would burn in a censer before his god and pray for my profit. Burn it sparingly for forty days I said and took his leave. Then I assembled my soldiers and servants and the three syces of the zarafa to ready ourselves for the Dakkhin.

33

CHANDRABHAGA

THEY ARE CLOSING IN ON HIM. MOTTLED OF FLESH, HOOKED OF beak, hopping and bounding on inverted feet. He plunges into a dense dark thicket. They know he is there. He must not look back. The forest floor is swarming with multitudes of hands like hungry red ants. With great effort of will, he lifts into the air. A tree creaks as it bends to grab him. He veers aside. Leaves brush his face. He is falling...!

He started awake with a hoarse cry.

The mosquito curtains shifted. Sitting up, he parted them roughly. The door of the bedchamber had blown ajar a narrow rectangle of half-light. The shape of a sentry passed outside. He counted the beats before the sentry crossed again.

Sixty beats. There ought to have been two men on vigil, left to right, right to left. So much for watching over their Sovereign. He climbed out of bed and waited. After the sentry had walked past a third time, he counted to twenty and slipped outside—the gallery was empty—and then soundlessly into the acacia thicket.

Somewhere, a horse whinnied. A sentry, further ahead, alerted by a movement between the trees, called, *Stop! Who goes there!* The wind carried his voice the wrong way; the figure continued in the direction of the sea. Grabbing his spear, the sentry set after the presence.

Sensing he was being followed, Narasimha stopped and turning, waved the man away with a sharp word which wasn't lost to the wind.

The sentry froze in his tracks. He will be taking defeat badly, the General had briefed them: he will display irregular behaviour and speech; keep your eyes on him night and day and never stray far from him.

Could it get more irregular than this? Not yet light, and there was the Sovereign, wandering bareheaded and bare-chested in the wind. The sentry knew whose word he must obey. With the Sovereign always in sight, he followed, keeping the acacias between them.

The windbreak.

The sentry heard the splash of urine. A hearty stream, befitting of a Sovereign. And there he was again, taking the steps two at a time against the silvering sky. The sentry shot forward into the shadows. His spearhead clinked against something; he bit his tongue and fell into a crouch but there was no retort from the Sovereign. He exhaled, broke wind and shuffled on his haunches up the steps. If he were challenged, '*I must guard you, Majesty*,' is what he would say, he couldn't be faulted for it. Crouched eye-level to the topmost step, he watched transfixed.

Narasimha stood in the middle of the windbreak looking at the sea. He scratched his chin and cheeks: he hadn't been shaved in weeks. He smelt himself: sleep, horse, dust, sweat. On an impulse, he undid his dhoti and—as much as the wind would permit—folded and patted it into a limp wad. Placing it at his feet, he weighted it down with a brick; there was no shortage here of loose bricks. He kicked off his sandals, clapped them together to shake out the sand and arranged them squarely on the brick. Straightening up and tightening his loincloth, he stepped forward and jumped clear off the windbreak into the sea.

Cursing himself for being the sole witness, the sentry raced down the steps and back through the acacias, shouting for help.

He had never properly learnt to swim.

What *had* possessed him? There was nothing for it now but to distance himself from the windbreak or risk being lacerated against the shell-pocked masonry. More than once, his head went under. It was a shock to not feel the bottom beneath his feet. More than once, something live grazed his ankles and shins. He tried not to imagine what it might be. His loincloth came undone and dissolved into the blackness. He began thrashing his arms and legs, and then told himself there was no reason for panic: he felt completely weightless and there was time yet for the tide to ebb and the waves to come crashing. He then submitted himself to the gentle swell, the while paddling slowly away towards the east.

Presently, he felt confident enough to attempt it. Right arm first, then the left, over and over, the way he'd seen them do it. The hard part was to breathe *and* not swallow the sea. And to kick.

Without knowing it, he made it past the mouth of the Chandrabhaga—miraculously skirting the currents lurking there and the vagrant skeins of a fisher's-net. A little beyond the temple-beach, his strength failed him. The sky was turning the colour of the sea, pale blue-pink, flecked with white. He let himself go limp. He couldn't care less if the singing was real or inside his head.

~

The beachcombers took the thing on the beach for another of the mysteries the surf spat up at them. Most, they left to the kites and the crabs and for the waves to reclaim. This one was neither sea-cow nor sea-maid, not bloated, yellow-grey, or oozing bubbles and slime.

A *man*! Breathing! The women shooed the waiting crows with their baskets.

All limbs and extremities in place, therefore not one of their ilk. Rings and an armlet. A prancing horse tattooed alongside the right heel. A merchant drifted from some ill-fated vessel? It was a first for the women. They turned him over on his back.

After their initial surprise—no, it couldn't *really* be, if only they could *keep* him—they lifted the Sovereign between them and giggling at his shrivelled sand-covered thing lugged him—fingers trailing, ankles dragging—up the soft sinking dunes to the village.

~

A hut. His eyes stayed on the shallow inverted cone of the thatch, counting the converging beams—twelve; no, fourteen—and the shorter…what was the word for them…? laddered between. The smell of burnt oil and turmeric was overpowering. He concentrated.

Their dialect made some but not much sense. Three, maybe five different voices, speaking softly. He rolled to his side. The murmuring ceased. A figure rose and moved over to the mat.

Against the light from the doorway, he could sense rather than see the face marred by the blight. He kept his eyes on the man's frizzed aura of hair.

This much he understood: You are safe here, Majesty. We have sent word to your men. They will be here presently. Your wounds have been dressed… Do not fear… You are safe.

He remembered saying to Parijatapuri—it felt like a different lifetime—do not fear, it does not transmit. Somewhere outside, someone sneezed, and then hacked and spat. To distract himself, he wondered what they, the *Arkaja*, were at.

～

They subjected him to a scalding bath in a bitter infusion of neem leaves and turmeric. Next, they purged him of the gruel he'd been fed, before force-feeding him a porridge of millet and turmeric, followed by turmeric-tea which seared. He let them have their way and then lost a full day to sleep.

'You cannot do such things,' said the General tersely. 'I will not have you wandering about without my leave.'

'I am twenty-four,' he murmured, 'not a child.'

'There is talk that you attempted to kill yourself. I've done what I can to control the damage; any more, I'll have their hide for my slippers.'

He winced. 'It is no one's fault. I only wished to swim. A harmless whim.'

'The next time you feel the *whim*, you will have a man by your side—'

'A sentry was present.'

'Just as well. Had he not come running… There are people waiting to see your end.'

'They shan't have *that* pleasure in a hurry. You've had your say. Leave.'

The door opened to admit the Secretary. 'Forgive the intrusion; the Chief Architect's boy is here to see His Majesty. He says it is urgent.'

'Send him away!' the General shouted. 'He shall have no visitors until I permit it!'

'Show him in,' Narasimha said.

'You will rest until I—'

He held up a warning finger. 'Enough.' To the Secretary, 'Show him in.'

The General stood back, muttering, 'A mistake, all a mistake…'

The Secretary ushered in the boy. 'Salutation,' Narasimha said with a smile. 'Forgive me if I am not my usual self. Even a prince has his bad moments.'

'I have those as well,' said Dharmapada.

'You wished to speak to me?'

The child remained silent. Narasimha nodded to the two men. The General threw the child a dark look and said, 'I'm outside if I am needed.' The door slammed behind the Secretary and him and then swung ajar again. He'd have them see to the hinges…

'Is it true what they're saying in the guilds?' asked Dharmapada.

'That I attempted to kill myself? No, pay no heed to it. Are you never seized by an urge to do something out of the ordinary?'

'Sometimes.'

'You are fortunate. I feel that way all the time.'

'They are saying you will never finish the chariot. They say the losses are too great. What does that mean?'

'Your father and the others must be readers of minds.'

'It is true, then?'

'With what am I to recompense the guilds, the models, the quarries…everyone else…?'

'It bodes ill to leave a temple unfinished.'

He laughed bitterly. 'What choice have I?'

'The fallen temple. Raise it in the same spot, but for the Sun God's consort the Goddess of Shade. By the time it is done, your fortunes will have changed. You may then resume work on the chariot. I only came to tell you this.'

A tear slid down Narasimha's cheek. He brushed it away; it wouldn't do for the child to see. An oracular child in a world bereft of oracles. 'I shall do as you deem fit,' he said. 'And you have my promise; when the time comes for it, it is you who must install the crowning ornament.'

'I remember,' Dharmapada nodded, 'In five years hence.' The Secretary reappeared. They were spared the General's company—for the present, at least.

'Dispatch a note to the palace,' Narasimha said in an undertone. 'Inform Her Majesty that I shall bide here a while longer and return after the rains. Bid her pay no heed to any ill-tidings which will doubtless reach her…if they haven't done already.' He sat up. 'No, fetch my writing frame. I must write to her myself.'

34

THE DAKKHIN

THREE DAYS MARCH HARD EAST OF GOPAKAPATNA WE CAME
upon a mountain like a wall risen north to south and no way
around to the other side but a road through a forest to which
we kept full seven days. Nor were there caravans faring east or
west and it was only my party of not one but six covered carts
and their paired oxen which I purchased for eight paired ivories
and in these are the tributes and provender for ourselves and the
animals. I have for my comforts one cart with one servant and
leading our way is the zarafa with her syces and walking on both
sides of our carts are the fire-throwers and archers and following
behind are my other servants. In this way our company made
safely through the forest of whose beasts of which we only saw
the dung of elephants and heard their calls. The nights were not
pleasant and despite our fires and the soldiers on watch I slept
in fear of death by some unknown cause. The forest mountain
released us the eighth day with none of our numbers diminished.
We are now two days upon flat country which is the Dakkhin
and the sun bears down with fierceness and there is not another
human to be seen as yet upon this road.

～

The Arab syces in their own wisdom conveyed to me through
the soldiers whose tongue they speak that we must rest by day
and march by starlight. This we did with torches in hands and
lanterns tied underneath our carts yet on the fifth night which
was moonless one of the soldiers was bit by a snake from stepping
on it. We performed his funeral by a river at daybreak. After his
ashes were immersed I made to bathe but was stopped by my
men for the rocks upon the near bank were in truth crocodiles
of great length. So it is that we no longer walk by night. At
noontime today we came upon an empty tollgate. Also a well

but it was dry. Then a village—but the dwellings were broken and fallen about in the dust were the bones of cattle with not a shred of skin to cover them. The ground was unploughed and where field had been they lay fallow as though the rains have forsaken this country forever. Even the sky is empty. Perhaps the nasrani walked on this road in another life.

Yet this much is true of what the nasrani said. The zarafa is lively and feeds well of the thorn trees we chance upon here and there. The sun which broils our skin does not trouble her it would seem and whereas our oxen and ourselves are beset by ticks and flies not one of those pests afflict Her Highness. This her syces say is from her scented sweat which covers her nethers like a dark oil. Its fragrance I shall say is not unlike musk crushed with some bitter leaf or flower and this scent is most strong by night. When the men bed down to sleep on the ground they must be careful for there are scorpions aplenty. One of the soldiers was stung one night and he is lesser of a toe for it was burnt away so that he may live. Now he sits in the cart with me until he becomes fit to march again. I have learnt that he like me hails from Malwa but unlike me was not orphaned by the black death. When I drew my flute he stilled me from playing for fear of it calling forth snakes.

35

KATAKA

The Consort's Council sat in session in the Privy Office. The Consort was not present. The sole item on the agenda was a dispatch from the General describing, in fair detail, the Chandrabhaga incident. It was agreed that the Second Secretary convey the deliberations of the meeting to the Consort in private to spare her undue distress. He made his way to the Observatory, deeply troubled by what he must say.

She was alone, and expecting him. The high-ceilinged hall felt oppressively quiet. She read the General's letter and handed it back. The Second Secretary struggled through his delivery, stepping around his words as though they were arrowheads. She said nothing. His awful task done, the Second Secretary left, uncertain if she had understood a thing.

The Consort's assistants reassembled and resumed their studies around an astrolabe. 'Did you girls know,' she said, 'that a child's horoscopes can be altered to render it suitable to the adoption instrument?'

'Whose child is being adopted and by whom?' asked one of the women.

'It shan't come to it,' she replied.

～

I wish to speak to you | A covered carriage will come for you in the morning | Pray present yourself at the private apartments |

The note had thrown the Courtesan into a panic. The messenger had had nothing to add. She had slept badly and risen late. And now the carriage awaited. Checking her reflection one more time, she removed the ruby drop from her parting and also three jewelled clips, pinched her cheeks, and with the gold box of saffron wrapped in a silk kerchief, bustled out the Hall of Enchantment. It was five years since the Sovereign's wedding;

she'd had no call to visit the palace since. Her thoughts were jangled as the carriage clattered up the streets. The note could mean only one thing: *something terrible had happened*. Not to my seafaring son, she prayed for the hundredth time.

She was received by the Consort herself. She didn't look a day older than twenty. Her indigo shift was faded sky-blue from washing. Pearl drops at the ears, a string of jet beads at the neck. Just as well that I pared down my finery, the Courtesan said to herself. Sitadevi accepted her gift and smiled. 'Ah, saffron. You ought not to have troubled yourself. Come; pray sit.'

The Courtesan took the only other chair. The Consort sat in the chair opposite, folding and refolding the kerchief into ever smaller squares. A maidservant brought in a tray and placed it on the low table between them: two goblets of spice-tea and a salver of sweetmeats—Lotus Breath. Suddenly conscious of her own commonness, the Courtesan blurted: 'It is my fasting day, my lady, I fast on Thursdays for my dear departed…'

'It was remiss of me to have not asked beforehand,' the Consort said, motioning to the servant to leave. 'I see the years have treated you well.'

So it wasn't about her precious lamb. 'Thank you, my lady,' the Courtesan breathed. 'One does what one can to preserve this wasted body. Forgive me—' She touched the edges of her eyes with a corner of her wrap, '…I am moved *beyond words* from revisiting this air. Ah, the old days…! I trust my successor to the dance hall gives no cause for complaint.'

'She is more than competent.' A beat. 'I shall come directly to the object of your visiting me. How it is to birth a child?'

The Courtesan's eyes grew wide and then disappeared in a smile. 'Felicitations, my lady! How long and hard we've prayed for this! I shall be on hand if you so bid it through your confinement—'

'No. Not yet.' the Consort said quickly. 'I only wished to know how it feels.'

She frowned. Oh you poor child, no mother for counsel, not

even a mother-by-marriage. 'It feels like evacuating a hot iron ball, if you *must* know it. Yes. That is how it feels.'

'That must pain.'

'Be that as it may, it passes and we forget. Or no creature of our sex would be birthing all the time.' Think of your sister-by-marriage, she almost added. Leaning forward, she said softly: 'You are not with child, my lady?'

The question seemed to shake her poise. 'No. It is for that reason that I called you. You see…there must…there *must* be some way before it is too late—' Her voice, level until then, faltered and dropped a pitch: 'Why must it be this way?'

They were silent for a long moment. 'Forgive me, my lady, but if I may presume to say this… All these years… It is said you are averse to it.'

'Me? Is that what you think?'

'It has been said.'

Her eyes flashed. 'Then you must be corrected. It is he who is averse to it. My courses began the night we were wed. He took fright and—' She stopped, squeezing the life out of the kerchief, 'Everyone knew it, everyone knows *everything*. You surprise me!'

The Courtesan sat back in her chair. 'It will not be easy,' she began, carefully. 'A frightened man can be hard to bring back. But it is known to happen. Had you sought my counsel sooner—'

'I have now. What must I do? Tell me. You've known him all his life, better than anyone else.'

She stared at the sweetmeats. It was years since she'd tasted Lotus Breath, a speciality of the palace. The teas sat untouched. Anything she suggested could be used against her someday, but she was beyond caring. 'You must frighten him some more,' she said sagely. 'You will know how in the fullness of time, only don't tarry any more than you have. That is all an old woman can offer you by way of advice.'

The Consort rose from the edge of her chair. Uncreasing the kerchief, she draped it over the salver of sweetmeats. 'For when you are done fasting,' she said, bidding the Courtesan farewell.

36

THE DAKKHIN

HER HIGHNESS FATHEMA BROKE FREE OF HER SYCES AND RAN today. Her running is unlike that of a common horse or deer but of great swiftness and grace and soon we lost her to the emptiness which makes a haze from the heat for as far as the eye can see. After much searching we came upon her drinking of a stream where there are thorn trees. The syces have asked that we rest here two days so their ward may eat and drink of her fill and we partake of the shade of the trees for we know not when we may be so fortunate again. Upon the lid of this box I have cut marks with an arrowhead of our days and today we are nine and twenty. It comes to me at times that we are lost but the syces in their wisdom aver it is towards the sea that we are walking and this brings some peace to my mind. I burn to see the sea again but there are as yet eleven days before the Port of Fish. Perhaps the nasrani walked this way after the rains when all was green and pleasing.

∼

We saw a flock of birds today which were like peacocks but without that plumage. The archers let fly their arrows and we made a feast of their flesh. I was reading of what I had writ after eating when the nine-toed fire-thrower asked what I had writ so neat. Of our journey from Khalakatapatna to Kilwa and now of this wasteland I said. Why so he asked and I replied so that I do not forget all that we have done and seen and remains to be done and seen. He asked where I had learned to write and I spoke for some time of your tutelage and of Pol and then of his and my different lives in Malwa in former times.

∼

Today the smell of burning flesh reached our nostrils before the sight of its source a mile ahead. There a pyre maybe a hundred

forearms in width was smouldering. About it were a great
number of women and children. At our approach the women
began to weep and did little to hold back the children who came
running to see the zarafa in our lead. Our servants meantime
went up to the women and brought word of what thad occurred
there. The Raja of this land had expired and in the tradition of his
clan his kinsmen who had partaken of their first meal with the
Raja upon his anointment were bound by honour to immolate
themselves upon his demise and this word of honour they had
kept leaving their women widowed and their children fatherless.
Many of the widows were little more than children themselves
and in pity of their plight I enquired if they wished to go in our
company. At this they smote their heads with their hands and
loudly wailing hurled stones at us and so we left. That sight and
smell will remain with me as the true marker of this wasteland.

~

I am fevered the past days and will write again after the fever
breaks. I must cut on the lid the four and fiftieth mark of our
days. My hand pains. Forgive me master for closing here for
there is nothing left—

~

*I am awake. From the slapping of oars, I know it is a boat. It's
dark inside, but daytime, so it must be a covered boat that I'm
lying in. Where am I? Where am I going? I hear men talking. Who
are they? My soldier has come in. I know it is him from his touch.
He's bathing my face and then my body. Let me sleep, I tell him
but I cannot speak. 'Do not fear,' he says, 'for we are on the river
to the sea.' Which river, I ask him in my head, and which sea?
'We're in a boat on the river Krishna,' he says. 'You, me, the Arabis
and the zarafi, and your servants and things. We're making good
progress.' Why are we not walking? 'We'll soon reach the port of
Machalipatna and buy a different boat to Khalakatapatna from
there. This one isn't big enough, the other soldiers are walking.' Is it
forty days yet? I ask him. He's lying down next to me and saying:*

'Sleep now, Master. You can write about this when we are on the sea again.' I will never write again, I tell him. After I'm dead, give me to the Kalingodhra for I have no wish to feed a crocodile.

37

CHANDRABHAGA

July passed, and then August. The rains washed the masonry of the temple clean of stone-dust and sand. The surroundings are covered again in a brilliance of new green. The quiet will last longer this year: the labour gangs are not back at work from their villages. Only the warriors from Aphrike and a small band of stonemasons have stayed through the rains. Them, and the Sovereign.

Southwest of the temple plinth, the stones of the old tumbled shrine are sorted and gathered in orderly stacks. Reassembly will be easy: the masonry is for the most part undamaged; what is beyond repair will be copied and replaced. The limestone votive image, unscathed, is left where it was lifted out from the sand. To protect it, a hut of palm-thatch is placed around it—to ward it also from curious eyes.

The Sun God sits cross-legged on a thousand-petalled lotus-seat. The lotus stalks in the god's hands coil about his forearms, curving away in the round at the elbows to bloom as full-blown lotuses on either side of his face. In the base of the pedestal, a minute, legless charioteer steers seven steeds.

Narasimha knelt before the image. In this light, the stone seemed to emanate an opalescent radiance. He turned to Dharmapada, standing eye-level by his side. 'How *did* you know?' he asked the Chief Architect's boy.

'I sculpted it,' Dharmapada said, 'long ago, in a previous life.'

~

The Master Draughtsman and his deaf-mute brother, the Master Sculptor, were irritable today. The Sovereign had gone and changed everything. Already, the heads of Dawn, Noontime and Eventide were placed in a crucible and melted back to wax: the greenstone figures for the terrace-shrines must now bear the likenesses of the image from the tumbled shrine. It will not be easy to achieve. That face is beautiful beyond belief.

But the brothers' troubles had only begun. The Sovereign wished to be depicted—together with the Consort, very small— kneeling at the booted feet of Dawn and Noontime and again beneath the leaping hooves of Eventide. It was just as well that the Master Sculptor and his principal apprentice had yet to release the figures from their stony confines. Any mistake in articulating the new brief, they would be compelled to start afresh, with new greenstone from Dwarasamudra. The brothers were grumbling in silence when they were summoned to the sanctum of the chariot.

The Sovereign stood in the middle of the sanctum, frowning down at the empty floor. 'A throne platform,' he said, swirling around, 'to surpass all throne platforms, one worthy of the—' He searched for a suitable word, '...*Him*. Let us begin.'

The Master Draughtsman looked to his brother; the older man had read the Sovereign's lips. He unravelled his measuring-string, marked with big knots and little knots into cubits and their segments.

The Sovereign got in the way—throwing instructions, tangling the string, changing measurements, starting over again. The brothers gave inward thanks that the Chief Architect's son was not witness to this; but for *him*, they had grudgingly conceded, the smithys would still be grappling with false science.

~

September. Notwithstanding their orders to stay away until they were summoned, the work gangs returned: you cannot keep a good worker from his chisels and plumb line. The tumbled shrine reassumed its original dimensions and profile. It barely surpassed the height of the chariot's plinth. The limestone image was moved to the assembly hall of the chariot, where a brickwork cell was built around it. There it would remain, untouched and unseen, until the chariot was finished.

After countless alterations, the scheme for the Sun God's throne platform was ready. The fine line drawings, rendered to scale and precise in every detail, were unrolled before the Sovereign: three large panels describing the platform's many-faceted and many-recessed sides and frontage.

A hand's span wide, the bottom-most register is a frieze of forest elephants, running from the left and the right to converge in the centre, head to head. Separated from the elephants by bands of lotus medallions and jewel-ornament, the middle register is peopled with two tiered ranks of worshippers in their hundreds. Hands together in prayer, they gaze upon the Sovereign and the Consort, themselves knelt in worship inside a central shrine. At the base of the shrine, a child feeds a caparisoned elephant. The corners of the platform are embellished with couchant elephants and leaping lions. 'You have excelled yourselves,' Narasimha said to the draughtsmen, placing his signature seal.

Late one evening a courier from Kataka galloped in with a message: the Sovereign's presence was required in the palace.

38

KATAKA

A BARGE FROM KHALAKATAPATNA MADE ITS WAY UP THE Kushabhadra and late that afternoon, touched the jetty of Kataka Palace. From advance word that the Crown Prince of Parijatapuri was no longer in their midst—indeed, that his mortal remains had been given to the sea seven months previously—it was a sombre welcome that awaited the returning party. No drums, no trumpets, no garlands. The Consort's cousin was the first to step off the barge. He scanned the gathering before bowing, a beat too late, to the Sovereign.

'You seem to have done well staying alive,' Narasimha said in spite of himself, stepping back and up the steps.

He stared at the retreating figure. 'Wait!'

Perhaps it was only the breeze that had changed: the reception party drew a sharp breath.

Narasimha swung around. 'What did you say?'

'Where is my master?'

'Your *master*?'

'Your amanuensis. He who taught me to read and write.'

'I threw him out. Your orders were to *remain with the cattle*. Who asked you to come back?'

'I had no such orders. The Sultan Splendid saw me off with his blessings for my safe return and so I did. Your soul brother died before we reached Kilwa and you have no one to blame, not even him, for doing so without your leave. Your ship got damaged, I am not responsible for it. Much else has happened, yet I am back whether you wished it or not and all I wish to do is eat and sleep. And *that*, if you haven't noticed, is your zarafa and those are my men. Treat them well.'

They had told him yesterday that the Consort's cousin was bringing with him a most unusual beast. Nothing had prepared him for the presence being led off the barge. For a brief moment, he felt himself to be a child again. But only for a moment. With a curt nod, he hurried up the steps.

~

'And those are the circumstances of your son's passing,' he said. 'No one *killed* him, to the best of my knowledge.' There was no call to repeat the fatuous claims of a mad man.

The Courtesan turned the signet ring in her hands. 'It belonged to his father,' she said. 'I thank you for safeguarding it. Did he ever speak of me?'

'Oh, not a day went by without his taking your name. Now… about the Sovereign's amanuensis…'

'Ah yes, your friend. He bided here a while, almost a month I believe. When his cat died—what would you expect, he kept the poor thing encaged day and night—he said it was time for him to leave and so he did.'

'I see.' He glanced around the Hall of Enchantment, beginning at the oval mirror and ending at it. 'No one seems to know where he is.'

'Everyone knows where. He is in Cadambagiri.'

'Cadambagiri?'

'Must you squawk like my parrot? He said it was to Chin he was sailing—a ruse, I could tell right away—so yes, in truth it was to Cadambagiri that he went. The Secretary confirmed it.'

'The *Secretary*? Who would imagine…'

'One as stone-faced visiting my palace? Men have their needs.' She eyed him archly. 'But you wouldn't understand. I heard what happened here the last time you visited.'

'A most engaging game of rhyming riddles. I could have kept at it all night!'

'Ah, such tact. The Sovereign is fortunate in having you for his emissary.'

He shrugged. 'An accidental appointment. And one likely not to be repeated, seeing as I have reappeared like a bad dream.'

He cast his eyes again over the mirror, the armillary sphere, the lacquered screen. 'But coming back to my master...'

'Yes. I hear he has made himself indispensible to the lady of Cadambagiri. The Secretary complained bitterly that his own work has doubled since.' She studied the signet ring on her hand. 'Did he tell you ...he was besotted with her but was made to wed the sister. If only he had spoken up then, none of this would have happened. But too late...'

'I had better leave. It is late.'

'Why don't you bide here a while?'

'I was hoping you would ask,' he said. 'After that cheerless welcome... I may have spoken harshly to him... He has forbidden my cousin from seeing me. And I am hungry. Perhaps I shall stay, just a few days, until his anger abates.'

'There speaks a sensible boy,' she said, reaching for a bell pull. 'You deserve a hero's welcome.'

~

The giraffe half-heartedly nibbled the bitter leaves of the neem. On the circular platform, her syces sat telling their beads, unmindful of the people gathered about the courtyard to stare. The Consort stood lost in thought at a window in the enclosing apartments.

Following the rains, her maids had reopened the old wing, cleaning and remedying years of neglect; the faded murals in a hallway had provided them hours of amusement. She had since taken to spending as much time here as she did in her observatory, appointing it with a bed and a writing desk, carpets and lamps. In a corner, a copper boiler for spice-tea gurgled and hissed steam.

'Happy?' said Narasimha, entering the hallway.

She turned from the window. 'Quite.'

He walked across and stood by her side.

In the courtyard, the giraffe sloped aside to sample a different bunch of leaves. His beads done, one of the syces knelt at the edge of the platform and began massaging the giraffe's calves and knees. 'Her eyelashes,' the Consort said, 'are the envy of my ladies. She is possessed also of a peculiar fragrance, between musk and something else.'

'Useless thing,' Narasimha said. 'Beautiful *and* useless. You cannot saddle it.'

'Did you know,' Sitadevi went on, 'her name is Fathema. I'm told it means *chaste*, it's perhaps why she has no voice. I've been here all afternoon, and neither a bleat nor lowing or a neigh. Only a strange humming, if you can call that a voice. And those amulets around her neck.' She shook her head. 'For her health, evidently.'

He smiled.

'What fools of men,' she said abruptly.

'Who?'

'The fool who asked for but one of her kind. The other who obliged with but one of her kind. For the foolishness of two men, the hapless creature must live up to her name bereft of a mate.'

'If men can go without, so too can beasts.'

'Men go without by choice,' she shot back.

He ran a hand over the window ledge and looked at his fingers. They were clean. 'I leave you to your musings. I must write to Kilwa.' He began to move away, and paused by the murals. 'I'd forgotten these.' He grinned. 'Wait till you see the carvings for the chariot.'

'To what end those carvings?'

He feigned surprise. 'To guard it from lightning, what else. But of course, you wouldn't agree with that belief.'

'You're correct,' she said. 'I don't. I'm of the belief their purpose is to teach people to *live*. The elements have as much to do with it as they do with these…these paintings. But of course, you wouldn't know it, busy as you are with letters to people you'll never meet.'

'I must go—'

'I am not done, Husband,' she said, surprising herself. So this was it. 'I have more to say and you will hear it. I am not a zarafa and my name is not Fathema. I was not born and named Sita to live out my days barren or chaste. If you do not fulfil my one need, I will leave for Malwa at first light and I will take the beauty with me.'

~

'We are travelling again,' Narasimha said, striding into the Morning Office. 'What is it that you have there?'

The Secretary looked up. 'The boy's chronicle of the voyage.'

'Ah! Have you finished perusing it?'

'I was waiting for your—'

'Of course. But where *is* our hero? He must be grateful to be back. I haven't had occasion to speak to him properly.'

'He took himself to the Courtesan's.' So soon after that sour reception, this turnabout could mean only one thing. Mischief. 'The fruit of his penmanship,' he added, 'conveys a most peculiar voice.'

'But you haven't read it.'

'Only the closing passages.' He drummed his knuckles on the sides of the box. 'Scarcely half the stock has been used for it.'

'May I read?'

'A wasted effort, in my opinion,' he said, passed him a sheaf.

Fanning the frayed papers on the table, Narasimha leant over them. 'Remarkable! From coming unlettered to *this* in—what was it? six months? I must commend him most heartily.'

'Forgive me for presuming, but if you read closely, the work in its entirety—' Of course he had read it, start to finish. He cleared his throat. 'It was meant to be a *chronicle*—not a personal missive to the half-breed.'

'Secretary! Secretary…! You heard what that soldier said. They almost lost him in the Dakkhin. It must have been more than *youth* which preserved him.' He swept the sheets together. 'Sequence these. I'll read them tonight.'

The Secretary's face was impassive. He held his gaze.

Narasimha sighed. 'Yes, I know. I've lost a cherished friend, nothing I do or say will bring *him* back. I've lost a ship, I've run scared of the Turk. My temple remains unfinished. One thing after another without respite. Are you not *tired* of it as I am? Set a destination of your choice—Kalinganagara, Kashi, anywhere—and return refreshed of heart and mind.' He smiled. 'You see, that's what I came to say. I'm granting *myself* a recess. Inform the Sovereign Lady of Cadambagiri of my imminent visit. They can expect me in a fortnight. But before that, a letter of commiseration to Parijatapuri—'

'*Cadambagiri*?'

'Yes, yes, most irregular, I concede. I might have written myself, but it being an imperial visit, it is better that you do it. The former Right Hand—I gather he is still in her employ— might even be pleased to see me. Either that, or drop dead of fright.' He paused, and then laughed. 'You are wondering what madness has possessed me?'

'It is not for me to—'

'No, so allow me. Do you recall the Right Hand speak of the zarafa as a harbinger of fortune and serenity? He was right. The creature has indeed served its calling, even the clouds have been munificent. Now the lady of Cadambagiri can have it, before her other friends furnish her with one of its kind; I'll deliver it myself and have her part with the Scrivener in exchange.' He beamed at the Secretary. 'Come, there's no call to look like you must lay an egg. You've been woefully overburdened ever since he left. As for the harbinger, I've promised the Consort a pair next time, and a better ship. I won't imperil her cousin's life again.'

'Forgive me, but I do not follow any of this.'

'For his second embassy to Kilwa. The bullion this time will serve in the interim, enough for us to recommence work in Chandrabhaga in earnest. And a new ship, and sixty-six Vamshadharas to Kilwa next time. Dharmapada has been proven correct yet again.'

'Dharmapada?'

'The one and only. My fortunes would change, he said. I believe they have.' He passed a quick hand over his face. 'Now, about our letter to the bereaved clan...'

39

PARIJATAPURI

THE MESSENGER WAS ANNOUNCED INTO THE PRESENCE OF the Princess Regent. The man's heart leapt to his mouth at the sight that greeted him. 'So this is what it has come to,' he said to himself.

She was half-seated-half-reclining in a daybed, surrounded by six or seven bejewelled young men. One of them was curled at her feet like a cat and toying with her anklets. Another, a peacock quill in his hair and two more in his hands, was performing a slow sinuous imitation of a snake. The rest were draped about the bed wearing expressions of mild weariness, mild petulance and mild nothingness. Perhaps it was the afternoon light: the air about the grouping seemed to shimmer like the heat haze of a mirage.

To something the Princess Regent said, her company turned as one to regard the intruder with stony eyes. Sensing neither threat to themselves nor to the one about whom they daily congregated, they gathered themselves and, blowing kisses to the air, slithered away in a loose tangle of arms and legs. 'Who are you?' the princess asked, sitting up and drawing a shawl across herself.

'I bear sad tidings from Kataka, Your Majesty,' the messenger said.

'Can anything from Kataka be otherwise?' she said. 'Come, hand me it, I do not bite.'

She unsealed the scroll case. The missive was stuck. She thrust a little-finger in and, with a deft twist, extricated the contents.

The Sovereign of Kalinga—she read—regrets to inform you of the passing of the Crown Prince of Parijatapuri at sea whilst accompanying a batch of *cows*—surely there was some mistake?—to the kingdom of Kilwa in the Sea of Hind. His kind-heartedness, refinement of speech, faultless deportment, flawless comportment, inimitable wit—she rolled her eyes—and unconditional friendship and affection of over two decades could never be replaced. The obsequies had been conducted at sea itself. The writer was bereft of words of solace to offer the bereaved kin and country. Would the recipient of this pitiable dispatch be so kind as to acknowledge the personal effects of our dear departed...

She glanced up.

An ivory box in the crook of his arm, the messenger was absently running a finger in the curves of a lamp standard and inspecting the dust on his fingertip. She almost flung the scroll case at him but restrained herself. 'Take that to the treasury,' she said instead. 'They will verify the contents...' She smiled. 'Ah, yes... You must take me for a cold insensate wife. I am too overwhelmed to display the normal reactions of a woman bereaved. Your sovereign officiated at my nuptials in Cadambagiri. With this—' she held up the letter by a corner as if it were a rag, '...he officially signs its end. Convey to him a widow's gratitude and blessings.'

After the messenger had left, she remained seated, looking at but not really reading the thing.

Kilwa. Ship. Cows. Inimitable wit.

She frowned.

Many months ago, a scrap of a message... All she *could* remember was having twisted a pigeon's neck... It had felt like the cracking of a knuckle, but soft, inside. If only she could see through the mist which clouded her senses without warning these days.

Some days she permitted her thoughts to wander into the nursery and peer into the empty crib. She had trained herself to pretend it had never happened. It behoves a ruler, she reminded herself, to be unfeeling. She reached for her opium horn. Working a large sticky pinch into a chickpea-sized fid, she slipped it behind her underlip and lay back—emptying her head of the voices inside.

∿

In the outhouse, the First and Second Princesses were paying their grandsire their quotidian visit.

Here they come, the Raja said to himself: the older is harmless, it is the younger I should like to slap.

The same ritual, every morning and evening. Climbing into the bed, the Second Princess pried open the Raja's left eyelid. 'Still alive,' she declared, proceeding to open his right eye.

Evil child, thought the Raja, rolling his eyeballs back. The Second Princess squealed with practiced fright at the yellowish whites cobwebbed in red veins—more frightening now in the flickering lamp light. She pressed shut his eyelids, whispering, 'Shall I tell you a little secret?'

Her breath was warm and milky upon his face. This wasn't the usual routine. The Raja opened his eyes and rose an eyebrow. 'Mother said our father has *died*,' she said hoarsely. 'A man came to tell her today. Our father fell off a boat into the sea and got swallowed by a fish…as big as this bed…is what Mother said.'

The Raja's eyes grew wide.

'Mother says you're next.' She stroked his face gravely. 'If you die, with whom shall we play?'

'Enough now, come away, let him be,' said the First Princess, standing at the foot of the bed. She disliked these visits, the air in this place, the smell of the grandparent.

'Don't tell *her* I told you,' whispered the Second Princess, pressing her lips to his cold cheeks and clambering off the bed. 'And don't die. We shall be back in the morning.'

∿

In the country of Parijatapuri, mused the Raja, there lives a canny Raja who, following an attempt on his life, lost the use of most of his faculties. Confined to this miserable cell by her with whom he begat a male heir, the Raja is nowadays attended upon by an army of servants. There is a chamber-pot servant.

Another to wash and bathe him. Two to powder and dress him. Two more to fan him. Two, sometimes four, to massage him. A physician to look in, morning, noon and night. Sentries in the gallery outside. There used to be a servant to feed him, until he convinced himself that he was being poisoned and refused to eat, unless it was Her Radiance who fed him personally. In this way, he not only insured himself against death by her hand, but also ensured she would be compelled to wait upon him—and not once but thrice each day for as long as he lived. Perhaps it was her presence, the touch of her spoon to his lips: unexpectedly one afternoon, the first of July to be precise, he had felt a prickle of sensation in his loins.

The prickle had travelled down his legs. He prudently kept the development to himself. When no one was watching, he twiddled his toes and arched his feet under the coverlets. That very night, he struggled out of bed and took his first faltering steps. He almost collapsed from the pain but clenching his teeth, willed himself to remain upright and soundless out of fear of alerting the sentries outside. The pain had slowly subsided, giving way to a sweeter, more bearable ache. There was no stopping him then.

At dead of night ever since, the Raja climbed out of bed and padded the length of the cell a hundred-and-eight times, silent as a jungle cat. In the coming weeks, he learned to strengthen his arms and shoulders by pressing himself off the walls, and then the floor, two-score times. His appetite, at the best of times sluggish, improved by the day; he took care not to display any enthusiasm for food to the hand that fed. One night, he succeeded in rousing and pleasuring himself. If ever there was a breakthrough in his vitality, this was it. The servants—surely they knew what he was doing—chose not to comment on his altering frame.

He heard the door open and shut softly. Her Radiance had come with his last meal of the day… and, for all he knew, his life. The mattress sank as she sat down by his side. He opened his eyes.

She smiled. 'I bear tidings enough to make you sing,' she

began, briskly stirring the bowl of porridge. Already, the bowl and the spoon had tarnished from an alien ingredient. 'Your precious son is on his way back,' she went on brightly, 'and not alone, for he has found *our* son as he promised. They should be here any day. Now, open wide…your favourite bitter gourd and green pepper tonight. I must hurry and prepare—'

He pressed his lips tight and pulled his head sideways and back.

She laughed, a whit shrilly. 'Why, what's the matter? Oh, I see… You *know* it's safe, it always is, I must finish here and go, I haven't all night…' She directed the spoon at his mouth again. A hand shot out from under the coverlets like a python's head and seized her wrist. She uttered a sharp cry. He pushed her hand back towards her face, forcing the spoon around to her lips. She resisted and then, changing tactic, let herself go limp, the better to throw the porridge in his face. But he had her by the other wrist, his spatulate fingernails biting into her skin. 'You are hurting me,' she gasped. His lips peeled away from his yellow teeth in a grimace; she lunged forward at him, snapping at the air. In the scrimmage, he shook the bowl and spoon free from her hands and thrust her off the bed with all his strength. She dropped to the floor in a heap, winded, but quickly pulled herself into a crouch like a cornered animal about to spring.

'You and I understand each other perfectly,' he said, lifting the coverlets and climbing out of the bed, 'I believe we had better keep it that way.'

She stared up at him.

'Surprised?'

She nodded mutely.

'And this?'

She turned her eyes away.

'It has come to my knowledge,' he said, taking a step, 'that your fool husband is dead.' She flinched, anticipating a blow to her head, but no: 'I shall grant you a day,' he went on, 'to consider the merits of what I am about to say. There is naught in the scriptures, nor even in the primer to statecraft, to proscribe a king from taking the widow of an adopted heir for his own wife. I am, as you can see, wholly alive. It is best that you do not fight me. Never again.'

Her mind raced. She always knew she was destined for greatness. The rewards for patience were within her reach. Rani today, Cadambagiri next. Her stars couldn't have shifted for the better than this. She remained where she was, scarcely daring to breathe.

There was a rap on the door just then. A servant rushed in, breathless, only to stop mid-step at the sight. He found his voice, 'Sire…my lady…forgive me; the baby…! *the baby prince*—' She scrambled to her feet and was out of the door in a flash, so she didn't hear him finish, '…in a well.'

Having delivered the awful tidings, the servant stood gaping at the erect figure by the bed. The Raja stared back. The servant averted his eyes—to the silver bowl fallen by the bed.

'What are you waiting for?' the Raja said. 'Clear up the mess and quit my sight.'

There was porridge everywhere—splashed to the legs of the bed and the night-stand, the chamber pot, the wall-skirting, he would need to take a mop to it. Collecting the bowl, he ducked for the spoon under the bed. There was some porridge congealed to it. Hurrying to the kitchens, he slyly licked the spoon clean and proceeded to scrape the bowl for the dregs. The bitter-peppery porridge had a metallic undertaste, some ingredient he couldn't at once place. His tongue turned heavy; the bowl fell and skipped across the dark paving. The servant dropped to his knees, clawing at his mouth and rasping for help.

∽

Months ago, a gardener, noticing the uncovered well, had replaced the planks and gone his way. With the rains gone, the disused courtyard was receiving its seasonal clearing of vines and weeds. One of the gardeners had shifted the planks. The pinched black hole had coughed up the stench of fermented death.

They sent down a kitten in a wicker basket and after it was drawn back, shaken but still alive, two men on ropes to investigate. It took them all evening to bring up the remains. The work gang and more servants stood in frightened silence, torches smoking in their hands.

It could have waited until daybreak. But no. A cloth pressed to her face, the Princess Regent sifted the small bones with a stick. There was no gold to be found in the mess. But for the skull, it could just as well be the remains of a pye.

The servants had thrown some sacking over the larger pile. They implored Her Radiance to not uncover it. Ignoring them, she flicked up an edge. The torchlights glanced off silver toe-rings; claw-like toenails; rotted sinew, purple-red. 'Whore-borns!' she spat, 'It is that milk mother and *her* baby—' But how were they to know it. She veered aside, retching up strings of bile.

~

Bathed and perfumed, the Princess Regent lay awake by the Raja's side. The gruesome discovery had stirred sediments which had settled to the darkest recesses of her mind. She'd suspected it all along: the wretch she had had rendered speechless for casting aspersions on the paternity of her son had stolen him in revenge. Stolen, but not drowned in a well. She sat up and reached for her opium, her one solace.

The voices in her head convinced her that her little prince was in Cadambagiri. Wrest him from that witch, they said. Avenge your ruined wedding night and your poor father's suicide. Plan your moves with the exactitude of a snake and like a snake, strike to kill.

She didn't know it yet, but this was to become the brief of her existence—her pulse, her reason for waking, her last wish before sleep, her life-juice. It scarcely diluted with time; rather, distilling to the potency of some rare illicit spirit. She glowed from it—like a small bright jewel. Through it all, she remained devoted to the man by her side. They coupled at will, turning more inventive with age. She was never again burdened with child.

40

CADAMBAGIRI

'The Heart of Light?' said the Scrivener. 'No, this is the first I've heard of it.'

'This big.' The envoy made a fist of his right hand and pressed it to his chest. His younger companion—he of the dark dancing eyes—nodded and touched his right fist to his chest. The three men were seated around the Scrivener's table in the archives. Outside in the courtyard, the Governor of Bharukachchha's latest gift of rare white peacocks were flaunting their luminescence. 'This big,' repeated the older envoy, 'and of the clearest water. You cannot *not* know of it. Originally the property of the Eighth Incarnation who was gifted it by a black bear, who in turn—'

'A *bear*?' the Scrivener snorted. 'Whatever next!' He held up a hand and shook his head. 'No, my dear man... I have been here ten months and have heard no mention, *ever*, of any such gem mined from our hill.' He looked at both men pleasantly. They looked back at him, pleasantly. 'Even assuming it had,' he continued, 'the chances of it leaving Cadambagiri are as likely as fish falling out of the sky—and do let us keep bears out of this— for Her Excellence's forebears would have guarded it with their lives.' He waved a hand towards the shelves, 'And no mention of Hearts of Light in the documents, I have perused every one of these, as well as the treasury inventories—' He took a deep breath and placed his hands on the table. 'So, really... There are no diamonds underneath our cadamba trees. Her Excellence is grateful as always—but to seek to *survey* the hill...to even assume we might entertain so...so *absurd* a request...'

'We only ask that she consider it,' said the younger envoy smoothly. 'We are in no hurry to force anyone's hand. Ultimately, it is for Her Excellence to agree or not, and for you only to place our petition before her eyes. How unreasonable can that be?' He smiled, before adding with a soft laugh, 'Forgive me for pointing it out, but in the past the minister in charge of these affairs was always accommodating of our every request, none of these obstacles to—'

'Alas,' said the Scrivener primly, 'I have an entirely new method in place.'

'And are entirely unaware of the full nature of our previous embassies?' He glanced at his older colleague before continuing, 'As there is much to be gained from cordiality, so too is much to be lost from imprudence. Our Governor, may God keep him well, is a most gracious man, educated and refined…in fact, much like yourself in diction and bearing. It would be most advantageous to all concerned if Her Excellence were to give him her consent.'

The older envoy, looking more than a little uncomfortable the past several minutes, asked to be excused to go to the privies. In the silence left in his wake, the Scrivener and the young Persian sat gazing at each with polite smiles. 'We heard you are from Siraf,' said the young man at length. 'I myself hail from Shiraz, my esteemed senior from Tabriz. There is much I have learnt from him.'

'Indeed,' the Scrivener said. Not wishing to linger on the subject of genealogies, he said in a sudden little rush of breath: 'May I seek your advice on a small private affair?'

The envoy rose an eyebrow and dazzled a white smile. 'I am honoured.'

'Oh, you are most kind. You see, there's a personal, not official, dispatch that I must reach to a friend. The trouble is, he happens to be deputed to Kilwa, to the court of the Sultan Kiswahili to be precise. You do see my predicament…?'

'Think no more of it. Have you it ready?'

'I shall have it so tonight.' He felt the blood rush to his face. 'Oh, thank you *most* kindly!'

The older envoy returned. The younger man rose. 'Our work here is done for the day,' he said to him, and turning to the Scrivener: 'I trust we can return tomorrow to a more favourable consideration of our request. Before we take your leave...' He reached into a side pocket, 'Pray accept this. A small token of our gratitude and lasting acquaintance.'

'What is it?' said the Scrivener, turning the gold-and-glass object in his hands.

'A most salutary contrivance for improving the sight.' He moved around the table in a whisper of muslin. 'Here, if you will allow me...'

~

After they had left, the Scrivener removed the ocular device and polished the paired glass discs on the edge of a sleeve. The visit had unsettled him. He ought to have probed deeper about that Heart of Light instead of making eyes at the Shirazi. If gemstones indeed lay under the cadambas, perhaps he could undertake a discreet survey? There were hundreds of trees, where would he begin? How would he convince Her Excellence of the merits of their burrowing into the hill? Why, oh why, did it have to be him? He repositioned the device on his nose and glumly took in the contents of the Muniments Room, close range and middle distance, and then through the doorway at the white peacocks twirling in the sunlight.

How other-worldly the pearly newcomers seemed and yet of this realm. He sighed. The way the Shirazi's knuckles had brushed his ears as he helped with the present, that whiff of perfume on his wrists... Perhaps he could be persuaded to bring him a phial of it next time... In due course, a white cat... A carpet or two for his austere apartments. Everything, ultimately, had happened for the best. But enough daydreaming. There was another matter he had deliberately kept pending the past week, and only because he was loath to address it. His eyes fell upon a silver scroll case that he had thrown to a shelf. With an annoyed grunt, he leant over for it.

There was no questioning the authenticity of the dispatch. The signature seal aside, he'd recognize his former colleague's handiwork from a mile. At the mere sight of it last Friday, his heart had leapt to his mouth and then, as he skimmed the writing, sunk like a stone to the pit of his groin; his hands had trembled and turned clammy. The sensations resurfaced manifold as he read the missive afresh with his newly sharpened eyes.

The Secretary's bland tone conveyed little, if anything, of the object of the Great Ganga's imminent visit. What could possibly be a *matter of urgent consequence to the future fortunes of Kalinga and Cadambagiri*? What matter could possibly merit a *personal* visit? Surely not that old affair of the crazed sister in Parijatapuri and her insipid husband? Surely *that* entity had by now returned from Kilwa—hopefully infused with some colour and spirit? Surely he, the Crown Misery, had entreated Narasimha to negotiate a settlement though marriage... Or perhaps...?

He gasped. How could he have been *so* blind! Of course Narasimha *himself* had at long last acquiesced to his Consort's entreaties to take another wife and produce an heir. All that covert correspondence between Kataka and Cadambagiri... It all fell into place. Clearly the imminent visit was in order to personally seek the Sovereign lady's hand...and therefore the *future fortunes...urgent consequence...* But what, then, of his, the Scrivener's, *own* consequence? He flung the letter across the table and sat back, nervously plucking at his sleeves—but only for a moment before leaping out of his chair with an anguished wail and striking his forehead in the manner of the natives with the palm of his hand.

Stupid, stupid, *stupid* mongrel! A response was awaited and all he had done was...*nothing*. For all he knew, Narasimha was already on his way—reply or no reply—with elephants, trumpets, priests and gifts. There was nothing for it but to act at once, or regret at leisure on the streets of Hind. Snatching up the letter, he flew through the halls and courtyards which separated the bleak north wing of the palace from the Sovereign's apartments.

AUTHOR'S NOTE

Narasimha I (ruled 1238-64) completed the eponymous Sun Temple of Konark c.1250. The presiding deity, Kona Arka, 'Corner Sun', was named for the first rays of dawn touching the easternmost outpost of Narasimha's empire. The finished temple is estimated by historians to have stood approximately 225 feet in height. Legend has it that Dharmapada installed the gold finial of the sanctuary tower.

Various causes, and dates, are attributed to the tower's collapse. The ruined monument, comprising the assembly hall and subsidiary structures, is now a UNESCO World Heritage Site. The green-chlorite images of Dawn, Noontime and Eventide are preserved in situ on the terrace. The sanctum, empty, is open to the sky.

A royal reception for a giraffe is the subject of a gorgeous sculptural panel on the southern façade of the basement-plinth. Narasimha, on elephant back with a parasol-bearer (damaged) seated behind him, approaches the exotic—itself accompanied by three robed figures (their upper quarters damaged) and seven other exulting men. The elephant's mahout wields a tiny elephant goad; a standard-bearer (damaged) follows a few paces away. A stylized night-blooming jasmine tree frames the otherwise naturalistic scene; peacocks roost in the luxuriant foliage.

In a separate panel alongside the giraffe's reception, the temple's Chief Architect and his wife have stepped through an archway to stand radiantly smiling under a banana tree. The lower half of the composition is vandalized.

Of the profusion of figural sculptures everywhere—divinities, animals, mythical creatures and mortals—the amorous couples and groupings number in the hundreds and demonstrate a raw, earthy vitality, devoid of artifice. It is tempting to imagine they, and the sculptured dancers and musicians, were modelled from life.

Narasimha was succeeded by his and Sitadevi's son and natural heir, Bhanudeva I (ruled 1264-79). Paramardideva died a hero in battle, c. December 1255. In memory of her husband, Chandrikadevi raised the Anantha Vasudeva temple, completed c.1278, in Ekamra (modern-day Bhubaneshwar). Tughral Tughan Khan enjoyed two terms, from 1236-46 and 1272-81, as the Mamluk Delhi Sultanate's governor in Bengal. Sultan ibn Bone Soleiman (ruled c.1225-63) was the penultimate ruler of the Persian Shirazi dynasty which founded the Kilwa Sultanate c.957.

While these historical figures appear as characters in this book, and while many of the historical settings exist under contemporary names, this story is a work of fiction and historical characters, settings and events are revisited in these pages in a fictional context; and so too the battles and journeys described.

A number of books provided me the frameworks to reimagining an India that was. My research has especially benefitted from K.C. Panigrahi's definitive *History of Orissa*, Sila Tripati's *Maritime Archaeology: Historical Descriptions of the Seafarings of the Kalingas* and George F. Hourani's *Arab Seafaring*. R.C. Majumdar's *Ancient Indian Colonies in the Far East* and S. Muhammad Husayn Nainar's *Southern India as Known to Arab Geographers* both make for rivetting, sometimes incredulous, reading. Percy Brown's *Indian Architecture: Buddhist and Hindu* has evocative descriptions and pictorial reconstructions of the Sun Temple complex. Heinrich Zimmer's *The Art of Indian Asia, Vols I and II*, and *Konarka: Chariot of the Sun God* by Bettina Bäumer and Masatoshi A. Konishi with extraordinary photographs by Morihino Oki have been constant touchstones. Thomas Donaldson's deceptively slim *Konark: Monumental Legacy* is an excellent companion to a physical visit of the site. George Michell's *Penguin Guide to the Monuments of India, Vol I* accompanied me to Odisha in 2001 and continues to inspire.

The verse from Yang Wan-li's poem (*Don't Read Books!*) quoted by the Scrivener in Chapter 5 is adapted from Jonathan Chaves' translations, *Heaven My Blanket, Earth My Pillow: Poems from Sung Dynasty China by Yang Wan-li*. Also in Chapter 5, the Scrivener's quote from the *Manteq at-Tair* of Farid ud-Din Attar is adapted from *The Conference of the Birds* by Dick Davis (tr.) and Afkham Darbandi.

The first month of the Hindu calendar roughly overlaps mid-March and mid-April. The Gregorian calendar is used in this novel for convenience.

ACKNOWLEDGEMENTS

MY FIRST THANKS ARE TO SREYA URS, AS ALWAYS, FOR HER FIRST reading of this work. Anil Ananthaswamy for an essential masterclass, even while he was completing his second book. Helen Clarkson and Anthony Goldie for Zheng He's qilin in Malacca. Brinda Datta, Sophie Gaur, Nirada Harendra, Sandhya Harendra, Sachindra Karanth, Eric Lavertu, Pradeep Narrain, Sandeep Reddy, Adil Sadiq, and Sarita Sundar for their many kindnesses. My editor Sudeshna Shome Ghosh for encouragement from the start and her expert hand in our second collaboration; but for her, Fathema may have wandered off course. Shalini Krishan and Anurag Basnet for the copy-edit. Ravi Singh for publishing this book: thank you. To the family, finally, for great patience and support.